THE WOUNDED THORN

THE WOUNDED THORN

Fay Sampson

This first world edition published 2015
in Great Britain and the USA by
SEVERN HOUSE PUBLISHERS LTD of
19 Cedar Road, Sutton, Surrey, England, SM2 5DA.
Trade paperback edition first published
in Great Britain and the USA 2015 by
SEVERN HOUSE PUBLISHERS LTD.

British Library Cataloguing in Publication Data

Sampson, Fay author.
  The Wounded Thorn.
  1. Historic sites–England–Glastonbury–Fiction.
  2. Chalice Well (Glastonbury, England)–Fiction.
  3. Criminal investigation–Fiction. 4. Detective and
  mystery stories.
  I. Title
  823.9'14-dc23

ISBN-13: 978-0-7278-8485-5 (cased)
ISBN-13: 978-1-84751-589-6 (trade paper)
ISBN-13: 978-1-78010-639-7 (e-book)

All Severn House titles are printed on acid-free paper.

Severn House Publishers support the Forest Stewardship Council™ [FSC™],
the leading international forest certification organisation. All our titles that
are printed on FSC certified paper carry the FSC logo.

MIX
Paper from
responsible sources
FSC   FSC® C013056

Typeset by Palimpsest Book Production Ltd.,
Falkirk, Stirlingshire, Scotland.
Printed and bound in Great Britain by
TJ International, Padstow, Cornwall.

AUTHOR'S NOTE

Most of the settings in this book, in and around Glastonbury, are real and well worth a visit. I have, however, added others which are fictional. You will not find the Bowes Hotel, the Copper Kettle teashop, the Archive of Avalon, the Spiritual Sphere, St Bridget's School, Sister Mary Magdalene's convent, the Baptist church hall, Straightway Farm or Arnold's DIY store. There is no industrial estate or sluice gate at the locations I have indicated.

All the characters are fictional. In particular, my apologies to the real-life staff of the Chalice Well, Glastonbury Abbey and the Avon and Somerset Constabulary. For the purposes of this novel, I have removed them from their jobs and substituted others who are entirely my own invention.

ONE

'You can see why they call it Wearyall Hill,' Hilary panted. 'I seem to remember David and me galloping up here when we were younger.'

They were following the path of beaten grass up the steep hillside. Hawthorn bushes foaming with blossom starred the green slope.

'It's not so bad if you take it steadily.' Veronica laughed. 'Someone told me to take smaller steps going uphill. But you just charge at everything, regardless of your age.'

'You needn't rub it in that I'm the wrong side of sixty now, and you're not. If it *is* the wrong side. I've often thought about that triple goddess thing: Maiden, Mother, Crone. You know, I quite fancy the Crone stage. Not having to bother what you look like, no squalling brats around your ankles, the licence to say what you want and to hell with what anybody thinks about you.'

They paused for breath as they reached the ridge. From here they would turn right. The spine of the hill would take them more gently to the summit. Hilary looked around her with appreciation. The ground fell away steeply on either side. To her left lay the little town of Glastonbury, the grey pillars of its ruined abbey standing out amid the contrasting red-brick houses. On their right was the broad farmland of the Somerset Levels. And, unmistakably piercing the skyline, the dramatic cone of Glastonbury Tor, surmounted by its solitary tower.

Hilary breathed a sigh of contentment. 'Glastonbury, Canterbury, Lindisfarne. Probably the three holiest places in England. Where it all began.'

'Do you think Joseph of Arimathea really did plant his staff here on this hill two thousand years ago?' Veronica asked. 'And it took root and flowered to become the Glastonbury Thorn?'

'Hmm. Well, you can take your pick from two legends. Either he brought the Christ child here, on a trading expedition. Or he came here after the crucifixion, bringing the Grail that caught Christ's blood.'

Veronica sang softly, '*And did those feet in ancient times walk upon England's mountains green?* Mind you, they could both be true, couldn't they? If Joseph was used to trading here, it might explain why he would bring the Grail here, when it grew too dangerous to stay in Palestine.'

'Hmm. I normally take these kind of legends with a pinch of salt. But there's an odd thing. Did you know that the Glastonbury Thorn isn't native to Britain? Apparently it's a species from the Middle East. It really could have come from Palestine. Makes you think, doesn't it?'

They set off again, along the steadily rising path, striding more easily now.

'Is that it up ahead? With the metal cage around it?' Veronica asked. 'Oh, the poor thing!'

'You do know some vandal cut it down?' Hilary asked.

'Yes, but I read that it had put out new shoots from the stump. And they planted another young one as well.'

Ahead of them, to the side of the path, stood not one but two wire cages. The first appeared to be empty, save for a wooden post. In the other stood an old tree – or rather, the ruin of one. Someone had hacked it off above head height. Every branch had been sawn through, where it sprang from the trunk.

But its nakedness had been transformed. Both cage and tree were hung about with multicoloured ribbons, medallions, and strips of paper bearing prayers.

'The Glastonbury Thorn,' Hilary said, stopping in front of it. 'I wish I knew who did that to it. Someone with a chainsaw and a grudge? Or some exhibitionist who wanted to see his handiwork splashed over the papers and TV?'

Veronica reached out a hand through the cage and stroked the bark. 'And to think it may have stood here since Joseph of Arimathea brought it from Palestine.'

'Hmm,' said Hilary more sceptically. 'Don't forget, these trees don't live for ever. From what I've heard, this one was planted by the council in 1951 for the Festival of Britain. The earlier one here was hacked down by the Puritans in the Civil War. But the faithful saved bits of it and planted them all over the town. This was grafted from one of those.' She bent closer to examine it. The old gnarled wood was spattered gold with lichen. The lower part was almost obscured by a rampant growth of nettles.

'I thought you said that new shoots were springing from the stump. I can't see anything, can you?'

Veronica walked around the ruined tree, studying it. 'No, you're right. There's nothing that looks like a green leaf to me.'

Hilary felt an unexpected pang of dismay. 'I was going to say all sorts of things like: "Hope springs eternal" and "You can't keep nature down". A symbol of Resurrection. But there's nothing, is there?'

'Do you think the shoots died? Or has the vandal been back? They never caught him, did they? Does he keep on destroying it?'

Hilary straightened up. 'There's that other cage. The one we walked straight past. That must be where they planted the replacement.'

Both women moved back to study it. This metal cage had been pushed sideways, so that it hung at a drunken angle. The protective wire netting around its base had been torn aside. There was nothing inside but the wooden post and the black collar that had once supported a young tree.

'It's gone too,' said Hilary bleakly. 'There's nothing left.'

She straightened up and surveyed the scene around them. The little town of Glastonbury, the striking landmark of the Tor. A centre of pilgrimage for thousands of years.

'The sacred heart of England, but there's evil even here.'

'Who does it?' Veronica said, coming to join her. 'Is it some pagan who wants to attack the Christian myths about the tree? Or a Christian who thinks the tree is pagan, with all these ribbons and stuff?'

'Or a mindless vandal, who'll destroy anything people value.'

Veronica stood looking down at the town.

'There's so much else holy that draws people to Glastonbury. The Abbey, King Arthur's grave, the Chalice Well, the Tor. Do you suppose any of that is under threat too? Is there someone here who'd like to destroy more of what we care about?'

Hilary came to join her. 'Nothing feels as safe as it used to. Or perhaps it's just me. It really never was a safe world. You know I said that the thorn tree really may have come from Palestine? Touching the bark just now – feeling it dead – I try not to think about David in that hospital in Gaza, but I can't help worrying.'

'It's not the first time he's gone out to help, is it? It's only for a month. He'll be fine.'

An expression of consternation came over Hilary's face. 'Oh, Veronica, I'm sorry! Here am I, worrying because my husband might be in danger, while yours . . .'

Veronica smiled, a little sadly. 'It's all right. It's been six months now. I still miss him terribly, but I'm learning to cope. And it was a kind idea of yours for us to come away here and take our minds off it.'

'And now I'm rubbing it in. Typical.'

'No. We came here years ago, Andrew and I. Visited the Abbey ruins, climbed the Tor. It's good to remember happier times.'

Hilary stood in silence for a while. Andrew had died so suddenly. A ruptured blood vessel. There had been no time for Veronica to prepare herself, to say goodbye. It had been Hilary's suggestion that the two of them should come to Glastonbury, to set aside their grief and worry in this most sacred of English towns.

'I sometimes think we take too much for granted. The things we care about. Even here there are people who would attack them, for reasons we probably can't even guess.'

As she turned back to the ravaged tree, something caught her eye. The glint of metal in the afternoon sun. She bent closer to look.

'Idiot!'

Someone had pushed a coin into a crevice of the gnarled bark.

'Look at that! It's not just vandals. Some devotee thinks this tree is precious, but they've done their best to kill it all the same.'

She lowered her knapsack and delved into it to find a Swiss army knife. Using one of the blades, she carefully prised the metal out of the bark.

'Two pounds! Expensive poison.'

She stood looking down at the stained coin in her hand. Then she grinned. 'Well, no point in throwing it away.' She slipped it into her purse.

'Come on, then. This should go some way towards a slice of gateau. Let's drown our sorrows with a pot of tea and some sinful cream cakes. We'll enjoy the rest of Glastonbury while we have it.'

They started to walk down the hill.

Presently, Veronica said, 'That character who destroyed the Holy Thorn . . . Do you really think he, or someone like him, might target something else?'

TWO

'**D**o you know,' Veronica said, gently stirring her Earl Grey teabag, 'I've never been to the Chalice Well. Andrew and I always meant to, but what with the Abbey and the Tor and the Thorn on Wearyall Hill, we never quite got around to it.'

'Me neither. Right, that's settled.'

They walked up the High Street, past St John the Baptist's church.

'Hang on a minute,' Hilary said.

Two large trees stood in the front corners of the churchyard. Half hidden behind the left-hand one was a flowering hawthorn tree. Hilary marched through the gates towards it.

'There is hope, after all.'

A wooden notice bore the information: A Glastonbury Holy Thorn.

'I told you the townspeople had sneaked cuttings of it when the Puritans cut it down. This was one of them. Apparently, it still flowers in spring and midwinter.'

'There's something magical about that. Is this the one they cut blossoms from to send to the Queen at Christmas?'

'That's right. Looks healthy, doesn't it? Not like that poor wreck on the Tor.'

'Let's hope it stays that way.'

Their route led them on through the town. For all the Christian history for which Glastonbury was famous, the shops they passed offered an eccentric mix of New Age wares and alternative religions. Crystal pendants alternated with seated Buddhas. Placards announced aromatherapy and deep soul cleansing.

At the end of the High Street they took the road that led towards the Tor. The traffic was busy, but when they turned in at the gatehouse of the Chalice Well gardens a noticeable peace fell. They walked up the cobbled path to the ticket office. The gate into the gardens was patterned with two overlapping circles, making a figure of eight.

'The Vesica Piscis,' Veronica read from the leaflet. 'It symbolizes a union of heaven and earth, or spirit and matter.'

'Hmm.' Hilary pushed the gate open and stepped into the gardens. She looked round, shrewdly appraising.

'It's like so much else at Glastonbury. The Christian myth is really strong – and by "myth" I don't mean it's false, but the deep story running underneath everything. The red spring, coloured by Christ's blood from the Grail. And there's all this other stuff – New Age paganism, Goddess worship, Kabbalah, you name it.'

'*Many Paths, One Source*,' Veronica read.

'What they mean is, whatever you care to believe in, you'll find something to attract you in the gift shop.'

'Don't be so cynical,' Veronica reproved her. 'These gardens are rather lovely. There's a real atmosphere of . . . peace.'

Hilary shot an apologetic look sideways. 'Sorry. You're right. I sound like a hardened old sceptic, don't I? Go ahead. I'll follow you.'

Veronica led the way. They came to the first pool, in the open sunshine. It was shaped again like the Vesica Piscis figure of eight. Water tumbled into the pool down a series of fluted cups, banked by flower beds. The water was a brownish red, staining the stones it flowed over. On benches around it people sat, drinking in the peace.

Veronica and Hilary sat down too, meditating companionably.

After a while, Veronica rose. She drifted past flower beds, touching the blossoms lightly as she passed, or bending to drink in their fragrance. Following behind, Hilary watched her. Whatever she had said about the Chalice Well, the gardens were doing her friend good. There was, she had to admit, a sense of healing.

They went up the steps to a rectangular pool, which invited visitors to bathe in the therapeutic waters. Again, the water tumbled through red-stained channels.

Giant yew trees stood sentinel before a higher gateway.

It led them to a spout of water issuing from a lion's head in the wall. Two circular stones, golden red, stood beneath it. Glasses set on the upper one invited the passer-by to drink. Hilary reached out a finger to investigate the red-slicked stone.

'A chalybeate spring. Iron. I suppose it's not surprising that people should jump to mystical conclusions about where the colour came from. Don't they say it was Christ's blood which Joseph of Arimathea collected in the chalice he used at the Last Supper?'

'Or rust from the nails with which he was crucified.'

They both drank from the water.

'It's refreshing,' Veronica said. 'A little bit metallic. They say you only need a few sips.'

'The iron might actually do us good.'

Hilary strode on uphill, past another Glastonbury Thorn, in the direction of the Chalice Well. When she reached the circular enclosure, she paused. She hadn't been sure what to expect. A stream gushing out of the hillside? Or bubbling up out of the ground?

The reality was neither. Within a circle of low walls, a vertical shaft was protected by a grating. Plants showed a vivid green below the rim. The well cover was thrown back, to reveal that same pattern of interlacing circles, this time pierced by a lance. The cobbled pavement around it was studded with ammonites.

But standing in front of it was a figure Hilary had least expected to see: a small woman covered by a blue burka, which hid everything but her eyes. Hilary stopped dead in surprise.

Hands emerged from within the blue cloth. From under the folds of her burka the woman drew a notebook. She looked at the well in front of her and the surrounding stonework and flower beds. She made rapid notes and sketches. Then she turned, almost bumping into Veronica and Hilary behind her. For a moment, the eyes in the slit of her veil looked startled.

'Sorry! Didn't hear you coming.'

The voice did not have the accent Hilary had anticipated. It bore the strong nasal twang that could only come from Birmingham. The eyes that regarded them through the narrow opening were blue.

She swept her skirts aside as she moved around them and hurried off down the path, brushing purple alliums and yellow tulips as she passed.

'Well!' Hilary let out a long breath. 'I didn't expect *that*.'

Veronica was only half-listening. She knelt down beside the well and dipped her fingers through the grille. 'It's too far down to reach, but they say the spring is warm.'

'Another indication of the mystical. Like the hot springs at Bath. Hot red water. Got to be a supernatural explanation. But tell me, what's a devout Muslim woman doing at a Christian and New Age shrine?'

'The same as we are?' Veronica sat back on her heels and smiled up at her. 'Satisfying her curiosity about one of the foremost sacred sites of Glastonbury? Enjoying the peace and beauty of the gardens? Why not?'

'Hmm,' Hilary snorted again. 'I'm not sure it fits. Whatever it was that brought her here, she was keen to make notes about it.'

'Perhaps she's a writer. Collecting ideas for an article.'

Hilary turned her head and watched the shapeless figure of the woman disappearing back down the path to the entrance.

Veronica knelt for a while before the spring. Hilary seated herself on the low wall.

Presently they took a more meandering way back to the exit, pausing in a meadow facing Glastonbury Tor. They found a bench and let the peace of the late afternoon sink into them.

As they rejoined the path, Hilary scanned the scattering of visitors still coming towards the well: foreign tourists, a family party, people she judged from their ethnic clothing and esoteric pendants to be New Age devotees, more conventionally dressed women about their own age, who seemed as interested in the planting of the flowers and shrubs as the sacred significance of the site.

'Oh, no!' she groaned. 'Spare us.'

Prancing along the path came a motley figure who would not have looked out of place on the fringes of a Morris dance. His multicoloured clothes hung in tatters. His battered tall black hat nodded with feathers. He wore a jester's shoes with up-curled toes. There were tattoos on his hands and his face was smudged with soot. He danced towards them to the sound of bells held between his fingers and his palms.

When he was a few paces away he swept off his hat and bowed deeply. Mockingly? Hilary wondered.

'So you're here to be blessed by the sacred spring? How does it make you feel? Rejuvenated? Uplifted? Did you see visions in the healing pool on your way here? Have you drunk the water yet? You really should. You can feel the power washing through you. The blood of Christ or the milk of the Goddess. Who's to say?'

'Thank you,' Hilary interrupted firmly. 'We've done everything we need to. Now, if you'll excuse us, we're on our way to the exit.'

'Don't forget the shop. They have, if I may be so immodest as to mention it, a book of mine. *Dancing with the Divine*. Rupert Honeydew at your service.' He flourished the feathered hat again.

'I'm sure we'll see it.' Hilary was aware that Veronica at her side was stifling giggles. 'Now, if you wouldn't mind . . .'

Rupert Honeydew stood aside with exaggerated politeness.

Veronica waited until he was out of earshot before she gurgled, 'Don't look so disapproving, Hilary. You should see yourself. It all adds to the gaiety of life, don't you think?'

Hilary turned to her with surprise. 'I should have thought you would be the one to resent having the peace disturbed by a self-important clown like him.'

'He's harmless. And certainly colourful. I think there has to be room for eccentrics. And if he's had a book published, he can't be completely mad.'

'Hmm. Nowadays any idiot with a word processor and a few spare quid can get themselves into print.'

The exit was, predictably, through the gift shop. Hilary looked around the narrow space at the crystal pendants, the Vesica

Piscis-themed jewellery, the gift cards with images of the Chalice
Well and its gardens, bottles of Chalice Well essence. Some of
it, she admitted grudgingly, was decent enough.

Veronica went straight to the bookshelves. The titles, as Hilary
had expected, covered a wide range of tastes and beliefs. *From
Arimathea to Avalon*; *The Moon and the Mother*; *Sacred Wells
of the British Isles*; *The Buddhist Way of Meditation.*

'Here it is,' Veronica cried. 'He wasn't joking.' She pulled off
a high shelf a rather larger and glossier hardback than Hilary
had imagined. The cover showed an ethereal woman in a flimsy
gown dancing beneath a full moon.

'Pagan rubbish!' said an unexpectedly deep voice beside her.
'Look at it! This place is full of it. Blasphemy!'

Hilary was startled to find a large red-faced man in tweeds
uncomfortably close to her as he peered forward at the book in
Veronica's hands. He waved at the rest of the merchandise with
a hand dangerously close to Hilary's nose.

'George!' said a small, square-faced woman behind him. 'Keep
your voice down.'

'It's a free country and I'll say what I like. It's *my* country. A
Christian land, or it used to be. I'll not have it fouled by all this
fancy foreign rubbish. Moon worship! Healing crystals! Eastern
mumbo-jumbo.'

His voice reverberated through the shop. People stopped to
listen. Hilary wished she could get Veronica away from him and
Rupert Honeydew's book.

Veronica was doing her best to argue. 'But the gardens here
are lovely. And the Chalice Well. Does it really matter if some
of the people who find peace here believe different things
from us?'

'Does it matter! Do you want them to go to hell? Glastonbury
used to be a Christian place, when I was a young man. The
streets weren't filled with all this nonsense. Now, I'd like to put
a bomb under the lot of it.'

'George.' His wife was tugging at his sleeve. 'You're making
a scene.'

A nervous-looking shop assistant was making her way towards
them. She flinched as George's fist collided with a glass-fronted
case of perfume bottles.

Hilary took the book from Veronica's hands and replaced it firmly on the shelf. She steered her friend away from the confrontation.

Out of the corner of her eye, a flicker of blue snagged her attention. The woman in the burka was watching from the card rack at the back of the shop.

The shop assistant was arguing with the man in the tweed jacket, trying to persuade him to leave quietly.

'I'll say what I like,' he roared at her. 'I'm an Englishman and a Christian. I've more right to my say than these pagan foreigners.'

His voice faded as Hilary tugged Veronica outside.

'Well!' she exploded. 'You thought *I* was sceptical, but it's really got under his skin. Why come here, if he feels that strongly?'

'I suppose he thinks that, underneath all the esoteric stuff, the Chalice Well is what it's always been. A sacred place in the Christian story of this country. I remember when these gardens weren't open. The spring flowed out to the street through a hole in the wall. But there was always something special about it.'

'Well, so much for peace and meditation. And I was beginning to get a fondness for the place.'

'Hilary.' Veronica's voice sounded tentative, but pleading. 'Would you mind very much? I did feel peace when I was kneeling at the Chalice Well. Now it feels – I don't know – shattered, dirtied somehow. Would it be too much trouble if I went back there for a few moments? Just to regain what I found? I won't be long, I promise.'

Hilary caught back the sceptical comment she had been about to make. It was only six months since Andrew had died. She tried to imagine the emptiness she would feel if she lost David.

'Of course.' Her voice softened. 'Take your time. We're not in a hurry to go anywhere else.'

She followed Veronica as the smaller woman made her way more rapidly this time up the sloping paths to the wellhead. She stood back to allow Veronica the privacy of communion with whatever she had found beside the pool. Steps led up to a seat within an arbour. She climbed them and sat down. Her eyes roamed over the gardens beyond. There was no one else in sight.

It was only when she allowed her gaze to drop again to the circular enclosure around the well that she saw it. From here, she was behind the well cover, which was thrown back to display its decoration. It was propped against a tall stone shaft.

Between the lid and this pillar was something that she had not seen before. A canvas strap with a buckle. She moved down a few steps to see further. It was attached to a small black knapsack, which had been pushed out of sight into the shadows. She stared at it idly for a moment before a lump rose in her throat, threatening to choke her.

'Veronica! Get back! Now!'

THREE

Veronica looked round, her small face startled. When she saw the urgency with which Hilary was rushing towards her, she scrambled to her feet. Hilary grabbed her arm and hauled her away.

'No, I'm not mad. You didn't see it. Someone's left a knapsack hidden behind the lid of the well.'

Veronica looked over her shoulder as Hilary dragged her further down the path.

'It's probably some kid who put it down and forgot it.'

'It's very neatly tucked away out of sight. I was looking at the scene around you for some time before I noticed a bit of the strap poking out.'

Veronica stopped and shook off the hand Hilary had clamped on her arm. 'You don't seriously think someone would plant a terrorist bomb at the Chalice Well? Why?'

'How do I know? Why would anyone destroy the Glastonbury Thorn? The world's full of nutters. Or people with a grudge against society. There was that loud-mouthed type in the shop. Didn't he say he'd like to put a bomb under the lot?'

'It was just a way of talking. If he really was a bomber, he'd hardly be likely to advertise the fact to everyone within hailing distance.'

'Could be a double bluff?'

Hilary had her phone out.

'What are you doing?'

'Calling nine-nine-nine.' She made the call and at the opera-tor's prompt said curtly, 'Police.'

A group of Japanese tourists was approaching along the path. Hilary covered the phone with her hand and snapped, 'Stop them.'

Against the background of Veronica's gentle remonstrations with the group leader, she explained briefly to the police her discovery of the abandoned knapsack behind the lid of the Chalice Well. The response from the other end was non-committal about the chances of it containing a bomb, but she was relieved that they were taking her seriously enough to send officers in response.

'How far do you think the blast from one of those would reach?' she muttered. The tour group was chattering with excite-ment and questions. Should she urge them further back?

It seemed a blessedly short time before she heard the whine of a police siren in the distance. It stopped out of sight at the entrance. In the silence that followed the Japanese leader began to herd his group away along the path by which they had come. He seemed to be communicating the news to others they met. Hilary and Veronica were left alone, a prudent distance from the wellhead but still within sight.

At last Hilary saw what she had been hoping for. Coming up the now-deserted path between the flower beds were two police officers in fluorescent jackets.

'Which of you is Hilary Masters?' the taller one asked, looking from Veronica to Hilary.

'I am. I phoned you. There's a very suspicious-looking bag hidden behind the lid of the Chalice Well.'

'Clear the area,' the policeman said to his colleague. 'And seal the entrance. If there's anything in this, we'll want to question everyone we can about what they saw.'

'Will do, Sarge. But I expect the bomber will have legged it by now.'

'Someone may have seen him with a knapsack.'

'Or her.'

'Now, if you wouldn't mind,' the police sergeant said to the two women, 'we've got an explosives specialist on the way. If you'd just follow my colleague back to the entrance, and wait in the shop, we'll need statements from both of you.'

'Certainly,' Hilary said.

She cast a regretful look over her shoulder as the officer began to unroll police tape and cordon off the area. She would have liked to see how the explosives expert dealt with the suspect package.

As they retraced their steps down the path the heady excitement of her discovery was beginning to fade. What if she were wrong? What if Veronica's innocent explanation of a child carelessly leaving a bag behind were true? She felt hot with embarrassment at the thought of all those police officers racing to the scene, the tape saying DO NOT CROSS, the penning of potential witnesses in the gift shop. All because of her over-dramatic imagination.

'You know,' Veronica was saying, 'I hate to sound as though I'm jumping to some sort of racial stereotype, but there *was* that woman in the burka. I wondered at the time what she could be doing here. Christians and pagans, yes. Or maybe Buddhists. But it seemed out of place for a Muslim.'

'I know,' Hilary agreed. 'I'm trying not to think in clichés. Islamic terrorists carrying knapsacks on board the Tube and letting off explosions. But you can't help wondering. She didn't leave straight away, though. I saw her again in the shop. And we'd spent quite a long time sitting on that bench in the meadow before we went back to the exit.'

'You think she might have been waiting to see what happened?'

'Criminals often do wait to see the effects of their crime.'

'If it *is* a bomb, would it be on a timer, do you think? Or triggered remotely?'

'How would I know? It might have gone off while you were kneeling there. Almost within reach of it. It makes me sick to think about it.'

'Or that couple with the two little children. Unless it was timed to go off after closing time, when nobody was about.'

'You're too innocent for your own good, Veronica. People who let off bombs are not going to worry about casualties. Too often, that seems to be the intention.'

They walked the rest of the way to the entrance in silence.

There were more police at the gatehouse. Hilary had been dimly aware of the repeated sound of sirens as she discussed the grim possibilities with Veronica. They were directed into the gift shop.

It was crowded now. Anyone still on the premises had been corralled here.

'I'm not going to be the world's favourite person if this is all a hoax,' Hilary muttered.

'The shop assistant is looking distinctly nervous. With this crowd, anything could vanish off the shelves.'

'At least our friend in the tweed jacket isn't here. He's made good his escape.'

'I really don't think he's a suspect. Too obvious. And he wasn't carrying a knapsack.'

'He could have dumped it before we met him. We took our time coming back. Anyone could have been up to the wellhead in the meantime.'

'She's still here,' Veronica whispered.

The young woman in the burka – Hilary felt sure from that glimpse of her eyes that she *was* young – was pressed uncomfortably against a display of Vesica-shaped jewellery. She looked as if she was trying unsuccessfully to avoid contact with the press of bodies around her.

'Madness and mayhem!' sang a voice above the noise of many people. 'It's full moon tonight. Beware the werewolves.'

'Saints preserve us. Not *him* again. That's all we need.' She could only glimpse the feathered hat of Rupert Honeydew above the crowd, but his exuberant presence seemed to fill the crowded shop. 'For heaven's sake, I hope they get him out of here first.'

But the voice of authority that called from the door summoned the first witness to be interviewed. 'Is there a Hilary Masters here, please?'

CID had taken over the meeting room in the stone and timber gatehouse. Two plain-clothes officers sat behind the desk.

'Mrs Masters? Or is it Miss?' asked the older one.

'Mrs Have you found out yet whether it is a bomb?'

Disregarding her question, he held up his warrant card. 'Detective Sergeant Wills, and this is Detective Constable Fielding. Please sit down.'

Hilary felt a surprised resentment that the case – *her* case – was being dealt with by a sergeant, and not a more senior detective. But perhaps there was an inspector somewhere, leaving his juniors the unglamorous job of taking witness statements.

'Now, Mrs Masters, if you'd take us through the events of this afternoon. Try to remember as much as you can. You never know what may prove relevant.'

Hilary thought back to their walk out of town and their arrival at the gatehouse. 'We weren't really paying much attention to the other visitors, I'm afraid. Not at that stage. So many people carry knapsacks nowadays, it wouldn't have seemed out of the ordinary. I've got one myself. It wasn't until we got to the wellhead and . . .' She hesitated.

'Go on.'

With a feeling of reluctance, Hilary told them about the woman in the blue burka. She felt a stab of guilt. 'I hate to think I'm perpetuating a stereotype. "Islamic dress equals terrorist suspect." But I was surprised to see her there. The Chalice Well attracts a pretty eclectic clientele, but it's not really a Muslim thing. And to be honest, she could have been carrying anything under those robes. But you can ask her for yourself. She's in the shop.'

'Was it after she'd gone that you spotted the rucksack?'

'No. Well, not immediately.'

Hilary's evidence was interrupted by a uniformed officer who came and whispered something in the detective sergeant's ear. DS Wills in turn passed it on to his constable, *sotto voce*.

Then he turned to Hilary with a lift of his eyebrows. 'It seems the bag did contain explosives. Well done, Mrs Masters.'

She felt her face flush with gratification. So she hadn't been making a fool of herself, springing to melodramatic conclusions. People really had been in danger.

'Now, you were saying . . .'

'You asked if I noticed the knapsack after the woman in the burka left. I said no. What I meant was that it wasn't right away. We stopped at the well for a while, then took a roundabout way back. When we got to the gift shop there was a man blowing his top about all the pagan connotations of the place. New Age pendants, books on Goddess worship. He thought it should be a purely Christian sanctuary. He even said he'd like to put a bomb under it.'

'Did he, indeed?' The two detectives exchanged glances.

'My friend, Veronica Taylor, said she didn't think that was significant. If he really was the bomber, he would have kept quiet about it.'

'Do you know this man's name? Is he in the shop now?'

'His wife called him George. That's all I can tell you. A big man in a tweed jacket. With a loud voice. And no, he's not there now. He must have left before we found the bag.'

'So how *did* you find it, if you'd come back from the well?'

'My friend was rather upset. This character was arguing with her over a book she was looking at. It shattered the peace she'd found beside the well. She's been through a bad time recently. She lost her husband. She asked if I'd mind going back to the well. It was then that I noticed it. But only just. There was a strap poking out from behind the open lid of the well. The knapsack itself was almost out of sight.'

'Well spotted. Tell me, on your way back to the well, did you notice anyone coming away from there who might have been suspicious?'

'Lord, no. I mean, you don't really look at everyone you pass in a place like this, do you? Not unless they stand out from the crowd. Like Rupert Honeydew.'

'Who?'

'You'll know him when you see him. Feathers in his hat and a jester's shoes.'

'Oh, *him*. The one dressed like a clown.'

'That's the one.'

The detective sighed. 'We have the pleasure of interviewing him to come. It should be an interesting experience. Did you see him anywhere near the well?'

'He was coming towards it as we were leaving, the first time.'

'Was he, indeed?'

'And if you want to know whether he was carrying a knapsack on that occasion, the answer is no. Not that I remember. But with all those fantastic rags and tatters he's wearing, I might have been mistaken.'

'Thank you.'

The detective constable at his side laid down his pen.

Hilary felt an obscure disappointment. 'I can go?'

'Unless you can think of anything else that's relevant. I'll have this typed up for you to sign, then you're free to leave. And thank you for your vigilance. We don't know yet how it was set to go off, but you've certainly saved one of Glastonbury's chief attractions and possibly lives as well.'

'My friend was kneeling right beside it,' Hilary said quietly.

She got up to go. She should have been feeling elated. Her keen eyes had spotted a potentially lethal bomb and had averted a disaster. But considering all the visitors who had roamed the paths and visited the well that afternoon, how was it possible to identify the one who had planted the bomb?

When her statement was ready, she signed it.

Veronica was next.

The mood in the shop was growing restive. There were at least twenty people waiting to be interviewed and the space in the shop was narrow. A number of them had slipped outside, to take refuge on the seats by the Vesica Pool. Hilary wondered whether Wills and Fielding were the only detectives on the job. The harassed shop assistant and the man from the ticket office were doing their best to keep the visitors calm. Rupert Honeydew was attempting to entertain them by singing a folk song about a fox and a blackbird while dancing to his bells. No one seemed to be appreciating this. People were trying to back out of range.

Hilary took advantage of a pause as he drew breath at the end of yet another verse. Her voice rang out above the hubbub.

'If it's any consolation, this is not a hoax. There really was a bomb at the well.'

The room fell silent. A mother drew her two little girls closer to her. The blonde shop assistant sucked in a sharp breath. The Japanese tour leader began talking in a low and urgent voice to his group.

There was no need for Hilary to stay. She made her excuses to the uniformed police guarding the exit and stepped outside towards the road.

At once, she regretted her decision. She should have waited on the other side, where there were benches with vistas of water and flower beds. She stood forlornly in the car park, watching the traffic hurrying past. Not far away, the distinctive slopes of Glastonbury Tor rose above the treetops, topped by the tower which was all that remained of St Michael's Church. Churches on hilltops, she recalled, were usually dedicated to St Michael, the warrior archangel portrayed in stained-glass windows with his mailed foot on a dragon. Perhaps these hilltops had once been pagan shrines, and St Michael was celebrated as conquering what Christians saw as the dragon of the old religion.

She looked behind her again. A building she had not noticed on their way in announced itself as Little St Michael's Retreat House. The gentleman in the tweed jacket had been unduly dismissive of this place's Christian associations.

The Chalice Well advocated *Many Paths, One Source*. It invited Christians and other faiths, including pagans, to enjoy it side by side. Was the person who had planted the bomb Christian or pagan? Or neither? Might an Islamic terrorist destroy anything held dear by a Western imperialist culture? She sighed. She had found the bomb, but it seemed unlikely that she would find the answer.

FOUR

'Excuse me! Have you just come from the well? Is it true what they're saying? There's a bomb inside?'

Hilary found herself looking into the eager face of a young woman with long untidy hair falling to her shoulders.

'I was in town, and all these police cars came racing past. They've cordoned off the place and they won't let me in.'

A uniformed police officer stood impassively within hearing.

'It has to be a bomb, hasn't it? Unless it's a murder.' Her eyes widened on the word. She looked almost as though she might be hoping for an even more sensational reason.

'No one's dead, thank God,' Hilary said shortly.

'But you were there. Why have they let you out? Did you see anything?'

'I've just told everything I know to the police. I'm not sure that I need to undergo a second interrogation.'

'Look, give me a break. I'm a reporter.' She fished in her capacious bag and drew out a dog-eared business card. 'Joan Townsend, journalist. At least, I want to be.' The plump face grew wistful. 'I've got a first-class degree in media studies. Couldn't get a job on the local rag, though. The nationals in London don't want to know. TV, useless. But I keep sending them stories. One day I'm going to make it big. This could be my chance.'

'An unexploded bomb?' Hilary said sceptically. 'Yes, all right, there *is* a bomb. It might make an inside column, but it's hardly front-page headlines . . .'

She flinched away as Joan Townsend's camera flashed in her face.

'Did you have to do that? You nearly blinded me.'

As her sight cleared, she recognized the offending camera as one of professional quality.

'One good picture is worth a page of text.' The young woman was looking happier now as she dropped the camera on its strap and scribbled in her notebook. 'Your name is?'

'I don't see what that has got to do with you. I've made my statement to the police. That's enough for one day.'

'Please,' begged Joan. 'I need a story.'

'Thank goodness that's over. I hope I haven't kept you waiting.'

Hilary was relieved to hear Veronica's voice. Her friend was looking flushed and rather nervous.

'Honestly, I felt such a fool. All those people we passed in the gardens, and I couldn't describe more than half a dozen of them. And as to whether any of them was carrying a rucksack . . .'

Joan seized on this new information with delight. 'A rucksack, was it? It had the bomb inside it? Could you describe it?'

Hilary groaned inwardly as the wannabe reporter turned her enthusiasm on Veronica.

'It was more of a knapsack, really. Quite small. Plain black canvas. It was Hilary who spotted it. She's the hero of the day.

If it hadn't been for her, goodness knows who might have been blown up, besides the Chalice Well.'

'*You* found it?' The reporter turned her delighted face back to Hilary. The loose lank hair swung over her eyes. She pushed it back as she grabbed her camera again. 'I really have got to get a good picture of you. Perhaps the two of you. You were there when she found it?' she asked Veronica.

'Indeed I was. Kneeling on the stones beside the well, almost within touching distance of the bag. I hadn't noticed it, you see. It was hidden behind the lid of the well.'

'The one with the fancy design on it? The circles and the lance and the leaves of Glastonbury Thorn?'

'That's right. They turn it back, so that it makes a decorative background to the pool.'

'Names, please.'

'Veronica Taylor. And this is Hilary Masters. Don't look like that, Hilary. If you must go around discovering bombs, you must expect a bit of limelight. It'll be on the TV next.' She laughed.

'I sincerely hope not. I want to get away from here before we encounter any more of this sort.'

'Just let me file my story before anyone else gets in on the act.' Joan Townsend was still scribbling frantically.

'I know how you feel,' Veronica sympathized. 'My daughter Morag is doing English and Media Studies at uni. She'd love to be a reporter like you.'

'She might not if she knew how tough it is. A good degree gets you nowhere. It's either luck or who you know. I'm just hoping this could be my piece of luck. Of course it would have been more of a front-page story if the bomb had actually gone off.'

'And killed a few people, you mean?' Hilary snapped.

The reporter paled. 'I didn't mean that. Of course not. It's just that bad stuff makes news. It's what people want to read about. I don't make the news. I just report it.'

Veronica laid a soothing hand on her arm. 'Of course you didn't mean that. We all know how it is. No news is good news, isn't that what they say? Is there anything else I can tell you?'

Hilary sighed exaggeratedly. The shock of the day was

beginning to get to her. She would have welcomed a strong coffee, or something even more stimulating. She had been standing in the car park rather longer than she wanted to.

Other people were dribbling out of the gatehouse in ones and twos. There must indeed be other officers taking statements. The mother with the two little girls appeared. Both of them carried diminutive knapsacks, one pink, one purple. For a few dazed moments, Hilary imagined them stuffed with explosives. She shook herself. She had seen the actual bag that contained the bomb. Not very big, but black. She could not help a shudder. She and Veronica had been so close. What would it have taken to set it off?

She turned briskly. 'Veronica.'

But her companion was busy racking her memory for anything more she could tell the aspiring journalist. Hilary would have to wait for her coffee.

She looked up to see Rupert Honeydew prancing his way from the gatehouse.

'Cheer up, my lovelies! The Goddess triumphs over death. An unexploded bomb. The Chalice Well survives.' He made to grab Hilary's hand, but she snatched it away.

'And who are you?' Joan Townsend's camera flashed at the extraordinary sight: the colourful tattered clothes, the soot-smeared face, the feathered hat. 'Were you at the well, too? Did you see the bomb? How did people react?'

Hilary took a firm hold of Veronica's arm. 'That's quite enough of *that* for one day. Let's make our escape while we can. I'm sure Mr Honeydew will welcome the publicity more than I do.'

'She's only trying to get her career off the ground. In a couple of years Morag will be doing the same. It seemed only kind to help her. It's not every day you can tell an out-of-work journalist that you've seen an unexploded bomb at one of the sacred sites of England. My good deed for the day.'

'I'll remind you of that if I see my face plastered over the papers tomorrow morning.'

'Don't be so curmudgeonly. You're a heroine. You deserve it.'

'It's the last thing I want. I came here to take my mind off murder and mayhem. All the stuff David has to deal with in that hospital in Gaza.'

'I'm sorry.' Veronica squeezed her hand. 'I didn't think.'

We came here for you as well, Hilary thought. *And if it's taken your mind off losing Andrew, then maybe it's not all bad.*

'She gave me this.' As they turned on to the pavement outside, Veronica held up another of the slightly crumpled business cards with Joan Townsend's contact details. 'She said to get in touch with her if we remembered anything else. Or if we saw the Marsdens.'

'Who?'

'That man in the tweed jacket who was shouting his head off in the gift shop. He and his wife had gone before the police arrived. The shop assistant knew who he was. Apparently he's a bit of a local character. Joan thinks there might be a story there. Why some people feel so upset about the well, while others love it. She asked me to ring her if we see him again.'

'I sincerely hope we don't. Once was more than enough. You didn't tell her about the woman in the burka, I hope.'

'Well, I did just mention it.'

'Oh, no! I can imagine what sort of headlines that's going to make. ISLAMIC BOMB THREAT? *Woman in burka seen at sacred well.* That's all we need.'

'You're really sure she didn't do it?'

'I'm not sure of anything right now, except that I'm dying for a cup of strong black coffee, preferably laced with a tot of rum.'

On the way back to their hotel, Hilary found herself scanning everyone they passed on the pavement. Her eyes were seeking that distinctive, quasi-military figure of a large man in a tweed jacket, with a more diminutive wife at his side.

Veronica gave her a sidelong glance and laughed affectionately. 'Relax, Hilary. You've done more than enough for today. It's not your job to hunt down missing witnesses. You've described the Marsdens to the police, and I was even able to give them a name, thanks to that assistant in the gift shop. I honestly don't think they're suspects, anyway, just *because* he talked about planting a bomb, but I'm sure the police will find him and check up on him, just in case. Just let them get on with it. You're on holiday.'

'I know. Sorry.'

She let the matter drop and tried to get back into the frame of mind that had brought them both to Glastonbury. It was steeped in Christian legends, going all the way back to Joseph of Arimathea and the Holy Grail. Yet as she walked its pavements, she could not help visualizing its busy streets and shops, its ancient abbey, the tower-crowned Tor, smashed and defaced by a terrorist bomb.

'You're right,' she said gruffly. 'I suppose I keep thinking of David in Gaza. A strip of land packed with refugees and looking like a gigantic bomb site. And still they keep lobbing their home-made rockets over the border, into the land their families fled from, and provoking retaliation all over again. I wish I could just get hold of both sides and tell them there has to be a better way to find peace.'

'Is that why you want to get hold of this bomber, even though it's nothing to do with the Middle East?'

'We don't know that it isn't. Until they arrest whoever planted the bomb, the police will have no idea of the motive. I certainly haven't.'

'I hate to think that it might have gone off. I know the Chalice Well is just a natural spring of water. It would have gone on flowing, and I'm sure it wouldn't have taken much to restore the setting. But it's a holy well. It's been a sacred site for centuries. I would have felt . . . violated.'

'What sickens me is that it might not have been just the well. You were kneeling almost within arm's reach of it. And there was that woman with the two little girls. Or that whole group of Japanese tourists. If the bomb had gone off then . . .'

'I'm beginning to see why you're so keen to put your finger on the bomber. We don't know whether he meant to kill people as well as damage the well. It makes me shiver to think of it.'

'It's ironic, isn't it? The streets of Glastonbury are full of people flaunting fifty different ways of finding peace. The Chalice Well itself was designated a World Peace Garden. And somewhere in the midst of all this is a bomber who may have set out to kill.'

'You've thwarted him once,' Veronica said softly. 'Do you think he'll try again?'

FIVE

Hilary was enjoying a full English breakfast, an indulgence which she only allowed herself on Sundays at home. Today was Tuesday, but since it was included in her hotel bill it seemed a shame not to take advantage.

She was just pouring herself a second cup of coffee when Veronica chortled. 'She really did make the nationals. It's here!'

She passed over the tabloid newspaper which had been laid on their breakfast table as a freebie. She had refolded it so that page five was uppermost. Hilary's coffee sloshed into her saucer as she saw the headline: *BOMB AT BRITAIN'S MOST SACRED SITE.*

'Hmm! I'm not sure the Chalice Well is *that* important.'

But her heart was sinking as she read on.

Sharp-eyed holidaymaker Hilary Masters, 61, spotted the bomb in a bag left unattended by the well.

'You told her my age!'

'Come on, Hilary. Only yesterday you said you were enjoying the Crone stage.'

There were two photographs. The larger was of the Chalice Well, displaying the ornamental cover as they had seen it yesterday afternoon. The smaller one showed Hilary looking belligerent, with a smiling Veronica at her side.

Hilary rescued her friend Veronica Taylor, 56, from a possible violent death.

She felt her stomach churn, threatening the breakfast she had just enjoyed. She had a sudden urge to get her hands on Joan Townsend's throat and throttle her.

'It was never my ambition to get my mug-shot in that rag. She might at least have sold it to the *Guardian* or the *Times*.'

'Still, you have to be glad for her, don't you? She's been trying to break into journalism big time. It's not the front page, but they've given her a decent spread.'

Hilary was trying to disguise the curiosity which made her

read on. It was not the sort of newspaper which gave in-depth coverage, but there was enough to show that the police had confirmed the finding of an unexploded bomb. She was disappointed that there were no further details about whether it was set to go off at a certain time or whether it was remotely controlled. Would the police tell her if she asked them?

She scanned the last paragraphs. Her heart sank further. There was, as she had feared there would be, a subheading: *MYSTERY ISLAMIST SEEN.*

Below was an account of the woman in the burka. Had Joan Townsend seen her for herself? Or was it just Veronica's incautious reference to meeting the young woman at the well?

There was no mention of George Marsden threatening to bomb the well. Did that mean that Joan had dismissed him as being less interesting, or had a sub-editor chopped off her story before the end?

She threw down the folded paper.

'What really frustrates me is that I have no way of knowing who the police have got as their prime suspect – assuming they haven't already made an arrest.'

Veronica's eyes twinkled at her across the table. She seemed to be enjoying her friend's discomfiture. 'How do we know *we're* not the suspects? After all, we're the only people the police saw at the well.'

'That's ridiculous. I was the one who phoned them.'

'Well, you know what you said about George Marsden shouting that he'd like to bomb the place? A double bluff? They might think we were trying to put ourselves above suspicion.'

Hilary sighed. 'Veronica. My calling the police meant that the bomb didn't go off. Would the police really think I was that stupid?'

'No.' Veronica fiddled with her teaspoon. 'I suppose not. But we still have no idea what *was* meant to happen. Or why.'

Rain spattered the pavements. Veronica stood on the steps of the hotel and frowned up at the lowering sky.

'I was going to suggest a morning at the abbey, but the forecast is for sun this afternoon. Should we switch plans?'

'As long as you're not going to suggest climbing the Tor in

the rain instead. I wouldn't mind a trawl around the bookshops. You have to wade through piles of New Age nonsense, but there's likely to be some solid historical stuff hidden away among all the rot. It's so long since I was last here, I'm out of date with the latest historical and archaeological research on just what Glastonbury was.'

'Do you think it really did have a connection with King Arthur? The real one in the fifth century, I mean, not the Hollywood version of knights in medieval shining armour.'

'If there *was* a real one. Plenty of people doubt it. Personally, I think there has to be a nugget of truth for the legends to latch on to. Like the grit in the oyster shell which is at the heart of every pearl. Still, it's the Christian history which interests me more. Whether the abbey church really does date back to Roman times, and whether a Celtic saint like Brigid might actually have come here.'

'Well then, that's settled. I might do some shopping myself. Holidays are a good time to pick up birthday and Christmas presents for people, don't you think? More time to drift around looking at lovely things, and less pressure.'

'If what you want is a healing crystal, you should be OK. I just hope not too many people here have seen that picture in the paper.'

'Hilary, don't be so conceited. It was just a small photograph on page five.'

'Hmm. We'll see.'

They walked along the main street of Glastonbury. Hilary's eyes went to the newsagents' stands. The billboards announced what she knew they must, but dreaded to see:

GLASTONBURY BOMB

It seemed to be only that one newspaper, so far. Joan Townsend really had got her scoop.

As they walked past, she surveyed the shops selling incense and sacred gemstones, the notices announcing séances and healing sessions, the rune stones and witches' balls.

She chuckled. 'You know what they say about Glastonbury: it's a great place for shopping if you want a pack of tarot cards, but if you need a pint of milk, you have to go to Bristol.'

'It's always like that. People falling over themselves to make money out of sacred places. It's the same at Lourdes, with shop after shop of religious tat; or Tintagel, where every other commercial outlet is named after Merlin. But you need to get beyond that – the real sanctuary at Lourdes, or the real castle at Tintagel. Once you leave the commercial bit behind, it's all still there.'

'Well, let's hope the abbey lives up to my memories of it this afternoon.'

They turned into the largest of the bookshops. Hilary made for the section on the early history of Glastonbury.

Veronica tugged at her sleeve. 'He's here again,' she said in a low voice. 'Rupert Honeydew.'

Hilary looked up in dismay, but Veronica was pointing to a book on a shelf they were passing. 'His book. *Dancing with the Divine.*'

'Hmm! I've seen enough of that already. You were looking at that when George Marsden accosted you. It seemed to set him off.'

Veronica looked slowly round at the other customers. 'I wonder if he lives here. That Marsden man, I mean. He must do, mustn't he, if they know him at the Chalice Well shop?'

'Well, he's not around this morning. He must have a home life. He's probably tending his roses. I'm assuming he's retired.'

Veronica touched the book again. 'I'm surprised Joan didn't put him into her article. Rupert Honeydew. He's such a colourful character, he'd make brilliant copy. And we were there when she took his photo.'

'She probably did write about him,' said Hilary. 'They'll have decided how many column inches to give her and chopped off anything that didn't fit. That left just us and that poor woman in the burka.'

Veronica turned from the bookshelves to give her a quizzical stare. 'You've changed your tune. When we first saw her, you were worried because you didn't want to stereotype her just because she was a Muslim in conservative dress, but you *did* suspect her.'

'Yes, well. We've met a few other possibilities since then.'

For a while, she busied herself among the books she had come to see. Veronica trawled the greetings cards and calendars and made some small purchases. They met at the cash desk.

'You know,' Hilary said as they stepped outside, 'the rain's blowing over. There isn't time to do the abbey before lunch, but I wouldn't mind a walk back to the Chalice Well. There are a few questions I'd like to ask that shop assistant. The one who told you about the Marsdens.'

'Hilary!' Veronica exploded, 'I keep telling you. Just because you found the bomb, it doesn't mean you have to find the bomber. You'll have half the police in Somerset following up the forensic evidence and the people they interviewed. There's nothing we can do.'

'Humour me. You talked to the shop assistant. I didn't.'

They retraced their steps from the day before, out towards the Tor. Cars swished past on the wet road. But by the time they reached the Chalice Well, the sun was breaking through.

Hilary stiffened. The entrance had changed. TV vans were parked outside: Sky, BBC. There was still a solitary police officer on duty, but the gatehouse was no longer cordoned off. Hilary marched up to it.

'We don't want an entrance ticket. We were here yesterday. We'd just like another look at the gift shop.'

'Did you get caught up in the bomb incident?' the ticket seller asked. 'That was a real picnic! They herded us up like cattle. I didn't get home until eight. As if I had time to go sneaking round the gardens planting bombs. Did you . . .?' He leaned closer, his eyes sparkling. 'My gosh! It's you, isn't it? You're the one in the paper. You found it!' He was holding out the same newspaper they had seen at breakfast.

Hilary backed away. 'I was only doing what anyone else would have done. I'm glad the police got there in time. So, it's OK if we just pay another visit to the gift shop? Things weren't exactly normal yesterday.'

'Of course, of course. Anything we can do to help you.'

'There, you see,' Veronica whispered as they walked away. 'You're famous.'

'I'd rather not be.'

There were two women behind the counter in the gift shop this morning. Veronica nudged Hilary and said softly, 'The older one wasn't here yesterday. But that's the young one I talked to.'

The assistant was a slender young woman in her twenties with a cap of smartly coiffed blonde hair. She stood examining her frosted fingernails as they approached.

'Excuse me,' Hilary said. 'You were here yesterday afternoon, weren't you?'

The young woman's eyes shot up to meet hers, startled. They were a surprising light green. Hilary wondered if they were natural, or tinted contact lenses. There was something about the assistant which resembled a glamorous doll.

'If you wouldn't mind . . .' Hilary made a sudden decision. 'I'm Hilary Masters. I was the one who found the bomb at the wellhead. I know the police will have asked you all sorts of questions, but, well, as you can imagine, I'm rather keen to find out a bit more myself.'

The woman's eyes went to her colleague, who stood nearby listening avidly.

'Go on, Mel,' the older woman said. 'She saved the Chalice Well, didn't she? The least you can do is tell her what she wants to know.'

'Thank you. Is there anywhere we can talk?'

'I can't leave the shop, can I?' The blonde young woman looked unhappy. 'And Beth's due for her lunch break.'

'I can wait,' said her colleague. 'I'll mind the till while you talk.'

From the look in her eyes, Hilary thought, she probably wants to listen in.

The shop was quieter than yesterday. There had been clusters of people watching curiously at the gatehouse, but it seemed the sensation of the day before had kept more people away from the gardens than it had attracted. The place had a subdued feel, as if still waiting for something to happen.

'I don't know what there is to say.'

The younger woman, whom her colleague had called Mel, interested Hilary. She sensed a reluctance to talk which surprised her. She would have expected the sales assistant to be falling over herself to talk about the dramatic happenings of day before. It was not every day one got caught up in a plot to blow up one of the major tourist attractions in a place like this. Yet Mel did not seem to want her fifteen minutes of fame.

But then, Hilary reminded herself, *neither did I.*

'Well then,' she took a deep breath, 'what can you tell me about George Marsden?'

SIX

Mel shot an appealing look past Hilary at Veronica. The assistant was a small-boned girlish figure who reminded Hilary of a shrew cornered by a cat and desperately seeking a means of escape. Hilary sensed something frightened in those light green eyes.

It seemed strange. From what Hilary remembered, the assistant had merely been passing on the news to Veronica that George Marsden was known at the Chalice Well, and that this was not the first time he had made a nuisance of himself by sounding off his views against the eclectic nature of the place.

So why does he keep coming? Hilary wondered.

And why does this young woman look as though she is afraid she has said too much?

The brightly painted pink lips twitched nervously. There was a sullen tone in the girl's voice as she replied.

'I can't really tell you that much. Only that he comes in here now and then with his wife. She never says much. Only "George!" or "Keep your voice down."' Her own voice rose. 'But he won't, will he? It's like there's something here that really gets under his skin. He's always banging on about it being a Christian place, only there are all these hippies and pagans and Buddhists, like, taking it over. He'd like to turn the lot of them out. Well, you can't, can you? I mean, live and let live. This is my job. The more of them that come, the better it is for me.'

'Does he live locally?' Hilary tried to steer Mel back to the Marsdens.

She shrugged. 'I suppose he must do. He comes in several times a year. It's not like he was from Liverpool or London, is it?'

'I've seen him a few times in the town,' the older assistant put in. 'There was a meeting about what to do about flooding in the Somerset Levels. He was shooting off his mouth about that too. He has some idea that the Bristol Channel used to come all the way up to Glastonbury and we ought to let it come back, not go on fighting nature. Well, you can guess how popular *that* makes him. There's people near here have had their homes underwater.'

'So I'm guessing he lives above the flood level.' Veronica laughed. 'In Glastonbury itself?'

'Search me. You could try the phone book.'

'Not everyone's in it,' Mel objected. 'Not if they've just got a mobile.'

'George Marsden didn't strike me as the sort who was into smartphones,' Hilary snorted. 'I'm not sure he isn't back in the era of messages in cleft sticks.'

'I did look him up,' Veronica said quietly. 'There's a telephone directory in the hotel. He's not there.'

Hilary paused. 'Hmm. Could have registered himself as ex-directory. Maybe he was getting too many calls from angry people he'd upset.'

'You don't really think he'd plant a bomb at the Chalice Well, though, do you?' Mel asked, wide-eyed. 'I mean, you don't like to think about it. I didn't like him very much, but when it's someone you know . . .'

'The police must have questioned you yesterday. Did you tell them about him? That he was here, and not too pleased about the Chalice Well?'

She shifted uncomfortably. 'I might have.'

'Well, I certainly did,' the older one joined in. 'Gave them as much as I could remember about everyone who came through the shop. Including you, I'm afraid.' She laughed at Hilary and Veronica.

'Fair enough. They knew about us, anyway. But the Marsdens had left before the police arrived.'

'And there was that idiot Rupert Honeybee,' Beth added.

'Honeydew.'

'Whatever. Prancing about like a clown at the circus, drawing attention to himself. We get all sorts in here, but really! Says the Goddess inspires him and he has to drink the water and dance for her. Poncey twit.'

'Is he another regular?'

The younger assistant stood examining her fingernails, but Beth responded vigorously.

'I'll say. He's what they call a Companion of the Well, so he can come here any time. Says he "needs to drink from the sacred waters to keep his spirit in tune with the divine".' Her voice took on a mocking tone, as if she was mimicking him.

'So you wouldn't expect *him* to blow up the well.'

The older assistant looked shocked. 'It never entered my mind!'

Mel had taken advantage of her colleague's intervention to slip away. A visitor was approaching with a sheaf of cards in her hand. Mel took them from her. Hilary watched her go, thinking that she looked glad of an excuse to escape. It seemed odd. She had painted her face and nails and done her hair to draw admiring attention to herself, yet now that she had the chance to be in the spotlight as a key witness, she seemed to be shrinking from it. Hilary had come here to find out more about George Marsden, but now it was the witness herself who interested her.

'What's her name?' she nodded towards the till. 'Mel what?'

'Fenwick. Why do you ask?'

'Oh, just want to get my notes in order.'

'I'm Beth Harkness, by the way.'

'Pleased to meet you, Beth. Has Mel been here long?'

'Ever since she left school, by all accounts. She's local. A real local, I mean, not like me. I'm just an incomer, but Mel's family have been in Glastonbury, or on the Levels, since the year dot. Her grandfather's got a farm somewhere near here.'

'And the Marsdens?'

'Couldn't tell you for sure. It was about six years ago when I first came across him. They were opening up a new shop in the High Street. Well, I say new, but it was only the sort of stuff you see everywhere. Witch balls, tarot cards. You know the sort of thing. He was standing outside holding up a placard saying it was the devil's work. And then he turned up at the well here, saying much the same things. Well, not exactly. He thinks it's been a sacred place since the time of Jesus. And everybody else should clear out and leave it for the Christians.'

'Which brings us back to where we started. If he feels that strongly about it, would he blow up the well itself? It might have made more sense to plant the bomb here at the shop. Strike at the commercialization of it.'

'God! I hope not!'

'Sorry. I didn't mean to scare you. But you get my point.'

Out of the corner of her eye, she was aware that Mel too had started at the suggestion. The fine-boned face behind the make-up looked pale.

Does she know something that she's hiding, Hilary wondered, or suspect it?

'Hilary, look!'

Hilary had been aware for some time that Veronica had been fidgeting at her elbow, wanting to say something, but she had resolutely pursued her questioning. Now she had gathered all she could, though she had an uneasy sense that, in one respect at least, the mystery was deepening. She turned at last to meet her friend's eager face.

'It's her. Joan. She's got herself on TV too.'

Hilary peered through the open doors that led to the gardens. One of the TV crews had set up its camera to show a background of the Vesica Pool, with the tumbling waterfall and a bank of spring flowers behind it. Posed in front of it was the female interviewer with a microphone, talking to the would-be journalist Joan Townsend.

'She looks happier this morning, doesn't she?'

'Which is more than can be said for me. It was not my intention to get my face plastered all over the gutter press.'

'It was only page five, Hilary. And quite a small photo.'

'Big enough.'

She waited until the interview was over. Joan Townsend seemed reluctant to leave the TV crew, but they folded up their equipment and moved off.

Hilary took a deep breath. Then she strode past a couple entering the shop, out into the gardens.

For a moment, Joan Townsend looked puzzled as Hilary marched towards her. Then enlightenment took over her sallow face.

'It's you! Did you see it? I made it into one of the biggies. Exclusive! I can't thank you enough.'

'That's what I wanted to see you about, young lady. Did you have to drag me into it? *Hilary Masters, sixty-one.*'

But Joan's attention had already slipped from her. She was looking over her shoulder at the departing camera crew. She broke into a run after them.

'What the . . .?'

'I think you've just made a really bad mistake,' said Veronica, behind her, with quiet enjoyment.

Before Hilary understood what she meant, the TV crew had turned and were hurrying back in Joan's wake.

'Oh, no!'

Hilary tried to push her way past Veronica and back into the gift shop, but her friend cornered her.

'Just a few minutes. Look, Joan's in her element. A column in the tabloids, and now she's fixed a story for the BBC. Give her a break.'

Hilary found a fluffy-headed microphone confronting her. The cameraman was crouching, to get a good angle on her in front of a bed of bright pink valerian, beside the water tumbling into the pool. Joan Townsend was sparkling with achievement.

Oh well, Hilary thought. In for a penny, in for a pound. She managed a strained smile for the camera.

The interviewer turned to face the camera too. 'Yesterday, one of Glastonbury's most precious sites was threatened by a terrorist bomb. Thankfully, it did not go off. For that we have to thank the keen eyes and quick thinking of visitor Hilary Masters.'

She swung round to face Hilary. The microphone was thrust towards her. 'Now, Hilary, tell us. What brought you to Glastonbury and the Chalice Well yesterday?'

Hilary stared at the microphone in disbelief. How could she tell the entire nation that she was worried sick about David working in Gaza, that Veronica had lost her much-loved husband, that it had seemed a good idea to take their minds off this by revisiting the holy places of Glastonbury?

'The same as most people,' she shortly.

'And that would be?'

'Ancient sacred history, of course. And I'd never got around to seeing the Chalice Well.'

A young man spoke over the presenter's shoulder. 'Hey, Gillian,

I've got a better idea. Why don't we all move on to the well and
do a retake there?'

'Last time I saw it, it was cordoned off with police tape,'
Hilary objected. 'It probably still is.'

'All the better. Adds to the drama.'

With a furious look at Veronica, Hilary found herself being
shepherded up the path she had taken yesterday.

She had been right about the police tape. They were halted
some distance from the wellhead. There was no police activity
at the Chalice Well now, but another lone policeman stood
guard.

'Sorry,' he said. 'No entry.'

Hilary looked past him. She could make out the lid of the
well, open as it had been yesterday. It was an eerie thought that
it might have been mangled wreckage today. Its very normality
seemed unreal.

The producer's face fell. He said to his cameraman, 'Get a
long lens on the wellhead, will you? And get that police tape in
shot. We'll have to take the interview from here.'

Gillian, the presenter, began again. 'Now, Hilary, tell us what
brought you to the Chalice Well . . .'

SEVEN

'Serves you right,' Veronica said over a salad lunch. 'You
didn't buy a ticket to go into the grounds. You should have
stayed in the shop. If you'd just let Joan enjoy her moment
in the sun, it wouldn't have happened.'

'There's no need to rub it in. I could kick myself. My friends
won't have read that rag this morning, but they will watch the
BBC news.'

'Hilary, dear. It's not a crime to stop someone blowing up the
Chalice Well. You don't have to be ashamed of it.'

'Hmm!'

'Look what they did to the Glastonbury Thorn. That was
terrible. It could have been the same at the well.' She paused, as

a thought struck her. 'You don't think it was the same person, do you?'

'How should I know? The Thorn was four years ago. If it was the same maniac, they've been sitting on their hands for quite some time. Well, apart from coming back to cut off all the new shoots. All the same, there's a big difference between a chainsaw and a homemade bomb.'

'You can find out all sorts of things on the internet nowadays. Including bomb-making. And a chainsaw wouldn't have been much use at the well. They could have attacked that rather nice cover, but not the spring itself.'

'I'm not sure even a bomb could do that. The spring comes from deep underground. The water would still have had to flow out somewhere.'

'It's more symbolic, isn't it? Shattering something that is precious to people.'

'I hate to think that religion is at the bottom of it. Somebody on one side or the other, Christian or pagan, who wanted to deny it to the opposition.'

'There are always fanatics. It's not the way most religious people think.'

'Or somebody with a grudge against Britain in general. Going for the things in our heritage that mean a lot to all of us.'

'If it *is* the same person, then it looks like someone local to Glastonbury.'

'Or, on the other hand, the two may have nothing to do with each other. Or perhaps the bomber got the idea from the Thorn vandal.'

'Very true.' Veronica laid down her knife and fork. 'You said you wanted to go to the abbey after lunch. Are you still up for it?'

'Why not? Of all the sacred places in Glastonbury, the abbey is at the heart of it.'

Sunshine lit the level grass around the abbey ruins. Tall shafts of columns soared into the summer sky, where once the transept had divided the nave of the great church from the magnificent choir. Hilary felt dizzy looking up at it.

She lowered her eyes. Far down the length of the demolished nave she could see the more complete remains of the Galilee porch and the Lady Chapel beyond. Stones set in the grass outside marked where the cloisters had once offered shady walks to the monks.

Veronica was dutifully following the guidebook, moving from site to site. Hilary stood in the sunshine letting the ripples of remembered history wash over her. The book she had bought this morning told her that there had been a wattle-and-daub church here, dating back, supposedly, to the second century, in the time of the Romans. She found the subsequent unbroken line of Christianity here in the south-west staggering. St Bridget of Ireland was said to have come here. By the time the Saxons reached Glastonbury, they too had been converted to Christianity. The Anglo-Saxon king Ine had built a stone church here, at the western end of this nave. The great abbot Dunstan, in the tenth century, had built one of the earliest cloistered monasteries in England. A shiver ran down her spine as she thought of all the centuries of veneration before the Normans had raised their soaring abbey church.

She was startled out of her reverie by a procession of miniature monks in black Benedictine habits, hands folded in prayer. Some walked in careful solemnity. Others had eyes dancing with mischief under their hoods.

Hilary gave the thumbs-up sign as a passing boy threw her a grin.

She watched Veronica come back and stop near the front of the grassy nave, not far from her. Hilary knew what the notice said. She raised her voice.

'Tomb of King Arthur and Queen Guinevere, supposedly. Their bones were found in the cemetery outside in 1190. Moved into a magnificent tomb in the nave by Edward the First in 1278. If the Welsh are giving you aggro, it's a good idea for the king to flaunt his Celtic credentials.'

Veronica paused and looked up. 'Terribly romantic, though, don't you think? Finding a deep grave in the cemetery with a hollowed-out log for a coffin and the bones of a gigantic man inside, with those of a lovely lady.'

'I don't know how you can tell she was beautiful from the bones.'

'And a lead cross saying *Here lies Arthur, the famous king, in the island of Avalon.*'

'If you can believe it. Mind you, they say the lettering on the cross is older than the twelfth century when it was found. It would have taken a very cunning monk to mock that up in those days. Still, there's no getting away from it – genuine or not, the find was huge for the pilgrimage business. And they'd just had an appalling fire.'

'Don't be such a cynic.'

'I'm not. In my opinion, they really did find something significant. Shall we take a look?'

They walked together down the length of the nave, towards the site of the ancient cemetery outside the Lady Chapel.

They were almost there when a flash of blue caught Hilary's eyes through the stone arches of the Galilee porch. Someone else was there in the space between the Lady Chapel and the great nave. Hardly surprising on a fine summer afternoon. Hilary took a few steps forward and halted, frozen in something like shock.

She could not be certain it was the same woman, but it was the same height, the same small build, as far as she could tell, shrouded in that burka, the same shade of deep sky blue.

'It's her, isn't it?' Veronica whispered.

Hilary shook herself. How ridiculous to be startled by seeing the woman again here at the abbey. If she was in Glastonbury, and interested enough in sacred sites to be making notes at the Chalice Well, why shouldn't she be here too? In fact, what could be more likely? She scolded herself for the base instinct which had made her stop dead as if she had seen something sinister.

'You don't think she's going to plant a bomb here too?' Veronica hissed.

'Veronica!'

'Sorry. But it brought it all back so vividly. Yesterday. Seeing her at the well. And then . . . Sorry,' she said again. 'I think it's upset me more than I realized.'

Hilary laid a hand briefly on her arm. 'I know what you mean. Half the time it seems unreal, what happened. It's all a whirl of police questioning, journalists, cameras. You think, *this can't be happening to me*. And then you remember. That horrible moment when I saw it behind the lid of the well. Then I know that it *was* real. Potentially deadly. And it happened to us.'

She brushed her face, as though swatting away the too-vivid

memory. She took a determined step forward, on to the stone paving of the Galilee.

'Hello,' she said, with forced brightness. 'I see we meet again.'

The woman turned. Hilary had forgotten about the unexpectedly blue eyes. They were surprised and curious. Then they narrowed.

'Yes, I was at the Chalice Well yesterday. Is that what you're getting at? The mystery bomber strikes again.' The Birmingham accent came across strongly.

'Well, no! We did see you there. But it's not a crime to go sightseeing in Glastonbury.'

'Isn't it? You wouldn't think so if you choose to dress like I do. I could see what everyone was thinking when we were banged up in that gift shop, waiting for the police to interview us. "Ooh, look. She's a Muslim. Must be the bomber." Never mind the police themselves. I bet they didn't take you apart the way they did me.'

'Well, no, actually. I spotted the bomb. That hardly makes me the prime suspect. Still, I take your point. Middle-class white Anglo-Saxon woman, turned sixty.'

'And Christian. As it happens I'm white too.'

'A convert?'

'Yes, praise be to Allah.' She paused, then forged on. 'Is that why you came charging in here to speak to me? You want to know what I'm doing here? Have I got another bomb hidden under all this?' A small hand emerged and twitched at her burka. 'If you must know, I'm Amina Haddad. I changed my name when I converted, but I'm still myself. I'm doing an MA in the survival of folk tradition in the south-west. King Arthur, sacred wells, you name it. I grew up with the stories of King Arthur and the Round Table, see? Just like you did. Doesn't mean I have to leave all that behind me when I put on the burka.' The eyes flashed.

Hilary held up a hand. 'No. I understand that. I'm sorry. And truly, I didn't believe . . .' Honesty stopped her. 'Well, to tell the truth, we went over everyone we met at the Chalice Well yesterday afternoon, asking ourselves if one of them could have been the bomber. You were on the list, naturally. But no more than anyone else.'

'We tried to remember if anyone was carrying a black knapsack,' Veronica added. 'And of course . . .'

'You think I put this on to hide it? *I wear it all the time!*'

'Yes, I'm sorry. We realize. Honestly. And we can think of far more suspicious people there yesterday.'

'Like that Guizer.'

'I'm sorry?' Veronica asked.

'Guizer. Someone who dresses up in disguise and pretends to be something they're not. Unlike me, who's dressed like this to show what I *am*. You'll see a Guizer prancing round the edges of a Morris dance, all rags and black-faced. Or the Teazer on May Day at Padstow, cavorting in front of the Obby Oss.'

'Oh, you mean Rupert Honeydew,' Hilary broke in. 'You think *he's* our suspect?'

'He's not what he pretends to be, that's for sure.'

'How can you know that?'

'A Guizer never is. Trust me. I doubt the Avon and Somerset police know as much about Guizers as they need to.'

Hilary and Veronica looked at each other. It had not seriously occurred to Hilary that Rupert Honeydew, for all his eccentricity, might be a suspect.

'But what would he have to gain by blowing up the well?'

The slim shoulders under the burka shrugged. 'Search me. Plaster it across the media? The Chalice Well. I mean, how many people in Britain have heard of it? Perhaps he wants to make it into something really big – supposing all that stuff about the Goddess and the sacred waters isn't just a fake.'

'We rather fancied George Marsden ourselves,' Veronica said. 'Oh, maybe you didn't meet him. Rather military type. Loud voice. And sounding off at full volume about Christian sites being befouled by pagans.'

Amina shook her head. 'And Muslims, no doubt. I'm sorry. I missed that one.'

'He legged it before the police arrived,' Hilary told her.

'They'll find him, though, won't they?'

'I'm sure they will.'

'Well, good luck to them. But they'll need to be sharper than I think they are to ditch their stereotypes and get behind the mask of the Guizer.'

She turned away. The notebook from yesterday was in her hand again.

Hilary looked at Veronica and raised her eyebrows. 'That's me put in my place,' she murmured.

'Do you think she's right?' Veronica asked softly as they walked away. 'I mean, Rupert Honeydew was the last person I would have suspected of harming the well.'

'It certainly hadn't occurred to me . . . Unless she's trying to shift suspicion somewhere else.'

'Hilary! You said we shouldn't suspect her.'

'Right now, I'm suspecting everybody.' She peered down from the walkway that replaced the floor of the Lady Chapel into the crypt chapel beneath. For a moment she stood deep in thought. Then she straightened up with a laugh.

'Right! Let's put that behind us. Who's for that splendid Abbot's kitchen?'

EIGHT

Hilary resolutely tried to push the encounter with Amina behind her. She had an obscure sense that she had behaved badly. She should not have pretended that it had been a chance encounter, when she had gone out of her way to speak to the young woman. The MA student had seen through her attempt at light conversation. She was astute enough to know that Hilary was as keen to question why she had been at the Chalice Well as any detective would have been.

Hilary winced. She did not like the sensation of being found to be at fault.

She marched rather faster than necessary towards the striking building with its octagonal roof rising to a spire.

The interior had been laid out to resemble its original function as a medieval abbot's kitchen. Four huge fireplaces occupied the corners, for roasting, baking, boiling and washing up. Boars and capons were skewered on spits over one. Cauldrons hung above another. The tables were spread with fake food and authentic-looking cooking ware. On a side table, a notice invited visitors to try their hands at working dough.

But Hilary found it hard to concentrate. The TV camera, the justly accusing stare of those blue eyes through the slit in the burka. The day was not going as she had planned.

She felt a stir of remembered longing for the predictability of the school timetable: the lesson bells, the ordered pattern of weekly classes. Yes, some of the pupils could be horrors, but by the end of her teaching career she had got things pretty much under control.

Now she was cast adrift in a world which was turning out to be a great deal more unpredictable than she had imagined. Veronica wanted to cast her as a hero, but Hilary felt she was not handling it as well as she should have done.

Veronica's silvery laugh came from where she was reading the guide book. 'They think there was a gallery up there, where the head cook could stand and direct operations. Like a medieval Gordon Ramsey.'

Hilary looked up at the metal gantry, which now housed a row of lights. 'Just as well they don't play a recording of what he might have said to his scullions.'

Even as she laughed, she had a sense of someone standing close behind her. A woman's voice spoke. Hilary recognized the tone of authority.

'Mrs Masters? If you wouldn't mind stepping outside for a moment.'

She turned. The woman wore a navy blue jacket and skirt and sensible shoes. Her black hair was caught back at the nape of her neck with a discreet ribbon. With a sinking heart, like a guilty schoolgirl, Hilary did not need to see the warrant card to know that she was being summoned by a police officer.

Her cheeks flamed as the other visitors in the kitchen turned to watch her follow the straight back in the navy jacket. She was glad of Veronica's presence behind her.

In the greater privacy of the outdoors, the woman held up the expected ID. 'Detective Sergeant Olive Petersen. Now, would you mind telling me what you were doing questioning Amina Haddad just now?'

'I wasn't *questioning* her! I happened to see her at the Chalice

Well yesterday. Given the circumstances, it seemed only natural to acknowledge the fact when I met her again today.'

'Mrs Masters, we are conducting a highly sensitive enquiry into a major security incident. Miss Haddad is a key witness, to put it no higher than that.'

'You mean you suspect her of planting that bomb because she's a Muslim.'

'That's none of your business. As I said, she's a witness. As are you. I should be extremely grateful if you could refrain from muddying the waters by trying to carry out some amateur investigation of your own. Do I make myself clear, or do I have to take you in for questioning and a formal warning from my DI?'

'Point taken,' Hilary replied through clenched jaws.

Veronica's voice came innocently over her shoulder. 'Does that mean you were outside the Lady Chapel listening to what Hilary and I were saying? If you're a detective on the case, that must mean you're following Amina. Did you think she was going to plant another bomb somewhere?'

An expression of annoyance crossed the detective's face, like a thunder shower sweeping across the sky.

'Thank you, Mrs Taylor. I see we have a second Miss Marple wannabe.'

Ouch. It was too near the bone. Hilary's sharp intelligence had certainly wanted to solve the puzzle, ever since the startling discovery of the knapsack at the Chalice Well. Her rational mind told her it was no more likely to go off when she and Veronica were there than at any other time, but there had seemed something personal about being the one to see it. She could hardly be expected to put it behind her and get on with normal life. Somewhere, in Glastonbury or beyond, there was still a potential killer who had threatened her own life and Veronica's.

'I think you're being unfair,' Veronica defended her. 'Hilary was the one who found the bomb. If she hadn't spotted it and called you, it might have gone off and killed people.'

'We are always grateful for the assistance of members of the public.' DS Petersen seemed to be speaking through stiff lips. 'But the matter is in police hands now. Not only do we not need your no doubt well-intentioned help, it could actually prejudice our enquiries. Interfering with a witness is an offence.'

'I wasn't interfering with her!' Hilary snorted. 'If you were listening, you must know I hardly needed to ask her any questions, even if I'd wanted to. She was the one volunteering information about herself.'

'And about Rupert Honeydew,' Veronica put in. 'The Guizer, she called him. Did you hear that?'

Hilary watched the detective sergeant's face keenly. There was no sign of a reaction.

'Is that it, then? Can we go?'

'If I have your word that you'll keep your curiosity to yourself in future.'

'I've spent a lifetime encouraging my pupils to be curious about everything around them.'

'As far as you're concerned, this investigation is out of bounds.'

Veronica took Hilary's arm. 'Really, I think you've made a mistake. Hilary was scolding me for stereotyping Amina just because she's a Muslim. It was meant to be a friendly conversation with her, nothing more.'

'I've made my point. I trust you've grasped it,' said DS Petersen.

As they walked away, Hilary was surprised how churned up she felt. She was used to being the one who reprimanded others. It wounded her self-image to be on the receiving end of reproof. She *hadn't* been questioning Amina Haddad like a suspect, had she? It was intended to be just a sociable recognition that they were caught up in the same situation.

Amina hadn't seen it that way.

And Hilary was not entirely sure she was being honest with herself.

Back in their hotel room, Veronica switched on the television for the early evening news. More trouble in the Middle East. Hilary listened intently for any mention of Gaza. There was none. She began to relax.

The national news was over. She expected Veronica to switch off the set, but the scene had switched to the local news studio. The two presenters were running through the list of stories to come.

'We have an interview with the woman who found the unexploded bomb in Glastonbury.'

Hilary groaned and threw herself back on the bed pillows.

Veronica threw her a half smile. 'I told you. You're famous.'

'Fame is the last thing I want. This was meant to be a holiday.'

She winced at the sight of her own face filling the screen. She had never bothered much about make-up or hair. If the interview had been in a studio, they might have tidied her up, powdered her shiny nose. But here she was, exposed as other people must see her all the time. She had not realized quite how unkempt she looked. Veronica managed to appear well-groomed, still pretty, even in her fifties.

She hardly listened to what she was telling the reporter.

The item was over. The programme shifted to the threat of local flooding.

Veronica sighed. 'Oh, dear. Poor Joan. I really thought she was going to get another moment in the limelight. But they've cut out the interview with her completely, and screened you instead.'

'She could have had it, and welcome. It was never my intention to make a public spectacle of myself.'

NINE

'Are you terribly hungry? I need to calm myself down. Would you mind if we eat later? I'd meant to leave the Tor until tomorrow, but right now I think it's what I need.'

'I know what you mean,' Veronica sympathized. 'When you're up there, with the whole of the Somerset Levels spread out below you, you get a different perspective on things. Especially at sunset.'

Hilary retrieved her stout walking stick from the boot of the car and they set out.

'I wish I could make up my mind about it,' she said. She lifted her head to the dramatically steep sides of the Tor. From the foot, the church tower had disappeared behind the shoulder of the hill. 'Religious or secular? Pagan or Christian? A place of ceremonial or a defensive fort?'

When Veronica did not reply, Hilary drew her gaze from the Tor to look at her companion. Veronica's own eyes were darting from one side of the street to the other. There was a little frown above her nose.

'Veronica. You're not listening.'

'Oh. Sorry! What did you say?'

'I was just musing about what sort of people originally settled on the Tor. And why.'

'Sorry. I missed that.'

'You were miles away. Or rather, you were more bothered about something in Glastonbury here and now than in what might have happened on the Tor in the Dark Ages.'

'Yes. I have to confess that I am. I know that detective sergeant said we ought to leave it to the police, but I can't help thinking that somewhere here there's a cold and calculating bomb maker. I might brush past him, or her, and I wouldn't even know it. It scares me.'

'Me too, if I'm honest. That's why I wanted to get away from it for an hour or two. Up there.'

'Besides,' Veronica sounded almost apologetic, 'there's Joan, poor soul. She'll have been so disappointed not to get her few minutes on the BBC. I know my Morag would have been gutted. I'd like to make it up to her. If I see the Marsdens again, I can give her a ring and she might catch him before he disappears again. I'm sure he's worth a follow-up story, with his views.'

Hilary forced a grin. 'You don't think that would count as interfering with another witness?'

Veronica chuckled. 'I wasn't actually thinking of accosting him myself. That's Joan's job.'

'And good luck to her!'

To reach the footpath up the Tor, they had to pass the Chalice Well, closed now for the night. Hilary gave it only a glance and strode resolutely past. She must put it behind her. She wished that yesterday had never happened. Then she pulled her thoughts up short. Did she really wish she hadn't seen that knapsack almost completely hidden behind the lid of the well? Surely someone else would have noticed it? But they hadn't, had they? And if Hilary hadn't seen it . . .

'Did you know there are no springs on the Tor?' She forced

her thoughts into different channels. 'Anyone living up there would have had to send folk with buckets all the way down here to the Chalice spring.'

'I don't suppose they washed very often.' Veronica laughed.

'No, but a lot of cooking went on. Middens piled high with animal bones. That's what makes people think it probably wasn't a Christian monastic site. Celtic monks and hermits lived a pretty frugal life. You can forget about fat Friar Tuck and medieval monks pigging themselves. What happened in the Celtic Church was different.'

'More like the Gospel in action?' Veronica suggested.

'Hmm. Saints are not always comfortable to live with. Still, I guess we're looking at some secular warlord camped out up there.'

They looked up at the steep profile of the Tor. Terraces seemed to have been cut into its slopes, giving it a stepped appearance.

Hilary grunted. 'At least we're spared the sight of New Age women dancing their way up. Some people think those aren't field terraces but a sacred maze.'

'I think I'll stick to the steps, myself.'

For a while conversation flagged as they made their way up the steep ascent. Hilary was glad of her stick. She was finding it necessary to stop and admire the view more often than she did when she was younger. There was only five years difference between them, but Veronica seemed to be tackling it more easily.

She stopped for the third time just below the summit. When she turned, the sun was sinking towards the horizon. Its level rays were flooding the channels of the Somerset Levels with golden light, picking out every river, stream and man-made drain. Hilary felt its beauty pierce her heart. This was why she had come. Now, at this time of day. She had needed this blessing, and now she had it.

She wished, selfishly, that when they reached the top, only a few steps away, they would have the summit to themselves.

One last heave, and she stood at the base of St Michael's tower. It was all that was left of the medieval church. Veronica had got there ahead of her and had moved on to stand looking out over a landscape washed with light.

She turned as Hilary came up. 'It's terrible to think that last winter all this was water, almost up to the Tor. All those poor people whose homes were flooded or their livestock marooned.'

'It's a miserable business, having flood water in your house. And it wasn't even clean water.'

'It looks so lovely now. Magical.'

'People don't believe in magic now. Fools!' came a masculine voice.

Both women started. Hilary had seen no one else enjoying the enchantment of Glastonbury Tor at sunset, and neither, it seemed, had Veronica. Her keen eyes sought the source of the voice, but she could find nobody.

'Oh, good evening!' Veronica said suddenly. 'I hope we haven't ruined it for you. I know what it's like when you've found the perfect place all by yourself and then some strangers come charging into it, breaking the spell and chattering away. We'll be quiet, I promise.'

She was looking down over the precipitous edge of the summit. On a grassy ledge just below them, an incredibly long-legged man in khaki shorts had folded his limbs into an angular crouch as he gazed out over the Levels. Rather like a grasshopper waiting to spring, Hilary thought.

'No problem,' he said, without looking round at them. 'As you say, magical. If you annoyed me, I could snap my finger and, hey presto, you'd be over the edge. Spellbinding.' His long mouth smiled, rather mirthlessly.

For a moment, Hilary felt cold inside. Glastonbury was full of nutters. It was the esoteric capital of England. This strange man might genuinely think he was a magician, with the power to cast two annoying women off the Tor if he chose. She drew Veronica gently back by the sleeve and nodded towards the other end of the summit platform.

'Leave him,' she mouthed.

'You think I'm mad.' With terrifying suddenness, the man was on his feet and up the slope. Alarmingly tall, he towered above them on his bare spindly legs. His eyes were cold, accusing. For a moment his features twisted into something very like hatred.

Veronica's hand flew to her mouth.

'I know who you are. Rupert Honeydew.'

The cogs of Hilary's brain clicked into place. Of course. Gone were the motley garb and the prancing gait that went with it. This was Rupert Honeydew without his costume. Amina's Guizer, she suddenly thought. You would never have known what lay behind the disguise. Now here he was, revealed like a hermit crab without its shell.

No, there was surely something more malevolent. She took a step back. She knew that she was genuinely afraid.

Veronica said soothingly, 'No one who comes up here to enjoy the sunset is mad. What could be saner?'

As Hilary watched in apprehension, a disconcerting change transformed Rupert Honeydew's face. It was as though he had passed his hand over his features and whipped away a mask. What he showed them now was a face in which his grey-blue eyes danced and the new moon of his mouth curved in what looked like genuine laughter.

'Well said! I see I am addressing someone who is in tune with the spiritual.' He swept her a profound bow. 'In today's world, believe me, that's uncommon. Be pleased to share my small domain.'

His long-fingered hand gestured regally around the summit of the Tor, with its sentinel tower behind them.

Hilary and Veronica exchanged uncertain looks.

'Thank you,' Hilary said. 'Veronica's right. We won't disturb you.'

'Go with the peace of the Goddess.' The eyes twinkled. 'You might even be inspired to dance for her. I shan't watch.'

As if to prove his assurance, he turned away from them, stepped down the steep slope to the ledge where he had been sitting and resumed that angular crouch. His eyes looked out over the evening plain, to the hills where Arthur was once said to have had his fort, and the glimpse of the western sea, bright along the horizon. It was as though he had turned time back and they were not there. As if they had never come, or as if he had indeed cast a spell and made them disappear.

Hilary had a strange feeling of insubstantiality, as if she doubted her own existence.

But the scary moment when she had indeed thought they were confronted by a madman had passed. She let out a long shuddering breath which told her how frightened she had been.

With a penetrating look at Veronica she turned and led the way to the other end of the narrow summit, where a compass pointed to landmarks in every direction. It was as far from Rupert Honeydew as it was possible to get.

Hilary settled herself on the low stone rim of the compass. Veronica stood with her back to her, above the precipitous drop to the plain.

'What a strange person,' she said softly.

'That's an understatement.' Hilary kept her own voice low.

'I thought he was just one of the more colourful characters of Glastonbury. Now I don't know what to think.'

'The Guizer. That's what Amina called him. But which is the real Rupert Honeydew? The laughing clown, who really believes he can dance with his Goddess? Or that horrible face he let us see for just a few moments?'

'I don't think I've ever seen such pure hatred.'

'You were very brave. And luckily you seemed to say the right thing. At least, it had the right effect. He turned back to – well, in his case you could hardly call it normal, but more like the Rupert Honeydew we first met.'

'You told me then he must be more than a fool to have a properly published book.'

'A professional fool, perhaps.'

'But with something terrifying underneath?'

Hilary looked over her shoulder. She could not see him from here. Was he still sitting where they had left him?

'I'm not going to let it spoil my evening,' she said with determination. 'I came here to enjoy the sunset, and I will.'

All the same, conflicting thoughts wrestled in her mind.

The sun was taking on a fiery red as it began to dip into the clouds above the horizon. The gold across the water channels of the Levels took on a bloodier hue. Dimly blue in the distance were the hills which may have held the stronghold of Arthur in his fight against the invading Saxons. The fabled Camelot. She thrilled to the thought that the hero of the west might have ridden his warhorse along the causeway that once had been the only route across the watery wastes to Glastonbury. The sacred island of Avalon.

Yet she felt a tension in her muscles that would not let her fully relax. She did not want to be sharing this sacred plateau with a man so dangerously unpredictable.

It was a partial success. She did feel the better for being up here, bathed in this light, letting all the history and legend of this remarkable place resonate through her blood. But another part of her would be glad to leave the summit unharmed.

More than half an hour had passed before Veronica turned to her with a quizzical look. The glow was fading.

'Do you think we ought to be getting back, before they stop taking orders for dinner?'

'Hmm. I suppose you're right. I shall be ready for a meal by the time we've hoofed it all the way there.'

They fell silent as they passed the place where they had come upon Rupert Honeydew. They were careful not to go too near the edge. Hilary could not see whether or not the clown was still squatting on the slope just below.

It was something of a relief to have passed the first flight of steps and know they were out of earshot of the summit. Hilary heard the false gaiety of Veronica's voice, a note or two higher than usual.

'Well! And I thought we could write him off the suspect list, because he was just a harmless fool.'

'He didn't actually do anything to us.'

'It was the expression in his eyes. I can still see it.'

The little town was becoming reassuringly clear and close as they descended. She could just make out the Abbey ruins, closed to visitors now. Grey stones rose in peaceful solitude among the dark green of the surrounding trees.

'But think about it,' Veronica said. 'Whoever planted that knapsack at the Chalice Well was sufficiently geared up to the twenty-first century to manufacture a credible bomb. The police haven't released any details, but I presume they believe it could have gone off. Dancing fool or psychopath, is Rupert Honeydew really up to it technically?'

'You said yourself, you can get all the instructions you need from the internet. And we can be pretty sure he's intelligent.'

'By that reckoning, half the people walking the streets of Glastonbury might qualify.'

'I don't think anyone else has given me such a shiver down my spine.'

TEN

Wednesday morning promised sunshine. Hilary raised her coffee cup thoughtfully and looked at Veronica over the rim.

'We seem to be galloping through the list of things we meant to do. Glastonbury Tor was on the menu for this morning. What shall we do instead?'

'I did think, if we had time, we might go out on to the Levels, where they found that ancient causeway.'

'The Sweet Track to Glastonbury? Wonderful name, isn't it? A length of wooden track six thousand years old, preserved because it was covered in waterlogged peat. Of course, it had to be shipped off to the British Museum to conserve it.'

'So there's nothing there now?'

'They used to have a replica at the Peat Moors Centre, but I think that's closed. Still, we can go and have a look. A walk in the marshes will give us a feel of the place. And, tell you what, we could stop off at the Abbot's Fish House in Meare.'

They donned their walking clothes and shouldered knapsacks for the day.

'You're sure you haven't got a bomb hidden inside that?' Hilary joked.

'I don't think it's a laughing matter. Somebody had.'

'I'm sorry. You're right. But we really must stop going around being afraid that the next person we bump into will be on their way to plant another one. Whoever did that at the Chalice Well is going to lie low for a while. There are police all over the place. If they do want a second go, they'll wait until things die down a bit.'

'Do you think it will be the Chalice Well again, or will they go for something else?'

'It depends on the reason for the first one, doesn't it? Someone with a grudge against the well, or are they wanting to make a bigger point? Remember the Baedeker raids the Nazis made on cathedral cities in the last World War? You can strike at the heart of a country by destroying its ancient heritage. And Glastonbury's got plenty of that.'

They stepped out on to the car park. Veronica turned towards Hilary's Vauxhall.

Hilary stopped her. 'Would you mind if I slipped off first and bought a newspaper? Not that trash they give us at breakfast. I should have ordered a decent one at reception.'

'There's a newsagent not far down the street.'

In the shop, Hilary handed over her money and turned from the counter, already scanning the front page.

'Oh, spare us!'

'What's wrong? It's not something about Gaza, is it?'

'No, thank God for that. But almost as bad. Look, the heavy-weights have got it now.'

The picture on the front page was the all-too-familiar photograph of the ornamental lid of the Chalice Well. An arrow directed the reader to page four.

The newsprint crackled as Hilary refolded the pages.

'It's there. Blast them, they've got my name, too.'

'That's hardly surprising, under the circumstances. You found the bomb, after all.'

'There are times when I wish I'd been a million miles away. I could wring Joan Townsend's neck.'

'If it hadn't been her, someone else would have fed them the story. She was just lucky that she happened upon you first.'

'I'm glad it's made somebody happy,' Hilary grunted, in a tone that belied her words.

Back in the hotel car park, she threw the offending paper on the back seat.

'Right. Let's put all that behind us. Got the map? Which way to Meare?'

Hilary turned off in the village and parked by a hedge. Across the gate, they could see an ecclesiastical-looking building of grey stone, standing alone in a field of buttercups.

'That's got to be it,' Hilary announced. 'The Abbot's Fish

House. They'd catch the fish in Meare Pool and store them in holding ponds until the abbey wanted them. The monks at Glastonbury must have got through an awful lot of fish, with all those fast days.'

Veronica read the notice beside the gate. 'It says that if you want the key, you have to fetch it from a house by the church.'

'Looks to me as if we may not need to. Someone's got there before us.'

Figures were beginning to emerge around the corner of the two-storeyed building. More followed.

'Just my luck,' said Hilary, halting on the narrow stone foot-path. 'A school field trip.'

'Do you miss it?' Veronica asked.

'Sometimes. But not as much as I thought I would.'

They were near enough now to see that the school group were all girls, dressed in checked skirts and purple blazers. Round the corner behind them came their teacher. She was quietly dressed in a grey skirt and a plain green jacket. There was something calmly cheerful about her round face. With a sudden insight, Hilary thought that she was probably a nun. It was hard to tell nowadays. They rarely wore black or grey habits and white wimples. She felt a twinge of envy for the serenity she read in that face. It was not an expression normally associated with running a field trip for a party of teenagers.

The teacher smiled at Hilary and Veronica as they met. 'Lovely day.'

'Great,' Hilary agreed.

'There's not a lot to see inside. Old beams, a stone fireplace. But you have to imagine how it used to be, when Meare Pool came right up to this field. It was a great lake, two miles long and a mile wide. They dug a channel to bring their boats up to the ponds and the fish house.'

Veronica looked out where she pointed, over the level pastures just beyond them. 'I'd have said it was hard to imagine all this underwater, if we hadn't had those terrible floods last winter'.

'Was that the same Meare Pool where they found those lake villages built on artificial islands?' Hilary asked. 'Two thousand years old?'

'That's the same. It's an old inhabited landscape.'

Hilary peered in through the metal lattices which protected the window spaces. As she turned back, she was aware of a stirring among the waiting schoolgirls, a ripple of excitement. She looked around blankly for its source, but saw nothing.

'Would you like the key? We're about done here. You need to return it to the house by the church.'

'Up there on the ridge, by what looks like the manor house? Right.' Hilary took the key from her.

They watched her shepherd her flock back through the gate to the road. Some of the girls turned their heads to stare back at them.

'What was all that about?' Veronica asked. 'Why are those girls looking at us?'

'Search me.'

'Well, the old Peat Marsh Centre may be closed, but it says "Avalon Marshes Centre" down this road. Shall we give it a try?'

They pulled into the car park, in front of a Portakabin which announced Visitor Information. A minibus was parked in the corner, but there was no sign of its occupants.

'Right. It's a fine day. The café's open. We're five miles out of Glastonbury. It's highly unlikely we'll meet anyone here who was at the Chalice Well on Monday, so we'd be daft to keep looking for suspicious individuals with bombs in their knapsacks. Let's enjoy ourselves.'

'Yes, Mrs Masters,' Veronica said demurely.

Hilary glared at her across the bonnet. 'You wouldn't be taking the mickey out of me, would you? I'm retired now.'

'Yes, Hilary. I'm sure you are.'

Hilary grinned, with a sudden release of tension. It really was true. Today felt like a holiday for the first time since she had seen that knapsack at the well.

Beyond a gate rose the conical roof of what appeared to be a reconstructed Iron Age roundhouse. Swirls of Celtic patterns in ochre paint decorated its low white walls. They settled for enjoying locally made fruit juice before tackling the visitor centre.

The Portakabin was empty. Around the walls were information boards about the Avalon Marshes. Photographic displays told them all about the wildlife and flora of the wetlands, the history of how the Levels came to be drained for agriculture, the bird sanctuary.

From outside, through the further door came the sound of voices. Young female voices.

Veronica stifled a giggle. 'It seems we can't get away from them.'

They stepped out into the sunshine. Through the trees, they saw the same party of schoolgirls they had met at the fish house. The girls had taken off their blazers and were hard at work. Under the guidance of a ranger, they seemed to be doing something with poles and planks of wood.

Hilary and Veronica stepped closer.

'It's the Sweet Track!' said Hilary. 'At least a replica of it.'

Poles forming X-shaped supports were being set in the peaty ground. A line of them led away through the bushes. Along them, other girls were laying rough-hewn planks.

Veronica gasped and clapped her hands. 'This is what you meant! They really did find this here on the Levels.'

'It was amazing to find wood surviving after six thousand years. That's three times as old as your lake villages at Meare. And long before King Arthur's time, or even Joseph of Arimathea – supposing he ever did come to Glastonbury.'

'Do you think they were peaceful people, out here in the marshes?' Veronica said. 'Or was the lake their defence?'

'Not much evidence of royal status or weapons, from the sound of it. Simple country folk, I should think. No shortage of fish, that's for certain.'

She could feel the tension flowing out of her as she left the violence of the twenty-first century behind her. If she could only get back to that simpler way of life. But perhaps it never was like that.

A sudden silence had fallen over the party of schoolgirls. Then there was a burst of excited chatter. Hilary suddenly realized they were staring at her again. The teacher she thought was a nun got to her feet and came over. Her eyes twinkled.

'They know who you are. You were on the telly, apparently. You found the bomb.'

Hilary's heart sank.

'Don't worry. I've forbidden them to ask for your autograph. You don't look as if you're enjoying your notoriety.'

'I'm not.'

'All the same, I'm truly grateful to you. Sister Mary Magdalene, by the way. St Bridget's School. I know a lot of what you hear at Glastonbury is fanciful legend, but there *is* an aura of sanctity about the place, don't you think? It would have grieved me if someone had blown up the Chalice Well. Let alone the thought of human casualties. We live in a terrible world. But the Lord's hand was over you that day.'

She smiled radiantly and moved back to the reconstruction, before Hilary could think of an answer. The girls were evidently badgering her with questions, but she shook her head.

'So we couldn't *quite* put it behind us,' Veronica said. 'But she was nice. I suppose she may have been imagining herself taking her girls to see the Chalice Well that afternoon. At least we don't have to worry about whether *she* was the bomber.'

'No, though it's probably no wilder than some of the speculations I've entertained. I even found myself wondering why that young woman in the gift shop was so reluctant to talk.'

'Let's forget about it, shall we? Why don't we get an early lunch here? Then I fancy a walk along one of those wetland trails they've signposted in the nature reserve. They say this is a great place for rare birds.'

'Not that I'd know one if I saw one. Still, we'd be walking over the course of the original Sweet Track, even if the path is made of recycled plastic bottles now.'

'Hilary!'

'Don't look like that. It's what it said on the display board.'

After their walk through the reed-fringed wetlands, they drove back over the Levels. To Hilary it felt strange to be down in this totally flat landscape, after the hills of her native Devon. Behind her lay the still pools of the nature reserve. On either side, a patchwork of pastures, ribboned with ditches of water that mirrored the brightness of the sky. The hedges were awash with may blossom.

Veronica was gazing out at it more thoughtfully. 'It's terrifying to think of this being all underwater last winter.'

'Nature getting its own back. It's made it easier to imagine what it used to be like two thousand years ago, when the Bristol

Channel came all the way up to the Tor. A wilderness of meres and marshes, with little islands here and there.'

'And then Glastonbury Tor, soaring up like a magic mountain. You can see why so many legends gathered around it.'

They looked ahead to the Tor. The tower of St Michael's church looked dramatically high from here. But Hilary did not want to think about that encounter with Rupert Honeydew the day before.

'The Isle of Avalon. Down here, there were people going about in coracles, or picking their way across boardwalks over the marshes. And everywhere you went, you could see that astonishing hill.'

The day had been, Hilary thought, like a magic island itself. Apart from that one hairy moment when she was in danger of being engulfed by curious schoolgirls, she had been able to put away the shock of what she had discovered, and its aftermath. They had met no one she needed to feel wary about as a potential bomb maker. No need to worry whether she had missed something vital, the way others had missed seeing that bomb at the well.

It was all very well for the police to tell her to keep out of it, but she couldn't, could she? Whoever planted that knapsack was still walking free. The police had made no arrest, taken nobody in for questioning, as far as she knew. DS Petersen had been shadowing Amina Haddad, though. Could Hilary be sure that it was only religious stereotyping which made the young woman in the burka a suspect? Did the police know something Hilary didn't?

She thought again of those curious blue eyes through the slit in the burka.

She felt the weight beginning to descend over her as the car neared Glastonbury.

They parked at the hotel.

'I don't know about you, but I fancy a nice old-fashioned teashop with gingham tablecloths and home-made cakes.' Veronica's smile was appealing.

'You're on.'

It seemed strange to walk along the crowded High Street of Glastonbury, after the solitude of the wetlands. Hilary tried to stop scanning everyone she passed and imagining that they were carrying a bomb. Vigilance was one thing; paranoia was something else.

She was aware that Veronica was no longer beside her. She looked back. Veronica had stopped further down the pavement. She too was looking behind her. Hilary was not sure what had caught her attention. It didn't seem to be anything in a shop window, nor the passers-by on the pavement.

In a few strides Hilary rejoined her.

Veronica spoke in a low voice. 'That woman. The one standing beside the grey car. Where have I seen her before?'

Hilary followed her gaze. A short middle-aged woman with clipped dark hair was standing by one of the cars parked at the kerbside. Nothing triggered a memory in Hilary's mind.

'Sorry. Can't help you. She looks a bit impatient. Hubby not turned up on time, do you guess?'

Veronica looked for a while longer, then sighed. 'No. I suppose we've got into the way of thinking that everyone we meet must have something to do with that awful thing at the well. I can't place her, but I don't suppose it would mean anything if I did.'

'So, do we find those home-made cakes or not?'

Hilary was savouring the particularly good coffee-and-walnut gateau. It was nearing the end of a healing day. This was more like the holiday she had planned. There had been that little upset at the Abbot's Fish House, when the schoolgirls had recognized her. But Sister Mary Magdalene had steered them away. No great harm had been done. On their wetland walk Veronica had been sure she had spotted a rare crane.

She would not let herself think too much about David in the Gaza hospital.

Veronica stared suddenly forward, spilling her tea on the gingham tablecloth.

'I know who it was!'

Hilary stared at her blankly.

'That woman standing beside the car. I knew I'd seen her before. It was Mrs Marsden. I'm sure it was.'

Hilary's brain was still taking time to catch up with Veronica's words. Then, slowly, the significance of that name penetrated.

'Marsden? . . . You mean George Marsden's wife? The little

woman who was standing next to him in the gift shop? Saying "George!" and "Keep your voice down"?'

'I had my hands full, fending off her husband about Rupert Honeydew's book, but I did spare a glance or two for her. Short, stocky. That rather severe haircut. Quick! I need to let Joan know.'

'Joan? Know what?'

Veronica had almost disappeared below the table as she fished in her handbag. She came up flushed and holding her mobile phone.

'Joan Townsend. The would-be journalist. Oh, don't be so obtuse, Hilary. She wanted to know more about George Marsden. They'd gone from the Chalice Well before she got there, and they're not in the phone book. I promised I'd let her know if I saw him. Only, where's the card with her number?'

Hilary watched her scrabble through her bag again. Then with a sigh she opened her own knapsack and took out her wallet. Slipped into one of the pockets was the little dog-eared card Joan Townsend had given her. She passed it across the table.

'Oh, bless you!' Veronica was already keying in the number.

'Though what good you think it will do beats me. The woman was waiting by the car as if she expected George to turn up at any moment. They'll be long gone before your cub reporter gets there. And she's a braver woman than I am if she's going to buttonhole him for an interview in the middle of the street.'

'It's worth a try, though . . . Joan! Oh, I'm glad I've caught you. It's Veronica Taylor . . . Yes, from the Chalice Well. I'm in the Copper Kettle in Glastonbury . . .'

Hilary listened as a breathless Veronica reeled off the information about seeing the Marsdens, or at least Mrs Marsden.

'Good. I do hope you catch her. We're just leaving. I'll keep my eyes open and let you know if I see him, or her, shall I?'

She put away the phone, beaming with satisfaction. 'That's my good deed for the day.'

Hilary pursued the last crumbs of the gateau with her finger. 'Did I gather you've volunteered us to do a street search for the missing George?'

Veronica coloured. 'Well, not exactly a *search*. But we'll be walking back down the street to the hotel, anyway. If they haven't driven off, it's just possible we'll see them.'

'Pigs might fly.'

Hilary heaved herself to her feet and swung the knapsack over her shoulder. 'Right, Sherlock, lead on.'

ELEVEN

It might have been the effect of a day in the sunshine, followed by a very satisfactory afternoon tea. Hilary found herself walking down the busy High Street in a more contented frame of mind. No longer was she watching anxiously for a potential bomber, but a cantankerous gentleman for the unsuccessful Joan to interview. She did not expect to find him.

Veronica clutched her elbow. 'There she is!'

'Who? Joan?'

'No. Mrs Marsden.'

The small woman in the green suit was no longer waiting impatiently by the car. She was making for the doorway of a shop that announced itself as the Archive of Avalon. Veronica had her phone out again, relaying the information to Joan.

'She's on her way,' she told Hilary, her eyes shining.

'Congratulations.' Hilary's tone was not entirely sincere. 'I hope it keeps fine for her.'

From the safety of the pavement, she could already hear George Marsden's remembered voice haranguing the shopkeeper at the counter inside. 'Sounds as if it's someone else's turn to be on the receiving end of one of his rants.'

She made to move on, but Veronica protested. 'We can't go now. What if he comes out and they disappear before Joan gets here?'

Hilary sighed. 'You can't act as wet nurse to that girl for the whole of her journalistic career – if she has one. You've done her a favour. Move on and leave it to her.'

'I know what you mean, but I keep thinking of Morag. Next year, she may be in the same position. It's a tough life. Joan needs a break.'

'And you think George Marsden may be it? Come on, he's a

loud-mouthed, self-opinionated bore. Not the Chalice Well bomber.'

'We don't know that, do we?'

'I'm sure the police will have found where he lives and questioned him by now. If they haven't arrested him, it's hardly likely he's going to spill the beans to an amateur reporter, is it?'

'It should still make a colourful interview. She needs to keep the story alive.'

Mrs Marsden had disappeared inside the shop. Through the open door came her voice. 'George! Please!'

Hilary grinned. 'Well, so long as we don't actually speak to him when he comes out, we're not interfering with a witness again, are we? DS Petersen can read the riot act to Miss Townsend instead.'

As she spoke, the couple appeared in the doorway. George Marsden was dressed as she remembered him from the gift shop, in a tweed jacket and cavalry twill trousers. His face was an alarming shade of red. She almost expected him, like the cartoon image of an angry colonel, to be shooting off drops of sweat from his balding head.

The smile on her face froze. From further down the street came a flash of light. There was the sparkle of flying glass, followed by an almighty roar. Clouds of smoke and dust billowed down the street towards them. Hilary grabbed Veronica and threw her to the ground.

She was choking for air in a fog of dust. Fragments of brick and splinters of wood were still raining down on her. She sheltered Veronica as well as she could and prayed that nothing larger would hit either of them.

The roar was rolling away from them, fading into the distance. Now she could hear the sharper sound of screams.

It was seconds more before she summoned the courage to get to her feet. She did not want to see what she knew must confront her. Then she was running towards the source of the explosion before she knew what had set her feet in motion.

Dust clouded the scene. She almost fell over a young man sprawled on the pavement. Blood was pumping from his leg, shockingly scarlet. A shard of glass had almost severed it. A voice Hilary did not recognize as her own had taken over the inside of her head, instructing her what to do. A tourniquet. That was what you had to do. Stop the flow of blood. She snatched the leather belt from her trousers and knelt to bind it tightly round the upper thigh. The man groaned as she lifted the limb enough to pass the strap underneath it. He was still alive.

'Hang on. Help's coming. You're going to be OK.'

She prayed it was true.

As if in answer to her prayer the street was filled with the urgent sound of sirens. Ambulance? Police? She couldn't tell.

She looked up. Veronica, covered in brick dust, was holding a screaming toddler in her arms, trying to soothe it. There was no blood on the child, but nor was there any sign of its mother. Hilary did not want to look past them through that fog of dust. The street had been busy. The young man she was kneeling beside was the only casualty she had seen yet. Who knew what carnage lay beyond him?

Blood had soaked her cream linen trousers. She thought, inappropriately, that she would have to throw them away. Odd how the brain occupied itself with trivialities at a time like this. She had been fond of this particular pair.

The flow of blood from the young man's leg was less now, wasn't it? He had fallen silent. A horrid fear gripped her. She slapped his face. It looked deathly pale under its mask of dirt.

'Wake up, sunshine!' Then more urgently, trying to shock him awake, 'Stay with us! What's your name?'

Relief broke over her, like a huge breaker lifting her up and washing her down again. He did not open his eyes, but a slurred sound escaped his caked lips.

'Baz.'

'That's great, Baz. I need you to make an effort to keep awake. Can you open your eyes?'

It seemed like an enormous effort, but the eyelids rose halfway. She glimpsed brown irises, bloodshot whites.

'Well done, son. I'm Hilary. And I'm going to stay with you until the medics arrive. You've got a nasty cut on your leg, but they'll see to it.'

It was a massive understatement. Short of a surgical miracle, he would lose the limb. How old was he? Mid-twenties? Was he local? A visitor? She thought about her own children, Bridget and Oliver, not much older. Then she forced the thought away. She could not bear to think of one of them here, caught in this mayhem, terribly hurt like this.

'Do you live in Glastonbury, Baz?' As if this was a chance encounter and they were chatting politely.

He was slipping away. His eyelids were closing. She slapped his face again.

'Not yet, Baz. Stay with me. They'll let you sleep in hospital once they've patched you up.'

A reassuring male voice spoke behind her. 'You're doing a great job, love. We'll take over now, shall we?'

She turned to find a pair of paramedics in green overalls. There was an ambulance close beside them, with its rear doors open. She had not heard it come.

The second paramedic, slighter, female, was helping her to her feet. Hilary felt astonishingly weak at the knees. There were spots like flies buzzing in front of her eyes. She wasn't going to faint, was she? Not now.

'Are you OK? No, of course you're not. Here, sit down.'

She let herself be led away to the edge of the road. She lowered herself to sit on the kerb and the paramedic pressed her head between her knees.

The blood soaking her trousers was cold against her legs now.

'Are you hurt too?'

Hilary shook her head, and then wished she hadn't. 'No, we were further up the road, thank God.'

She had a sudden clear memory. Standing outside a shop that bore the name in Gothic lettering: The Archive of Avalon. There was someone else there too, besides herself and Veronica stepping out of the shop. A trim little woman in a green suit with clipped black hair. And in the doorway, George Marsden. The name flew back to her. Red-faced, tweed jacket. Flushed from shouting invective at the shopkeeper. But just before the bomb went off he had fallen silent. He was already looking down the street to where the explosion would happen a second later.

She hadn't imagined that, had she? She could see it in such sharp-edged detail. She must check with Veronica.

Veronica! Her mind leaped back to the here and now. The aftermath of the bomb. The clamour of voices. People in pain. Police shouting orders. The dust was still settling. The paramedics were stretchering Baz into the back of the ambulance.

How many more?

Veronica?

For a heart-churning moment, she could not remember when she had last seen her friend. Then the fog in her mind cleared. It was OK. Veronica had run to help, just as Hilary had. She had been holding a sobbing child. Hilary got to her feet and looked around. There was a huge number of uniforms at the scene. Enough, she was glad, to form a protective wall, so that she did not have to see what had happened further down the street.

Had Veronica found the child's mother?

A straggle of schoolgirls was coming towards her. Some of them were bloodied. Their uniforms, though dirt-caked, looked somehow familiar. Those purple blazers. And then a voice, calm but firm among the chaos.

'Well done, girls. It wasn't an easy thing to see, but you've acquitted yourselves splendidly. The school will be proud of you.'

Sister Mary Magdalene was shepherding her charges away from the epicentre of the explosion. Some of them looked dazed, others were crying silently. The nun's plain grey skirt was soaked in blood, like Hilary's trousers. For a moment, they stopped and stared at each other. Then Sister Mary Magdalene smiled, with a genuine joy Hilary could only envy.

'I love teenagers, don't you? You think their heads are full of trivialities – what they look like, what their boyfriend said last night, who posted that photo on Facebook – and then something really serious happens and their true quality comes out, when older people are going to pieces.'

'Yes.' Hilary avoided imagining what the girls and their teacher had been doing. 'Will you excuse me? I'm still looking for my friend.'

'The pretty woman with fair hair? She's by the Tibetan boutique across the road, being buttonholed by a journalist, I think. She doesn't look as if she's been hurt.'

Again that reassuring smile.

Hilary threaded her way between the ambulances and police

cars. There was a cacophony around her of which she had only dimly been aware. It looked as though the police were trying to clear the street of all but the wounded and the emergency services. Hilary felt suddenly anonymous and unneeded, and was glad of it. She had done her bit. She could only pray that Baz would live. Now all she wanted was to get back to the hotel, have a large whisky, a shower and sleep.

The way to the Tibetan shop was blocked. A young woman in a baggy beige jumper was accosting a dazed-looking woman with a scared toddler clinging to her skirts.

'How close were you when the bomb went off? Did you see anyone going into the shop or coming out just before?'

Joan Townsend.

Hilary looked back. She could now make out that the explosion had ripped apart one of the shops and damaged others. There were still people on the pavement being tended to. She felt an unreasonable anger surge up inside her.

'Have you got nothing better to do with yourself? People are dying over there.'

Joan swung round. In a single glance she took in Hilary's blood-soaked clothes, the grit that snagged her hair.

'You were there too! Just like at the Chalice Well.'

Hilary saw the eager flash in the reporter's brown eyes.

'And what's that supposed to mean? Of course I was there. Veronica phoned you, didn't she? We were coming down the street because Veronica had seen the Marsdens and she wanted to be able to tell you where George was, before they got away.'

The reporter's eyes grew wider.

'George! Of course. The Marsdens! You told me at the Chalice Well they'd been there when you found the first bomb. Veronica thought there might be a possible story there. And now . . . Oh, thank you!'

The woman with the toddler had made good her escape.

'There must have been a hundred people on the street and in the shops,' Hilary snapped. 'And who's to say the bomber hadn't legged it long before his bomb went off?'

'But that's what they do, isn't it? Hang around. Just far enough away not to be hurt, but close enough to see the result . . . Unless it's a suicide bomber, of course. I can't thank Veronica enough for bringing me in on this. I mean, who else from TV or the dailies is right here on the spot? I had my camera out seconds after it went off. Here, take one of me, will you? Just for the record. I need it to be professional quality.'

She thrust her expensive-looking camera into Hilary's hands.

'You really want me to take a picture of you? Like a holiday snap? Not "me outside Buckingham Palace", but "me after an atrocity, with people dying in the background"?'

The sallow face flushed. 'You're not being fair. All the really bad cases have been taken off to hospital. It's mostly police now. Please!'

Hilary's finger was shaking as it hovered over the button. She lifted the camera, though what she really wanted to do was fling it away across the littered street, as so much else had been flung by the force of the explosion.

Instead, obediently, she framed the shot, with Joan smiling into the lens, and snapped it.

She handed back the camera silently.

'You're an angel! This time I really will make the front page.'

Hilary walked past her. Veronica was watching from the doorway of the shop, framed by knitted hats and multi-coloured bags.

'They gave me a cup of hot sweet tea. Would you like one?'

'I'd rather have a whisky back at the hotel. Let's get out of here as fast as we can.'

TWELVE

The hotel bar was abuzz with news of the explosion in the High Street. The chatter died instantly when Hilary and Veronica appeared. It took a couple of seconds for Hilary to realize why everyone was staring at her in horror. Slowly she became aware of the shocking figure she must present. Her cream trousers drenched in blood. Debris and dust in her hair. Her face no doubt grimed or smeared where she had passed her bloodied hands over it. Veronica was similarly dirty and dishevelled, if not caked in blood.

Ignoring the outbreak of concern and curiosity which followed, she spun rapidly on her heel and made for the stairs. Halfway across the foyer she stopped. The hotel manager, who had been serving behind the bar, was in sympathetic pursuit.

'I'm terribly sorry. If there's anything we can do . . .'

'Two large whiskies and a pot of strong coffee. In our room.'

The stairs seemed higher and harder to climb than she remembered. She found herself clutching the rail for support. A turn on the landing, then one last shorter flight. Veronica was there before her, unlocking the door and holding it open. It was wonderful to collapse into the armchair.

'You can have first crack at the shower,' Veronica said firmly. 'I'm going to try and brush some of this masonry out of my hair.'

It was luxury to let the hot water pour over her. Perhaps a soak in a hot bath might have been a better idea, but there was no reason why she shouldn't do that as well later on. The blood on her legs turned from scarlet to pink and trickled away around her feet. Her hair began to feel clean at last.

Fragments of memory kept coming back to her, jagged as shards of glass. The words 'flesh' and 'blood' made all too visible in Baz's partly severed leg. The flash of white bone. The screams from further down the street, where the fog of dust and falling debris was thickest. She did not think she would ever forget it.

She longed for David to be home from Gaza so that she could cry against his chest. It was not something she often did.

She was gradually feeling more human again. At least . . . surely what she had felt before was deeply human. The vulnerability of human flesh and blood. The pain of other people's suffering. It would have been inhuman not to feel as she had.

There was the comfort of the large fluffy white bath towel. The glow of hot water still on her skin. She looked down at the filthy clothes at her feet. She must not leave them for Veronica to deal with. But the little waste bin in the corner hardly seemed adequate. Perhaps there would be a plastic laundry bag in one of the drawers, which she must then dispose of. She picked them up in an armful and shuffled towards the door.

Veronica looked up swiftly. A smile eased the tension in her face. 'You look better. It's put some colour back in your cheeks. Here, coffee and scotch. And a tin of shortbread, on the house.'

'Let me make myself decent and I'll be right there.'

Fresh underwear, a clean pair of trousers and a warmer jumper than she would normally have worn at this time of year. Cleanliness had never felt such a blessing.

'There's a hair drier in the wardrobe,' Veronica volunteered.

'Later. Just let me get my hands on that scotch. I think I've left the bathroom habitable for you.'

Veronica nursed her hands around her cup of coffee. 'I can't get over the way some people behave at times like that. I'd have thought the normal human instinct was to run and do what you could to help. Or run the other way if you're scared and can't stand the sight of blood. But you'd be amazed at the number of people who turned up on the pavement opposite taking photographs on their mobile phones. It makes me sick to think of them posting their snaps on Facebook and making themselves out to be some sort of celebrity because they were there.'

'To say nothing of your pet journalist, Joan Townsend. Typical of the trade. More concerned about getting her story than seeing if there was anything she could do to help.'

Veronica was silent for a moment. Then she said quietly, 'Yes, I know what you mean. I suppose somebody has to do it – report on awful things like that. I never thought when I phoned her . . . I mean, I only wanted to help her get her interview with George Marsden . . . What happened to him, by the way? I didn't see him or his wife afterwards and they'd been standing right next to us. No, what upset me about Joan was that she didn't seem in the least concerned that I was only about fifty yards away when it happened. I've been thinking about that ever since. A few seconds more, and we'd have been outside that shop when the bomb exploded.'

'What shop was it? Do you know?'

'According to the women in the Tibetan shop, it was what you'd expect in Glastonbury. Like every other shop on the High Street. Crystals, joss sticks, charms. What I mean is, Joan knew I was in the High Street even before she got there. When she heard the bomb go off, she must have known we could be right in the firing line. But when she saw me, all she wanted to know was what I'd seen, where I'd been standing, had I seen any dead people. I like to think that if it had been Morag, she'd have shown a bit more humanity. She might at least have sounded as if she was a tiny bit concerned for us and thankful we were safe.'

'I take it your sympathy for her career prospects is wearing off.'

Veronica pulled a rueful face. 'I suppose none of us knows how we'll react to catastrophe until it happens.'

'You did well enough. I saw you with a child in your arms. Did you find its mother?'

'Thankfully, yes. I was terribly afraid . . .'

'So was I.'

'I wonder how many people died. There must have been some, mustn't there?'

'We could put the BBC news channel on. They have news twenty-four/seven.'

There was an unreality about seeing the drama reported on the screen. It was becoming harder for Hilary to realize that what she was watching was happening in Glastonbury, further down this same street. Television put it in the same category as disasters in the Philippines or Syria or the Central African Republic. But it had happened here, on the streets of an English town. *This* English town. She had been there. Clean and warm and freshly dressed, it was increasingly difficult to believe it.

'Seven people are believed to be dead, and a number of casualties have been taken to hospital, some with life-threatening injuries.'

Veronica sucked in her breath. 'That many! I'd hoped it would be less.'

'Fewer,' Hilary corrected her automatically. Then, shamefacedly, 'Sorry.'

'The police would make no comment about the possible perpetrator, but there is, understandably, speculation here about whether there is any connection between today's atrocity and the discovery earlier this week of an unexploded bomb at the Chalice Well, also in Glastonbury. We'll be interviewing a forensic psychologist later about a possible motive. The shop where the bomb was planted was the Spiritual Sphere. It specialized in the esoteric and supposedly magical goods for which many people come to Glastonbury. Could it be someone with a grudge against that kind of commerce?'

'George Marsden,' Hilary muttered. 'He was right on cue. Near enough to the explosion to see what happened, but not close enough to get hurt.'

'There was plenty of debris flying about in the blast,' Veronica corrected her. 'His wife was standing out on the pavement like us.'

Hilary groaned. 'Right now, all I want to do is snuggle down under a duvet and have a nap. But my conscience is telling me we ought to brave the wrath of the local constabulary and go back and tell them we saw him there.'

Veronica's cheeks grew pinker. 'I already have. I phoned them while you were in the shower.'

THIRTEEN

Hilary and Veronica stepped outside the comparative safety of the Bowes Hotel. Hilary drew her jacket closer around her in spite of the sweater underneath. It felt unexpectedly cold for May. Shock, she told herself. Hot coffee and whisky and a steaming shower could only do so much.

'Apparently there's no police station in Glastonbury,' Veronica informed her. 'They've set up an incident room at the other end of town.'

Hilary was alarmed to find herself wondering if she could walk that far.

She told herself that she had seen just one of the casualties. What about David, who was doing his stint in the hospital in Gaza? She had not realized quite so vividly what shocking things he must see.

'No hope of getting through the High Street,' Veronica said.

Police tape barred their way. The street beyond was swarming with uniformed officers, investigators in white forensic suits and others in plain clothes that Hilary guessed to be CID.

A huddle of people watched from behind the tape.

'Catastrophe tourists,' Hilary growled. 'Come to see if there's still blood on the pavements.'

'You don't know,' Veronica scolded her. 'They may just as well be locals who know people who were in the street. They may even live in one of those houses, and have been turned out until the police are sure it's safe.'

'Hmmph.'

They threaded their way around the side streets. When they came in sight of the incident room there was no mistaking their destination. The grey stone Baptist church hall struck Hilary as like a disturbed ants' nest. Police officers were scurrying in and out. A BT van she guessed must be setting up more phone lines. Just as they reached the steps a people carrier drew up and more uniformed officers leaped out.

'They must have raided the whole of the Avon and Somerset Constabulary to track the bomber down. Cancelled leave.'

'It looks a bit daunting,' Veronica agreed. She stepped back hastily as half a dozen young constables charged up the steps. 'Do you think they'll really want to talk to us?'

'It was your idea.'

They made their way with difficulty through the crowded doorway, feeling uncomfortably out of place.

'We've come to see DI Fellows,' Veronica told the harassed-looking desk sergeant inside the door. 'Mrs Taylor and Mrs Masters. We have an appointment.'

'Was that before or after the bomb went off? Things aren't exactly running as normal, you know.'

'After,' Veronica said firmly. 'Why else would we be here? We have information which may be significant.'

The sergeant ran his finger down the page of a ledger in front of him. He picked up a phone. After a brief consultation he laid it down again. 'Right. So you do. Jenny!' He hailed a passing policewoman. 'Take these good ladies to number six.'

It was hard not to lose sight of the diminutive officer as they followed her across the crowded room. Screens had been set up along one wall, dividing off cubicles with chairs and tables. Hilary glimpsed other interviews being conducted in some of them.

The space they were allocated was cramped. They squeezed into the chairs on one side of the table. There was no one facing them.

They waited.

'There's something about the police,' Hilary murmured. 'Even if you're innocent, they can give you the feeling that you must have done something wrong.'

It was a long time before the screen was moved aside. When Hilary and Veronica turned, rather too quickly, it was not the DI they were expecting. They met the stern features of DS Olive Petersen, who had challenged them at the abbey for interfering with the witness Amina Haddad. Her face held the same unfriendly stare.

'You two again? What is it this time? Can't you see we're rushed off our feet?'

'We have an appointment with DI Fellows,' Veronica told her more politely than Hilary would have. 'He seemed rather more keen to hear what we have to tell him than you do. I should have thought that any information which might lead to arresting whoever did this was what you wanted.'

'As long as it's hard information this time, and not more Miss Marple lookalikes wanting to be in on the action.'

'I think we'll ignore that,' Hilary said. 'We can wait for your senior officer.'

Detective Inspector Robert Fellows looked as harassed as the desk sergeant. But he forced a smile for them as he advanced swiftly, his hand held out.

'Mrs Taylor, Mrs Masters? Good of you to come. Sorry to keep you waiting. It's bedlam here.'

A slim, youngish man she guessed to be still in his thirties. Fast-tracked for promotion. *Yes*, she thought shrewdly, *your investigation into the unexploded bomb I found at the Chalice Well will have been taken out of your hands. This is for the big boys now. A detective chief superintendent, probably, not a lowly inspector.*

'It was the coincidence that struck us. Seeing him at the Chalice Well before I found the bomb there, and now this afternoon. Right at the time when the second bomb went off, he was there. He and his wife. Just far enough to be out of range of the blast . . .'

'Only just,' Veronica said softly. 'We were in line on the pavement. So was his wife. He was still in the shop doorway.'

'Fair enough,' Hilary said. 'We could have been hit by the debris. So could she. Well, we were pretty much showered with it, but nothing big, thank God.'

'Let's start from the beginning, shall we?' The inspector sat down opposite them. DS Petersen seated herself beside him with her notepad ready. 'Now, just for the record, suppose you tell me who you're talking about.'

'George Marsden, of course. At least, that's who the assistant at the Chalice Well gift shop said he was. We've not exactly been introduced. We've been looking for him ever since.'

'For the reporter,' Veronica put in. 'Joan Townsend. She needed more of a story.'

'She's got one now,' snapped the DS.

'Yes, well. That's why we followed his wife down the High Street.'

'First things first. This began when you saw his wife? Mrs Marsden? Not Mr? When and where?'

He took them through Veronica's sense that she had seen the woman by the parked car before, tea at the Copper Kettle, the sudden memory of who the woman was. Then Veronica phoning Joan Townsend and the two of them rushing out on to the pavement. Tracking their quarry down to find the irate George Marsden pouring out an earful to the owner of the Archive of Avalon.

'And just the same sort of shop as the one which was blown up,' Hilary finished triumphantly. 'He really does seem to have a grudge against that sort of stuff.'

'All those poor people,' Veronica said softly.

DI Fellows looked sideways at his sergeant. 'You tracked him down didn't you, Olive? After the Chalice Well thing?'

'There were dozens of visitors at the well that day. Marsden was no more suspicious than any of the others. He'd gone before the knapsack was discovered. Not hanging around like they're trying to say he was today.'

'Fair point.' The detective inspector's fingers played lightly over the table top, as if they remembered a passage of music.

Then he sighed. 'Right, thank you.' He gave them a tired smile. 'As you can see, this is a major enquiry now. Any information may be useful. Thank you for your time.'

He rose to dismiss them.

Hilary found herself reluctant to let the matter go. 'Do you think it's significant? Could he be your bomber?'

'At this moment, half of Glastonbury could be.'

'You were in both places yourselves,' DS Petersen said, rather more tartly than was necessary.

They were back out on the streets, which were swarming with black ants. Diverted past the shattered section of the High Street, where the forensic white ants were busy at work. Nothing to do now, Hilary realized sombrely, but to remember the scene she did not want to.

FOURTEEN

'Hilary,' Veronica ventured, 'we don't have to stay. It's not exactly turning out to be the holiday we planned.'

A hush seemed to have fallen over the little town as they walked back to the hotel. Hilary struggled to remember what time of day it was, or even what day. She looked at her watch. Five o'clock. Wednesday. It seemed incredible that earlier this afternoon they had been strolling contentedly through the wetlands of the nature reserve.

'Is that what you want to do? Go home?'

For her own part, she was aware of the loneliness of the empty house that awaited her without David.

'Or we could finish the week somewhere else. Wells, perhaps. It's got a lovely cathedral.'

'Hmm.'

'What's that supposed to mean? Hilary! You're not going to let go, are you? You still think that because you found that bag you've got to be the one who discovers who did it. That's ridiculous. The whole police force is on to it now. What can you do that they can't?'

'I still have this feeling there must be something I missed. We were so close. We must have seen whoever planted it.'

'Nonsense. There's no saying when it was left at the well. Let alone the one in the High Street. The bomber was probably gone long before we came on the scene.'

'I can't answer for the second one, but the one at the Chalice Well can't have been there long. Somebody else would have seen it.'

'Do you think it wasn't meant to go off? Someone wanted it found?'

'I'm not a criminal psychologist.'

'But today changes everything. Seven people killed. That's terrible.'

'I wish I could phone the hospital and ask them if Baz is still alive. But they wouldn't tell me. I'm not a relative.'

She pictured the young man's pale face as she had stood aside, rather shakily, and relinquished him to the care of the paramedics. She wanted desperately to believe that she had saved his life, but she could not be sure.

They turned in at the hotel. Veronica dropped her bag on the bed. She started to tidy her hair in front of the mirror, when suddenly she dropped the comb.

'Goodness me! I never thought. The children! If they get news of this . . . I'd better phone them.'

She snatched her mobile from the bag and switched it on.

'Too late! Oh, dear, I'm in big trouble. That's three text messages from Morag and two from Penny. Thank goodness Robert is abroad. It'll take him a day or two to catch up with this . . . Penny, dear . . . Yes, I'm really sorry . . . Of course I'm all right. It's been a terrible thing, but we were nowhere near at the time.'

Hilary raised her eyebrows. Veronica made a rueful face at the half-lie.

'Yes, we're still in Glastonbury. Anyway, I must go. I've got Morag breathing down my neck too. Love you. Bye.'

She smiled apologetically at Hilary. 'Penny's just finished A-levels. She and her best friend are camping in Wales. You wouldn't think the news would catch up with them that fast in Snowdonia, would you?'

'Nobody's switched off nowadays.'

'Except us. You'd better try your own phone. Oliver and Bridget are probably going mad as well.'

'As long as nobody's told David.'

Did she really wish that?

Mercifully, her married son had not yet switched on the TV to catch up with news of the catastrophe in Glastonbury, but he had seen her face in the morning papers about the Chalice Well.

'Yes, I'm sorry about that. Monday was nothing much. I didn't think I needed to alarm the family. I'm afraid it's got much worse today. You haven't heard? Another bomb, only this one went off. In the High Street. Seven killed . . . Yes, we heard the explosion, but we're both OK. Shocking, isn't it?'

Veronica was making her own peace with Morag at her university. Hilary made similar apologies to her daughter Bridget.

The two women switched off their phones and looked at each other.

'I have to say,' Veronica said, 'Morag wasn't only concerned for my welfare. She wanted to hear every last detail of what happened. I didn't tell her, of course. She got the edited version. But it made me think how journalists, you know, have to switch something off. Change their priorities. All Penny wanted to hear was whether I was safe.'

'Must be girls. Oliver caught the morning's headlines about the Chalice Well. Said he was dashing off to work then, but meant to ring me this evening. Hadn't heard about today, luckily. But Bridget scolded me as though it was all my fault. Said she'd been trying to get in touch with me ever since.'

'I think we're moving into that stage when our children are becoming more worried about us than we are about them. I never thought to ring them straight away.'

'You could say we had more important things on our minds.'

Hilary was becoming aware of a strange, insistent sound coming towards them. A high whistling and the thump of drums. She strode to the window.

Her ears had not deceived her. Coming along the street below was a strange procession. Women in white gowns, with wreaths of flowers in their hair. Some were playing pipes. Others held hands in fours and danced in circles as they advanced. At the rear tabors and tambourines kept up a steady blood-beat.

At the head of them all, like the Pied Piper, pranced the impossibly long-legged figure of Rupert Honeydew in his motley garb.

'What day is it today?' she asked Veronica sharply.

'May the thirteenth.'

'Hmm! I suppose by the old calendar this would have been May Day. Those certainly look like may blossoms they're wearing in their hair.'

'Don't you think it's a bit inappropriate for them to be dancing in the streets? Today of all days.'

'Mmm.' Hilary studied the procession as it jigged beneath her. 'Our mad Rupert is always on about the healing power of the Goddess. Maybe this is his contribution to today's mayhem. A dance for life.'

Veronica had joined her. 'You sound surprisingly sympathetic. After that do on Glastonbury Tor.'

'At least I can put out of my mind the idea that *he* might have been behind the bombing. From the sound of it, the shop that was attacked was just the sort he might have frequented himself. Probably selling his book.'

'Oh, look!' Veronica cried. 'That's someone I never expected to see with him.'

'Who? Where?'

'The fourth circle of dancers from the front. Do you see that one with the short blonde hair? I'm almost sure it's her.

'Who? Stop being so maddeningly obscure.'

'Mel, I think her name was. The young woman behind the counter in the Chalice Well gift shop.'

'Are you sure?' Hilary pushed the window wider open and leaned out. It was hard to tell from above. 'You could be right. But she's the last person . . . I mean, she didn't seem at all sympathetic when we were asking questions about Honeydew. She pushed off as soon as she spotted a customer.'

She stared down for a moment longer, then spun on her heel. In swift strides she was down the stairs, across the lobby and out on the street.

The dancing procession had met the same obstacle as Hilary and Veronica had. The police had cordoned off that section of the High Street where debris from the bomb still littered the ground. The shop that had borne the brunt of it hung drunkenly out from its neighbours.

The drums faltered and died to an almost inaudible tapping. The dancers slowed and stopped. Rupert Honeydew, the Guizer, Hilary remembered, tossed a padded stick in the air. He twirled about and set off along one of the side streets, just as Veronica and Hilary had done. As the line of dancers changed direction, Hilary caught a clear view of the blonde woman Veronica had pointed out. It was true. Seen clearly as she spun, right hand linked to her companions in a star shape, it was undoubtedly Mel from the gift shop.

'A dark horse. She let her friend do all the talking about our Mr Honeydew. You wouldn't have thought Mel had ever seen him before, let alone be one of his dancing troupe.'

'It's probably some sort of esoteric society. Not exactly secret, but what they get up to when they're dressed up like this is quite separate from their everyday life.'

'I wonder where they're going.'

'Let them alone, Hilary. It's got nothing to do with us.'

'Right now, I feel that everything that happens in Glastonbury has to do with us. I'll get my coat. Do you want yours?'

Veronica sighed. 'I suppose so.'

It was not hard to follow the sound of the distant music when Hilary reappeared at the hotel gate with both their jackets. A brisk walk soon brought them in view of the dancers. They had threaded their way round the centre of the town, and seemed to be heading out towards the Chalice Well.

'I can guess where they're bound for,' Hilary said. 'The Tor.'

'They say the terraces round the slopes are really a sacred maze. People dance it to honour the Goddess.'

'Well, this is as far as I feel like going. It's been a long day.'

They stood on the street leading out of town, watching the retreating troupe of dancers. The Tor was hidden from them here, but Hilary could imagine the flashes of white on the grassy cone, as Rupert Honeydew led his dance up the spiralling terraces that encircled the hill.

'I wonder what they'll do when they get to the top,' Veronica mused.

'Some hare-brained ceremony, cooked up in the belief that it's what the ancient Celts did. Victorian romanticism, most of it. An idea of druids and such dreamed up by an overheated imagination. I bet the real Druids were nothing like that.'

'More terrifying,' Veronica agreed.

'Just for a moment yesterday, Rupert Honeydew terrified me, but I don't suppose that makes him genuine.'

'But fancy Mel getting caught up in stuff like that. She seemed such a . . . modern young lady.'

'Not too modern to have fallen under the spell of the Guizer, apparently.'

'So you remembered. About the Guizer.' The words came from an unexpected voice.

Both women turned. Blue eyes surveyed them through a slit in the burka. Amina Haddad held a notebook covered in her swift writing.

Hilary registered a feeling of shock.

'You're still taking notes for your thesis, on a day like today?'

The eyes narrowed thoughtfully. 'Who's to say that what happened in the High Street isn't connected with the deep old traditions of a place like this? I know you laugh at Rupert Honeydew and his kind as a comic sideshow, but there are dark and strong beliefs under what he does. Don't underestimate their power.'

Amina was in her twenties, still a post-graduate student. Hilary had just retired from a lifetime in the teaching profession. But she felt rebuked by the younger woman's authority.

'If you say so,' she said abruptly. 'Not my field.'

'Excuse me,' Amina said, smiling through the slit now. 'You may not feel like climbing the Tor after them, but I think I have to. I can only guess what today's ritual is about.'

'Will they want you there?' Hilary remembered the flash of hatred in Rupert Honeydew's eyes. 'It might be more dangerous than it looks to muscle in on their secret ceremonies.'

'That's OK. I can look after myself. I'll be discreet.'

They watched her blue-gowned figure dwindle along the road towards the Tor.

FIFTEEN

The hotel dining room had an air of desolation. There was only one other table occupied, seemingly by a pair of businessmen. They were talking sombrely, heads bent close together.

'I'm beginning to wish we'd gone out to a local pub,' Hilary said. 'There might have been a jollier atmosphere.'

'Hardly. The locals are bound to have known people involved. I should have thought the atmosphere would be the opposite of jolly.'

'I didn't mean to be crass,' Hilary said gruffly. 'Just, you know, the Blitz spirit. Don't let the rotters get you down.'

A young waiter with a receding chin approached their table. 'Good evening, ladies. Glad to see you're still with us. Not like some.'

'Rats? Sinking ship?'

'Most of them have packed up their bags and gone. Can't really blame them, can you? These things tend to come in threes.'

Hilary turned to stare him in the face. He was a spotted youth with a lugubrious expression.

'Really? You think there's still another bomb to come?'

'My gran says it'll get worse before it gets better.' He placed the menus before them. 'Chef says to tell you the turbot with asparagus is very good.'

'Hmm.' It had not occurred to Hilary that it might not be over yet.

It seemed strange to be pondering what she wanted to eat. Strange to be interested in eating at all. There was an air of unreality that things should go on as before. Of course, for seven families it would not. Eight. If Baz survived, he would have what the press called 'life-changing injuries'.

Hilary attacked her spiced red pepper soup with gusto, but before long she found her appetite waning. Soup was comfort food, like the whisky. The main course was proving harder to

swallow than she had expected. She laid her knife and fork
aside.

'Do you think Amina will be all right?' Veronica asked.

It was an unexpected interruption to Hilary's train of thought.

'I don't see why not. She looks a competent young woman.
Well, *sounds* like one. We haven't seen more than her eyes. And
I've pretty much ruled Rupert Honeydew off the list of suspects
now. If it had been just an exploded bomb at the well then, yes,
I could have dreamed up a rationale for him to do it. But bombing
the crystal shop . . . It doesn't fit. No, I really think he has taken
his acolytes up the Tor to dance before his goddess and perform
some sort of healing. He's a freak, but harmless.'

Veronica twisted her fork but said nothing.

'Yes, well, he did look a bit malevolent yesterday evening,'
Hilary agreed. 'But that could just have been because we'd
invaded his sacred space.'

'He might think that's what Amina is doing if she follows
them, taking notes.'

Hilary sighed. 'We've got a mass murderer in our midst. I
hardly think there's going to be a separate murder of a post-
graduate student with too sharp a nose under that veil.'

'I hope you're right.'

'You may be in trouble with your children for not ringing
them, but you've still got the maternal instinct. Amina, the
Townsend girl, that crying toddler this afternoon.'

'I do hope things worked out for Joan. Somebody must have
taken her big story, mustn't they? It's terrible to think that what
happened today could actually do somebody good, but she *was*
in a prime position to get the first impression.'

'Thanks to you.'

'That was sheer accident. I rang her to tell her we'd found the
Marsdens. I had no idea what was going to happen next.'

'I should hope not. Look, I don't know about you, but I think
I'll skip dessert. We might still be in time to catch the news.'

'It's almost eight o'clock.'

'There's the BBC news channel, or Channel Four Plus One.
We could pick up their seven o'clock news an hour late.'

'If you really want to. I'm not sure I want to hear any more
about disaster and death today.'

'Stay and have your coffee in the lounge, then. I'm going up.'

But Veronica followed her up the stairs.

They were in time to catch the headlines. That repeated figure. Seven dead.

Hilary let out a glad cry of relief. 'That must mean Baz is still alive, surely?'

'I'm glad there's some good news.'

There were pictures of the shattered High Street, speculation about who might have perpetrated the horror. 'No one has claimed responsibility,' a police spokeswoman said. 'The police are currently pursuing several lines of investigation. We have an open mind at this stage, but two local people are currently helping us with our enquiries. A woman of forty-three and a man of sixty-two. I should stress that so far no charges have been made.'

Hilary half leaped out of her chair. 'It's them! It's got to be! The Marsdens.'

'Do you really think so? The police can't have had much to go on. We told them the Marsdens were in the High Street at the time. And at the Chalice Well not long before you found that knapsack. But that's just circumstantial.'

'Never mind.' Hilary sat back with a glow of satisfaction. 'We pointed them in the right direction. They'll have taken it from there. Questioned them, searched the house. That sort of thing.'

'There are thousands of other couples in the Glastonbury area. It may not be them.'

'You mark my words. It's the Marsdens.'

She almost failed to hear the newscaster's next announcement. 'There are reports, too, that the police are keeping an armed guard on one of the seriously injured survivors in hospital. He is thought to be a young man of Eastern Mediterranean origin.

'Baz!' Hilary was on the edge of her seat, her eyes incredulous. 'Oh, no! Surely it can't be him?'

Her impressions of that terrible afternoon somersaulted. Had she made all that effort to keep the bomber alive?

They were woken before midnight. Hilary opened her eyes to find moonlight streaming in through a gap in the curtains. It had a more ethereal quality than the security lights in the hotel car park.

It was not the light which had woken her. An eerie noise was penetrating the bedroom. The window was shut now, but her suddenly sharpened mind recognized the notes of pipes and drums, more ghostly this time, muted by the double glazing. She padded across to the window to see.

'What is it?' Veronica's voice came sleepily from the further bed.

'It's them again. Rupert Honeydew and his circus.'

'What are they doing this time? At this time of night?'

'I rather think it's *particularly* at this time of night. Don't you remember what he said, about dancing to the Goddess at full moon? There's one tonight. The whole countryside's washed with silver. Rather beautiful, really, and a bit eerie.'

'Leave them to it, Hilary. Come back to bed.'

But something nagged at Hilary's brain. 'I can't think they're going up the Tor again. If so, why do it in daylight earlier?'

Before she really knew what she was doing, she had crossed to the wardrobe and was pulling out clothes: trousers, sweatshirt, jacket.

'You're not going out, are you? Don't be an idiot, Hilary. Leave them alone. If it makes them happy to do their dances to their deity, let them get on with it.'

'I want to know what's going on.'

Without waiting to see if Veronica would follow her, she hurried downstairs, patted her pocket to make sure she had remembered the hotel keys, and stepped outside.

The music was suddenly loud, the moonlight brilliant.

The procession it illuminated was not the same as before. There were more men this time. Hilary saw animal masks, as well as the ghostly flowers in the women's hair.

She found herself drawing back into the shadows. She did not understand what was going on, but she sensed that this was more than the sunlit May-time dance she had witnessed earlier. There was a darker element. She watched the light flash on eyes glimpsed through the holes in the masks. She was reminded, incongruously, of Amina's burka, though the student's eyes had looked nothing like this. Was it the evil that had erupted in the High Street which had called forth this darker response? What did Rupert Honeydew mean by leading this dance through the streets of Glastonbury at midnight?

She looked up at the other houses along the road. Here and there, curtains had been tweaked aside and the occupants peered out. But few other people had come out to stand at the roadside, as she had.

She looked over her shoulder and was more relieved than she had expected to find Veronica standing behind her. The slighter woman had her hands in her pockets and her shoulders hunched, as if against the cold, though the night air was mild.

'That drumming gets into your blood, doesn't it?' she murmured. 'Like Padstow at May Day.'

'I wonder what they're doing. It can't be the Tor again, surely?'

Past St John the Baptist's church, the procession of dancers had halted as before where the police tape barred the way to the central High Street and the epicentre of the explosion. The figure of a policeman loomed against the light on the other side. The drums were beating insistently. Was Rupert Honeydew going to stage a confrontation? Break through the tape and lead his dancers to reclaim the wounded heart of the town?

He held out his long arms sideways, palms down. The drumming subsided to a gentler rhythm. The pipers keened and a singing rose from the ranks of stationary dancers. It was an eerie sound in the moonlight. A shiver ran down Hilary's spine. It was piercingly beautiful, and yet it scared her. She had an uneasy feeling that the singing might be conjuring up something she did not want to believe existed. Foolish, really. Just the effect of the moonlight and the darker shadows, the unearthly singing, the relentless rhythm of the drums. It must be calling to something buried thousands of years deep in her past.

'Can you see Amina?' Veronica whispered.

Surprised, Hilary peered through the tricking shadows that barred the moonlight. The street lighting fell only in intermittent pools.

'No. Why? Should I?'

'She was here before. I should have thought this was even more relevant to her thesis. There's much more going on here than women in white, dancing with flowers in their hair.'

'She's probably tucked up safely in bed somewhere. Doesn't

know what she's missing. We wouldn't have known ourselves if they hadn't come prancing past our window, with their drums a-drumming and their pipes a-piping.'

'I hope nothing's happened to her.'

The chanting from further up the street was growing. It had a hypnotic quality. The lone policeman had been joined by a female colleague. Lamplight showed her high-visibility jacket a lurid yellow. They were conferring together, but seemed uncertain what to do.

The women were plucking flowers from their hair now, throwing them across the cordon into the damaged street. White blossoms snowed down on the road, where a crueller debris had fallen earlier. Hilary shuddered, remembering. And still the sweetness of the singing went on. Rupert was chanting something in a deeper voice, though Hilary could not hear the words, or if she could, they were in a language she did not understand.

'I think it's a healing ceremony,' Veronica whispered. 'For all those dead or injured. Isn't that what he talked about? The healing Goddess?'

'That sounds benign. I'd like to think that's all it is, but it gives me goose pimples.'

'That's because your brain can't understand what's going on. Just take your intellect out of the way and *feel* it.'

A brilliant flash lit up the ranks of singers and musicians. Startled faces turned. Rupert Honeydew spun round, his long face caught in a second explosion of light.

He strode forward, thrusting the startled dancers aside. A long arm shot out and seized the camera from a dark-clad figure which had crept up to the back of the group. Something went sailing across the lamplight to land with a crash in the road.

A wail rose. A woman's voice. 'My camera! You filthy beast!'

'Goodness me! It's Joan!' Veronica cried.

'The little idiot. What did she *think* would happen?'

The young woman was a dark animal now, down on all fours, scrabbling underneath the police tape to lunge for her shattered camera. She seemed to be shovelling the fragments into a white bag. The police officers came running towards her. She was lifted bodily by the elbows and hustled back towards the tape. Moonlight sparkled in the tears on her cheeks.

The dancers drew back in silence to let her pass. Rupert
Honeydew drew a sign in the air over her head that Hilary feared
meant her no good.

Joan Townsend stumbled towards them, not seeing them,
clutching her plastic bag. Veronica stepped out into her path.

'Joan! I'm so sorry. Is it badly damaged?'

Joan halted and looked up at them, blankly at first.

'Oh. Mrs Taylor, it's you. Of course it's damaged! Three
hundred pounds, that cost me. I only hope the memory card is
all right. It's just my luck. This was going to be another exclusive.
Black Magic in Bomb-hit Town. I'd got a couple of mega shots,
but I don't even know if the card is still usable. How am I going
to get more pictures without a camera?'

'Have you got the memory card in that bag? If you have, I'm
sure you'll do brilliantly with what you've got. You really think
this is black magic, do you? Not some healing ceremony?'

'With those masks?'

'Yes, well, they do look a bit scary in the moonlight, don't
they? But this afternoon you were the first reporter on the spot.
You must have got someone to take your story then.'

'You'd think so, wouldn't you? I was *hours* ahead of most of
the competition. But I haven't got a big name for a by-line, have
I? They'll just take anything I've filed and mix it in with a whole
jumble of other stuff. It'll be a front-page story, all right, but I
won't be the one who gets the credit. Nothing I do is enough.'

'Poor you,' Veronica soothed.

Selfish little brat, Hilary thought. *Seven people dead. Two
children. Baz has probably lost a leg.* And then the thought hit
her: Baz himself might be the bomber.

*And all you can think of is whether you get your name in the
papers.*

She did not say this.

The singing beyond them seemed to have entered a new phase.
The dancers were holding hands in a long chain, beginning to
sway to the music as the pipes and drums summoned them. They
were revolving now into the side streets, encircling the damaged
heart. And still the drums beat out a mournful rhythm and the
voices called down a litany of grief.

The sound faded into the distance.

'Will you be all right?' Veronica asked Joan. 'Would you like us to walk you home?'

'It's OK,' the girl said dully. 'I'd better get back and write up what I've got. See if I've got any salvageable pictures. It's too late for the morning paper now, anyway. Just my luck.'

'Poor girl,' Veronica sympathized as Joan trudged away down the street. 'It must be heartbreaking to be at the centre of things and not be able to make her voice heard.'

'She might start thinking about other people for a change, and not how a thing like this affects her career prospects.'

'Did you see Mel there among the dancers?' Veronica asked as they turned in at the hotel gate.

'No. But I wasn't really looking. Why? Does it matter?'

'It was just something you said. After that do at the Chalice Well. You started to question her and you said afterwards that she looked scared.'

'Did I?'

'At first, while they were piping and dancing, there was something rather enchanting about it. But now, well, I keep remembering those animal masks, and how frightening Rupert Honeydew can be. I'm pretty sure Mel wasn't there this time. I can't help wondering why.'

'Amina Haddad. Joan Townsend. And now the girl from the gift shop. You should start a Society for the Protection of Young Females in Glastonbury.'

'I expect it's just my imagination.' Veronica laughed uncertainly.

SIXTEEN

'There's a memorial service at the parish church this morning. Do you want to go?'

'Need you ask?'

Veronica looked at her friend with concern. 'I worry about you. You're too caught up in this. It's not entirely reasonable. We don't know any of the people who died or were injured.'

'I do!'

Hilary had a sudden vivid memory of using her belt to strap a tourniquet round Baz's thigh. Trying desperately to keep him conscious. Seeing him stretchered away into an ambulance. Later that afternoon she had taken the laundry bag with her ruined trousers and dumped it in a rubbish bin at the back of the hotel. She had washed away all Baz's blood – so *much* blood – in the shower, but she could not erase him from her imagination. She wished she knew what had happened to him.

The cold was coming back to her. The police were keeping a guard on Baz. Was that because he was a vital witness? Or . . . She must not let herself think about the alternative.

'Anyway, I rather thought you might like to go. It's eleven o'clock.'

'I always bring a skirt on these holidays, thinking I might dress up a bit in the evening, but I never do. This time I might actually get to wear it. It seems more respectful for a memorial service than trousers, don't you think?'

The skirt in question was a deep green. Hilary did not feel the need to dress in black for mourning. A sober green would suit the occasion well enough. Services like this were expressions of loss, but also of hope in eternal life. She hoped it would comfort her, as well as the families.

The streets were alive with people again. They clustered thickly in front of the church of St John the Baptist, with its elegantly tall tower.

'I should have known the TV cameras would be out in force. Ghouls.'

'They're just doing their job. There hasn't been such a loss of life since the bombings on the Underground. Of course the nation wants to know.'

They had left the hotel prudently early. They just squeezed into one of the back pews in the north aisle. The church interior was heavy with the scent of white lilies.

Hilary studied the ranks of mourners in the pews at the front of the church. The first seats would, of course, be relatives of the dead, some of those tragically young. There were rows of uniforms, representing the police, the rescue services. Outside, work was still going on in the High Street, making the buildings safe. The town was swarming with police officers. Were they still questioning that couple, almost certainly the Marsdens? Or had they been released?

She looked round for Joan Townsend and did not see her. Hers was probably one of the battery of cameras waiting outside. Then she remembered: Joan's expensive camera had been shattered when Rupert Honeydew tore it out of her hands last night. Was it insured? Would she have been able to buy another?

Veronica dug her suddenly in the ribs. 'I didn't expect to see *him* here.'

Hilary followed the turn of her head. Across the nave, in the opposite aisle and a little behind them, an exceptionally tall man was making his way into one of the last seats. Today he wore a sober brown jacket and grey flannels. It seemed almost impossible to equate him with the figure clad in motley-coloured rags prancing through the moonlit streets at the head of drummers and dancers in animal masks, tossing his padded club in the air. But it was him, without a doubt. Rupert Honeydew, Amina's Guizer.

The thought sent Hilary's eyes darting round the packed church again. There was no sign of Amina in her blue burka. But then, why should there be? The service would no doubt be designed to appeal to a wide range of beliefs, but Amina's strict Muslim faith was unlikely to find a place in it. This would not form part of her folkloric research.

It was foolish to feel a prick of anxiety on her behalf. She should leave that sort of thing to Veronica.

The memory of those small hands busy taking notes at the well came back to her.

The congregation was rising as the organ music swelled. A small procession was coming up the aisle. The mayor and mayoress of Glastonbury in their gold chains took their seats in one of the front pews. Then came the clergy and choristers of the parish church, followed by the bishop in a purple mitre and cope.

Anglicanism did this sort of thing rather well, Hilary thought. The grave ceremonial. Young voices rising in the piercing beauty of music from Fauré's Requiem Mass. The centuries-old beauty of the architecture, which had seen so many mournings and celebrations and outlived them all. She felt for the relatives of the dead she could only see from the back, and hoped they were deriving some comfort from this loveliness, this majesty.

The words of resurrection uplifted her.

The Bishop of Bath and Wells gave a short but rather fine address on the transcendence of hope.

And then it was over. Veronica and Hilary waited patiently for the crush to subside before leaving their short side pew.

Outside, spring sunshine welcomed them, and the flash of batteries of cameras.

'She isn't here,' Veronica said. 'I thought she would be, even if her camera's broken.'

'Amina isn't either, though that's hardly such a surprise. Who was the third one of your chicks?'

'Mel from the gift shop, if you must know. And no, she isn't here either. I'm really not being a broody hen, Hilary. Mel's probably at work, unless they've closed the Chalice Well for the occasion.'

'It seems a bit incongruous to think of people coming here for the usual tourist visit to the well, on a day like this.'

'People do such strange things. They'll come to stare at the place where people died, and then go off and enjoy themselves for the rest of the day.'

'Though come to think of it,' Hilary mused, 'the Chalice Well gardens might actually be a good place to find peace.'

'Is that what we're going to do?'

'I hadn't thought. Perhaps we should have left by now, as that hotel waiter thought we would have.'

Veronica had her mobile out. She was frowning as she keyed in the number and held the device to her ear.

'She isn't answering.'

'Who are you phoning?'

'Joan, poor soul. I wanted to make sure she's all right.'

'I thought it was Amina you were worried about, after she insisted on chasing Rupert Honeydew's lot up the Tor.'

'Did I hear someone taking my name in vain? Ladies!'

Hilary was not a tall woman at the best of times, but she felt intimidatingly dwarfed by the unnatural height of the man who had come up behind her. He did not need the black top hat of his Guizer's costume to make him toweringly tall. His lean face surveyed them coolly.

'For two strangers to Glastonbury, you seem to turn up at remarkably sensitive times.'

'The Chalice Well was pure coincidence. And yesterday we were in the High Street when the bomb went off. We have an interest in today's service. I rather hope I may have saved one of the casualties' life.'

'Quite the heroine, aren't you?'

'That wasn't what I meant!' Indignation was growing. 'I was just trying to point out that we have reason to be here. We're not just rubber-necking.'

'I certainly thought it was more than that.'

'What are you getting at?'

She was rescued by a party of five coming down the church-yard path towards them. With a flash of gladness she recognized Sister Mary Magdalene stepping off on to the grass to by-pass them. Behind her came four of her pupils in purple uniform. They looked sombre. One of them had the traces of tears on her cheeks. Hilary remembered how they too had been caught up in the horror of yesterday's bombing, how Sister Mary Magdalene had praised the girls' courage in helping the wounded.

'It was a fine service, wasn't it?' the nun said. 'The bishop always does rise well to the occasion.'

'Establishment flummery!' Rupert Honeydew almost spat. 'I could show them where real healing lies. It's not here, but right up there.' He gestured to the Tor. 'Or at the red spring.'

'We all find our own paths to peace.' Sister Mary Magdalene smiled. 'May the Lord bless you on yours.'

She forged on towards the gate, and Hilary was glad to let herself be towed in the wake of the slight figure in her neat grey suit.

She looked sideways at the schoolgirls accompanying the nun. A twinge of nostalgia overcame her. Forty years. She would not stand in front of a classroom of pupils like that again.

She was jolted out of memories of the past by the sound of a furious argument on the pavement ahead.

'It's a disgrace! My home town is attacked by bloody foreigners and I can't even get into my own parish church to show my respect for the dead.'

'It's Marsden!' Hilary exclaimed. 'The police have let him go.'

'And Joan!' exclaimed Veronica. 'She's got her interview.'

The stocky journalist was almost overwhelmed by the thickening crowd. Other reporters and photographers were homing in on the scene. Bulbs were flashing.

Marsden swung round at Hilary's words. The bulging eyes caught hers. 'Not like some! They let strangers into the service, but not me.'

To her dismay, Hilary found the attention of the crowd turning on her. She held up her hands. 'We just wanted to pray for the bereaved and the injured.'

'Mark my words,' George Marsden was shouting, 'it's what comes of letting Muslims into this country. They should turn them back at the ports and airports, the whole lot of them. Jibberjabbering in their heathen language, building mosques.'

Ugly shouts of agreement rose from some of the bystanders.

'I've even seen one of their women dressed up in one of those – what do you call 'em? Like a tent.'

'A burka,' someone shouted out.

'Call it what you like, I've seen one of them right here in Glastonbury. And don't tell me that's got nothing to do with this bomb. I ask you, what honest woman is going to go around covered up in one of those, so you can't see what's underneath. How do we even know it *is* a woman?'

The sound of unrest was growing louder. Hilary was beginning to feel alarmed.

'She is. We've spoken to her.' Veronica ventured to raise her voice, but no one listened to her. Microphones were being thrust forward, questions shouted.

'Oh dear,' Hilary sighed. 'Maybe it's a good thing Amina isn't here this morning.'

'But she will be other mornings, unless she's packed up and gone.'

George Marsden was in full flow, but one question stopped him dead.

'Mr Marsden, is it true that you and your wife were held for questioning by the police?'

'That's an infamous suggestion! We were doing our public duty, helping the police with their enquiries into a dastardly murder. We were key witnesses, Sonia and I. We were right there on the High Street when that bomb went off. Another few yards and it could have killed us.'

'So why did the police detain you? Did it have anything to do with the fact that you were bawling out the owner of a shop very like the one which was bombed?'

There was a sudden tumult among the barrage of microphones held out towards him. George Marsden seized one of them and clouted the owner over the head.

'George, no!' his wife's voice commanded above the shouts of surprise. 'That's not the way to deal with these idiots.'

Today, the small dark-haired woman wore a black dress and jacket, against which a large silver cross glistened. She was almost engulfed by the press pack and the angry crowd of onlookers, but she stood her ground.

Her husband glared at her. 'I'll decide for myself what's the right way to deal with louts who say I'm not an upright God-fearing Englishman.'

From the thick of the mêlée a policeman appeared, working his way authoritatively through the struggling ranks of reporters and photographers. He laid a firm hand on George Marsden's shoulder and fended off the press pack with the other.

'Let's have a little order here, shall we? Show some respect. There's a funeral service going on here today.'

'Not a funeral,' Hilary muttered, 'a memorial service.'

But the uniform was having an effect. The misused microphone was restored to its owner. A policewoman had arrived and was shepherding Sonia and George Marsden away. Reporters were eagerly recording the event to camera or scribbling in notebooks. Out of the throng emerged a figure in a sagging brown cardigan.

'Joan!' Veronica cried. 'You're OK. I couldn't get you on your phone.'

'If you call this OK.' As so often, the would-be journalist was close to tears. 'This was *my* interview. Then everyone else muscled in. Not that it would have done me any good. I was right there in the High Street yesterday, for heaven's sake. The first journalist on the scene by miles. And what do I get? A couple of lines in one of the dailies, as if I was just any other passer-by. They just binned the article I wrote myself. A terrorist bomb. Seven people blown up. What more do I have to do?'

Veronica looked shocked. 'Joan, dear, those people are dead. I hardly think who gets the credit for reporting it is the most important thing.'

'Maybe not to you.'

The street was quieting around them. George Marsden, still arguing, was being urged further down the road by the police, followed by his wife. The bishop, the grieving families, the mayor and mayoress, Rupert Honeydew, Sister Mary Magdalene and her schoolgirls had all long since gone.

Hilary pulled Veronica's arm. 'Leave her. She's not worth bothering with. Let's restore a bit of sanity and go and find lunch.'

SEVENTEEN

'I tell you what,' Hilary said. 'You may be right about Wells. We don't have to change hotels, but let's leave this madhouse behind us and treat ourselves to an afternoon at the cathedral.'

'Good idea,' Veronica said. 'That was a lovely service, but that Marsden bigot has left rather a sour taste in the mouth, and as for Joan . . .'

'I take it your sympathy for our tyro journalist has diminished.'

'If not completely evaporated. I know they have to be single-minded, but there really are limits.'

They drove northwards away from the Levels through the gently rising hills. After the grief and devastation of Glastonbury, Wells received them with joyful arms.

'I do think it's such a jolly thing to have a moat round your bishop's palace.' Hilary laughed.

The water sparkled under the grey walls. Visitors were feeding swans. There was even a rowing boat. They crossed over into the cathedral close.

'It really is gorgeous, isn't it?' Veronica said happily.

'I like the chapter house best.'

They climbed the shallow stone steps to the octagonal chamber where the canons of the cathedral had gathered, each in his own seat around the walls, for cathedral business.

Afterwards, they wandered through the cathedral's forest of pillars, where masons had used their imaginations to carve foliage and surprising figures.

'There he is!' Hilary pointed with glee. 'The man nursing a toothache. And those naughty boys over there are being belaboured by the farmer for scrumping fruit. The Gothic is so much more fun than the classical, don't you think? Giving craftsmen and women the choice to show what they could do individually, not just repeating the same austere formula by the yard.'

It was only when they stepped back out into the water-ringed sunshine that the smile faded.

'So the police don't think the Marsdens did it. Or if they do, they haven't got enough proof to hold them.'

'Hilary! This was supposed to be an afternoon off.'

'It was meant to be a whole week off when we came to Glastonbury. But something happened to change that and we can't pretend that it didn't.'

'It's almost certain that the bombs were left by someone we've never even met and wouldn't recognize if we saw them.'

'Hmm.'

There were new arrivals at the Bowes Hotel. A van in the car park bore a logo in a script that Hilary decided was probably Japanese.

'A television crew. You mark my words.'

The van's Asian-looking occupants were chatting in the bar.

'So we really are world news.'

'It looks like it.'

Back in their room, Hilary switched on the early-evening local news. There were shots of the memorial service: the bishop in his mitre, a young friend of one of the dead reading a poem. Nothing about the altercation with George Marsden outside.

'The police have today confirmed earlier reports that they are mounting an armed guard on a young man in a local hospital who was critically injured by the blast. A spokeswoman said that officers are standing by to interview him, but it is not yet certain whether he will recover. Police sources would not reveal the name.'

'Baz!' Hilary's hand flew to her mouth. 'It has to be. So he's not out of danger yet. I tried ringing the hospital again this morning, but it was as I expected. They wouldn't release any information to someone who wasn't family. I don't even know his second name.

'Even if it is him, we still don't know why the police are guarding him. It doesn't have to mean he's a suspect. You said yourself, he could have vital information.'

'But if it *was* him . . .'

The scene in the immediate aftermath of the explosion came back to Hilary with shattering clarity. The pale young man with his almost-severed leg, herself willing him to cling on to life, the pumping blood, the tourniquet. All for what? She felt sick at the possibility.

'Hilary, I don't want to worry you, but thinking about that television crew downstairs. If the news has got as far as Japan, there's a chance that David may have caught up with it in Gaza. You really should switch your phone on more often.'

'Do you really think so?' Hilary felt a sinking feeling of dread. She had not wanted to burden David with this. He was facing enough trauma. She had made the children promise not to tell him. Now she switched on her mobile with a feeling of guilt.

The text message was terse. *Ring me. David.* And all the more urgent because of that.

It was both a joy and a chastisement to hear the urgency in his voice. 'Hilary! Why in heaven's name didn't you phone me?'

'I didn't want to worry you.'

Veronica got up with an apologetic finger to her lips and left the room.

'Worry me! For heaven's sake, woman! What was I supposed to think when I hear there's been a terrorist attack on Glastonbury, and there's no message from you?'

'I'm OK, really. Well, that is . . .'

It all came tumbling out: their proximity to the explosion, the casualties on the pavement, desperately trying to save Baz's life. 'And now they say he's under police guard in hospital. They must think it's him. What if all the time I was trying to save his life, he was . . .?'

'Love,' David's voice came gently. 'What do you think it's like in Gaza? I may find a militant on the operating table who's fired a homemade rocket at civilians in a futile attempt to regain his former homeland. Or it may be a child here who was hit in the retaliation. A human life is a human life. You had Baz's life in your hands, and you did what you had to. What any of us would have done in your place.'

'Thank you.' It would take some time to decide whether his words really made her feel better.

'But all the more reason you should have rung me straight away. I was going mad here, trying to find out what I could from the kids. When are you going to get past the stage of believing that a mobile phone is just something you carry in your handbag in case the car breaks down and you need to ring the AA? It's a means of communication, dammit. It's meant to keep people in touch. Did it have to be the children who told me you'd found another bomb before this one? What have you got yourself into?'

'I'm sorry,' she said, more meekly than was usual for her. 'I will try to remember to keep it switched on. Only then I have to be sure to charge the dratted thing. We seemed to manage perfectly well before they invented the things.'

'Well, it's not going to be un-invented. Use it.'

'I will. Look, sorry.' It was so good to hear his voice, to feel the love disguised as anger. She did not want to let him go. 'I really should ring off. This call must be costing a week's pension.'

'Of course. You're a lady of leisure now. I keep forgetting. You're free to go where you like. Well, all I can say is, leave Glastonbury. If it turns out your Baz is not the bomber, then the real one is still at large. I'd be happier if you were a hundred miles away.'

'Veronica and I have talked about that. I'll keep you posted.'

'Make sure you do this time.'

Their expressions of love sounded trite over the phone. Hilary was not very good at this sort of thing. But she was more comforted than she thought she would be by the knowledge that there was someone who cared so much about her, even if he was halfway round the world.

She went downstairs and found Veronica in the bar. The younger woman's eyebrows rose.

'All right?'

'Yes and no. I got a fair bollocking from his lordship. I've promised I'll keep my phone switched on in future. But it was good to hear his voice.'

The words were out before she could stop them. Veronica would never hear Andrew's voice again.

'I wonder if we should phone her.' Hilary put down her coffee cup and tapped her fingers on the arm of the leather chair.

'Who?'

'Amina. To let her know George Marsden may have unleashed a lynch mob on her. I wish I'd thought of it before.'

'Do you have her number?'

'No.'

'Well, then, there's nothing we can do. Unless you want to tell the police that she may need protection. They know about her, anyway. She was detained in the gift shop at the Chalice Well when they were interviewing potential witnesses.'

'Hmm. Everybody's always telling me I ought to be more connected. Maybe I will.'

She hoisted herself out of the chair and strode across to the bar. In the farther corner the Japanese TV crew were enjoying an after-dinner pot of tea.

'Excuse me. I see you've got your laptop with you. Would you mind terribly if I borrowed it for a few minutes?'

The young reporter looked startled, but flashed her a polite smile. 'Yes. Go ahead.'

He had to tell her the hotel's Wi-Fi password and show her how to use it to access the internet. Hilary felt more than ever out of touch with the modern world. It was a relief to see the familiar Google logo come up on the screen.

She entered 'Amina Haddad'.

'Bingo!' As she had expected, there was a flush of results. Amina was an active member of the academic community. Her name came up in association with university projects and published papers.

'Bristol University,' Hilary said, half to herself.

She made a note of other researchers working with Amina in the same field.

'There! We should strike gold with at least one of these.'

She handed the laptop back to its owner with a beaming smile. He bowed his acknowledgement.

'Now it's down to directory enquiries,' she said as she returned to Veronica. 'Keep your fingers crossed.'

She struck lucky with the first attempt. Professor Robert Hadley, anthropology. She listened to his home number ring.

'Hello. Hilary Masters here. I'm sorry to disturb you outside college hours, but I'm concerned about one of your students. Amina Haddad?'

'Yes. Why? Has something happened to her?'

'Not yet, as far as I know. But I need to warn her. Did you know she was in Glastonbury?'

'No. Well, not exactly. I knew it was on her list for field research, but . . . My God, the bombing! Don't say she was caught up in that?'

'Well, yes and no. As far as I'm aware, she was nowhere near it. But, well, you know she's adopted the burka, and that sort of thing doesn't go down too well at a time like this. Religious stereotype. Islamic terrorists.' She tried to suppress the thought that those suspicions might indeed be well founded. 'Anyway, you know the sort of thing.'

'I do indeed. She ought to get out of there.'

'That's what I want to tell her. There's a rather unpleasant character going around stoking up hatred against her in particular. It seems he's seen her around the town. And at the Chalice Well where the first bomb was found. Do you have her phone number?'

At first she thought he wasn't going to tell her.

'I'll ring her myself. I can see why you're concerned.'

'I'd like to tell her specifically what was said and by whom.'

To her relief, Professor Hadley looked up his records and read out the number to her.

'Thank you. I'll warn her straight away. I just hope I haven't left it too late.'

'Hang on. I've got an address here. One of my other students used it before. I think I recommended it to Amina for when she got around to going to Glastonbury. It's a guest house. Not too expensive for a research student budget.'

With growing elation, Hilary copied it down. This was more than she had hoped for.

'Well, thank you, Mrs Masters. It's good that someone's concerned about Amina at a time like this. I wouldn't want anything to happen to her.'

'Nor would I. Thank you too.'

She turned to Veronica in triumph, waving her slip of paper.

'There you are. Chick number one located. We'd better check up on her straight away. Fingers crossed. It worries me that George Marsden and his ilk have had most of the day to get ahead of us.'

EIGHTEEN

Hilary showed the address to the receptionist, who directed her which way to go. It lay on the other side of town. At the far end of the High Street, they picked up the now-familiar road that skirted the far side of the abbey grounds and led out to the Chalice Well and the Tor. But before long, they turned off it into a residential area of red-brick houses with flower-filled gardens.

'It seems strange,' Veronica said quietly, 'after all that's happened. This could be a suburban road in any English town. Glastonbury has always seemed remarkable in so many ways. So much astonishing Christian history, and now all the New Age stuff. And yet it's also full of ordinary people, living ordinary lives, just like anywhere else.'

'A little ordinariness wouldn't come amiss. It's got too remarkable for comfort just now.'

'This is number forty-seven.'

Veronica let Hilary go ahead up the narrow path past the blue hydrangea bush to the front door. A sharp-faced woman in spectacles opened it.

'Excuse me, I'm wondering if you could help us. We're looking for a young woman called Amina Haddad. Is she lodging here?'

'That one! Of course, I knew from the name on the booking she had to be a foreigner. I'm not prejudiced. But when she turned up in that tent-thing they wear, you could have knocked me down with a feather. I was all for shutting the door in her face. But she said I'd agreed to rent her a room, and it was against the law to turn her away because of her religion. Little madam!'

The whiskered face of her husband appeared behind her, tugging his pullover down over his ample chest.

'It's all this human rights nonsense. A man's not boss in his own home. I wouldn't have given her house room.'

'Not that she wasn't a quiet enough tenant. No bother. Only thing, she wouldn't eat downstairs with the others. She used to take her meals up to her room on a tray.'

'Beats me how they can eat at all with that ruddy great blanket over them.'

'I expect she takes it off in private,' Hilary said. 'But you talk about her in the past. Isn't she staying here now?'

'She is and she isn't, as you might say. Her stuff's still here, but she's scarpered. Went out yesterday and didn't come back. And it looks as if she won't be in tonight, either. The least she might have done is told me. Here's me not knowing whether to cook her supper or not.'

'No pork,' her husband said over her shoulder. 'Not even bacon for breakfast. What a life.'

'Thank you, anyway. You've been very helpful.'

Her heart was falling. It seemed as if Veronica's worst fears were coming true. She started to turn away, but the landlady's voice stopped her.

'She's not in trouble, is she? All those bombs. It scared the life out of me. And then this morning . . . I thought they'd have the door down.'

'Who?' Hilary's voice was suddenly sharp. 'Has someone else been here asking for her?'

'More than asking for her. A whole mob of them, there was, shouting their heads off. "Murderer! Terrorist!" And the language! If I'd seen her again, I'd have told her. This is a respectable house. I can't have things like that going on here. I've my other guests to think about. She'll have to leave.'

'But she never came back,' came Veronica's quiet voice.

'Maybe she got the hint that she wasn't welcome and took the next bus back to Bristol,' said her husband.

'Leaving all her possessions behind?'

'Yes, well. Likely she'll come back for them when all the fuss has died down.'

'Tell you something, though,' his wife added. 'She did give me a pot of flowers before she went. Sort of thank-you present, like.'

'Thank you,' Hilary repeated, and turned to go.

Her face felt frozen. She had laughed indulgently over Veronica's maternal concern for the young women caught up in this case: Amina, Mel from the gift shop, and the unfortunate Joan. Now, in one case, those fears were taking concrete and disturbing form.

They walked back down the road in a shocked silence.

'What do we do now?' Veronica asked as they turned the corner. 'Report it to the police? Do you think she had a reason of her own to leave in a hurry? But I don't like the sound of that gang of thugs. They sound just the sort of people George Marsden was trying to whip up against her. I only hope she got away before they found her.'

'Yesterday it was Rupert Honeydew you were afraid of. You thought she was asking for trouble, following them up the Tor to make notes of their ceremonies.'

'I really don't know what to think.'

'But you're right. We really do have to report this to the police. I'm terribly afraid something nasty may have happened to her. Yet I've no idea whether it's connected to the bombing or something else. If it isn't, they probably won't thank us for loading a different problem on their plates. And I can just imagine their faces if we tell them what Rupert Honeydew's lot were up to and suggest that a young woman in a burka may have been a Druid sacrifice.'

'Don't! They were just folk dancers! Rupert Honeydew may be odd, but you can't think . . .'

'Sorry. But very little of this is making sense.'

Or if it is, Hilary thought, *it's a sense I don't want to contemplate.*

The clouds were low. The street lights had not yet come on, but dusk was thickening early. There was a glimpse of a car park through an arched stone gateway. Otherwise, the tree-hung road alongside the abbey grounds was deserted.

'It's as if the whole town is in mourning,' Hilary said.

'It probably is.'

'I dare say the holidaymakers are keeping away. They may come and stare in the daytime, but they don't want to stay here overnight.'

A solitary car swept by, leaving a deeper silence behind.

Presently, the hairs on Hilary's skin began to prickle. She listened carefully. Above the sound of her and Veronica's footsteps she thought she heard a third pair following them. She glanced at Veronica, but her companion seemed not to have noticed.

It's probably nothing, she thought. *We can't be the only* people *in Glastonbury out this evening, even if it felt like that a few minutes ago.*

But there had been no one in the road when they rounded the corner from the residential estate. There were a few houses ahead to the right, and the long grey stone wall surrounding the abbey on their left. She was having to fight hard to prevent herself from turning her head and confronting her fear.

The footsteps were coming nearer. Not loud, but steadily determined. Whoever was following was gaining on them. Hilary wished the street lights would come on.

She could stand it no longer. She stopped dead and swung round.

The figure overtaking them in the half-light was one she recognized.

'Sister Mary Magdalene!'

The nun looked startled. Then she smiled.

'Mrs Masters? Mrs Taylor. I've got that right, haven't I? I'm glad to see that we haven't scared you away from Glastonbury altogether.'

'We've been in on so much, we thought we ought to see it

through. Not, mind you, that there's anything more that we can do.'

'No. We must trust the police to find the truth.'

Sister Mary Magdalene fell into step beside them. Hilary looked at her curiously.

'If you don't mind me asking, where did you spring from? We had the street to ourselves, and suddenly there you were behind us. For a few moments, it gave me the creeps.'

The nun gave a gentle laugh. 'I'm sorry! I didn't mean to frighten you. There's a retreat house in the abbey grounds. For people seeking a spiritual quiet time. They sometimes ask me to lead a meditation session for their guests – or pilgrims, I prefer to call them. You obviously didn't notice, but you passed the gateway to it when you turned on to this road.'

'That big stone arch, with the carvings over it?' Veronica asked.

'That's it.'

'Sorry. Now that you mention it, it rings a bell. But tonight I must have walked straight past it,' Hilary said.

'A few moments later, and you'd have seen me coming out of it.'

Hilary's strung nerves were beginning to relax. A nun on her way back to her convent after a session of spiritual counselling had not been what her imagination had feared.

'If we'd known the abbey had a guest house, we might have thought of staying there ourselves.'

'It's simple, but there are forms of comfort they do better than the best hotel, and the food's actually rather good. Plus, if you join one of their retreats, you get private access to the abbey ruins. They have their own gate in their back garden, so you can come and go as you please, even after closing time. Tonight, though, was different. I was sharing in a prayer vigil for the lives that have been shattered this week.'

The three of them walked on in silence.

As the houses closed round them again, Sister Mary Magdalene said, 'I must leave you here. My community house is down this road. God go with you.'

'And with you,' they both replied.

The lights were coming on now, the traffic more frequent, as they reached the centre of the town. Their hotel was at the other end of the High Street, but first they turned away towards the police incident room.

The commandeered church hall was less frenetic than the day before, but there were still a number of officers at work.

The outcome was what Hilary had feared. DI Fellows was unavailable. Instead, they were ushered into a cubicle to meet Detective Sergeant Petersen. She looked them up and down with a scornful resignation.

'Oh, spare us! What now?'

Hilary explained, as firmly and succinctly as she could, about Amina's disappearance and the varied reasons they had to fear for her.

Petersen sighed. 'You really are the story-book detectives, aren't you? *Of course* we know about Miss Haddad. She was one of the witnesses at the Chalice Well. And *of course* we know about Mr Honeydew. Did you think twenty people could go dancing through the streets of Glastonbury after a bomb attack and the police wouldn't notice? And they were back at midnight too. You didn't mention that. Are your detective skills switched off after lights out?'

'Amina wasn't there then,' Hilary said curtly.

The detective sergeant's eyes narrowed with sudden interest. 'But you were? My, you have been busy.'

'We were woken up. They passed right under our window with their drums and pipes.'

'And their animal masks,' Veronica put in. 'It was scarier that time.'

'And you went out to investigate? Why?'

'Never mind that,' Hilary said. 'The point is, as far as we know, no one has seen Amina since we left her heading for the Tor about five-thirty yesterday.'

'Since you're evidently so concerned about her, you haven't thought to check whether she simply left Glastonbury and went home for a break? After everything that's happened, that would hardly be surprising.'

'No.' Hilary coloured. 'I suppose I could have got back to her professor and asked for her home address.'

'She's not answering her phone,' Veronica said. 'I tried.'

'Unfortunately, not everyone is switched on twenty-four/ seven.'

Ouch, Hilary thought. *That could be me.*

Detective Sergeant Petersen laid down her pen. 'This is not a matter for CID. All we need now is a missing-persons enquiry in the middle of a terrorist bomb case. Amina Haddad is a grown woman. Don't you think it's a bit early to get the search dogs out?'

'She's not just any young woman. You must know that. She's a woman in a burka at a time and in a place where a bomb went off. We know she's in danger. I shudder to think what would have happened if she'd been in her digs when that vigilante mob got there this morning.'

'I thought you were afraid she'd been sacrificed by some New Age cult on Glastonbury Tor?'

'Yes, well.' It was Hilary's turn to sigh. 'It's complicated, I'll give you that.'

'Now, if you'll excuse me, I have a mass murder to investigate. We're working round the clock.'

Hilary had turned to go. 'That man you're guarding in the hospital. His name isn't Basil, is it?'

'I'm sure Detective Chief Superintendent Allenby will disclose that information to the public when she sees fit.'

Hilary was not used to feeling like a scolded child. She set her lips in a grim line and strode for the door.

'Well!' said Veronica, visibly relaxing on the steps of the Baptist church hall. 'That's us told. It doesn't sound as if she's going to take Amina's disappearance seriously. And if she's not, is there anything we can do?'

NINETEEN

Rain had washed the town overnight. It beaded the rose bushes outside the dining-room windows.

Veronica turned the pages of her complimentary copy of Friday's newspaper and gave a cry of delight.

'At last! She's made it!'

She swung the paper round so that Hilary could see the double page of the tabloid with its startling photographs and column of text.

OCCULT CEREMONY IN MURDER TOWN the headline screamed. Beneath it, the byline read: *Joan Townsend, exclusive.*

The main photograph was certainly striking. It showed the animal masks of Rupert Honeydew's followers swinging round to confront the camera's flashbulb, and the startled eyes of the white-clad dancers behind.

Hilary ran her finger over the women's faces crowned with flowers. 'You're right. Mel from the gift shop's not here. Or at least, not within camera shot.'

Veronica folded the newspaper happily. 'I'm so glad for Joan. She's not only got the credit this time, she's got an exclusive. No other reporters were on the street at midnight. And the public love all this black magic nonsense. She'll probably be able to sell her pictures in other places too.'

'Not if it's an exclusive.'

'Oh, I'm sure there are ways round that. It must mean she managed to salvage the memory card from her broken camera. This will pay for a new one, and a lot more besides, I should think.'

'Hmm. I don't know why you're sounding so pleased. I thought we'd agreed she was a self-centred little brat. And the last thing the police will want is to get a serious bomb enquiry mixed up in this New Age occult business.'

'Perhaps it *is* mixed up. I know I was sceptical yesterday, but nobody's come up with an obvious motive yet, have they? How do we know it's not connected with Rupert Honeydew and his followers?'

'I hardly think he'd be sticking his neck out by prancing through the streets the next day, drawing attention to himself.'

'He might have enough cheek. Hiding in plain sight. Besides, I'm not sure he's . . . normal.' She shuddered. 'I can't get rid of the memory of his eyes, that evening on Glastonbury Tor.'

'Well, we'll just have to see what the police make of this. Though it's not as if they didn't already know about it. There were officers on the spot.'

Veronica opened the pages again. 'It makes you wonder, doesn't it? Who were the dancers behind the masks? There are people here, men in particular, who we didn't see in the daytime, dancing out to Glastonbury Tor.'

'I don't suppose we'll ever find out. The police may wring it out of Rupert Honeydew, but they won't tell us.'

'It's creepy. We could be walking through the streets of Glastonbury and brush past one of them, and we'd never know.'

'*By the pricking of my thumbs, something wicked this way comes.* It would be very handy if good and evil signalled themselves as clearly as that. But we're not talking good and evil here, are we? Just New Age flummery. I still think it's nothing to do with the bomb.'

'So you say.'

'Though having said that . . .' Hilary grew thoughtful. 'I am scared for Amina Haddad. This had put her out of my head for the moment, but she's missing, and we last saw her following Rupert Honeydew's dancers towards the Tor.'

'Do you think the police will find her?'

'Will they even take us seriously? You heard what the detective sergeant said. She's a grown woman. There are any number of reasons she could go AWOL.'

'Leaving all her possessions behind?'

'Hmm, well. We're not the police. For us, it's likely to remain just another of those maddening loose ends.'

'Which leaves us with the question: what would you like to do today? We've covered just about all of Glastonbury's sights.' She gave a sudden peal of laughter. 'That is, except the obvious one, as far as my children are concerned. When they heard I was coming here, the first thing that entered their heads was the Glastonbury Festival. I don't suppose you want to see the hallowed site? Didn't they say the Rolling Stones were there last year for the first time?'

'It was certainly *not* on my itinerary. What would there be to see anyway? Just a lot of muddy fields. For my money, I'd rather join the Glastonbury Pilgrimage, when the town is flooded every June with worshippers from all over Europe. They process down the High Street with banners flying and gather in the ruined abbey church. No, the weather looks a bit dodgy this morning, and there's something I've been saving for a rainy day. We've passed it several times, as it happens. It's in the Tribunal, that rather fine fifteenth-century merchant's house at the start of the High Street. The Glastonbury Lake Village Museum. We saw a bit of that at the Avalon Marshes Centre, but if you could bear to spend another hour or so on our ancient marsh dwellers . . .'

'Not at all. I find it quite romantic, really. The idea of most of the Levels covered with water and just those few villages built up above the floods.'

'Yes, well, if we have a repeat of the rains of last winter, we'll be back to that way of living again.'

As they moved away from the table, Veronica gathered up the tabloid with Joan's photo-spread. 'You know, I really ought to ring and congratulate her. She must be feeling so pleased, after all those frustrations.'

'Suit yourself. Personally, I've had as much of the little madam as I want.'

Hilary sauntered across the lobby and ascended the stairs. She was just opening the room door when Veronica caught up with her.

'No joy, I'm afraid. She's not answering her phone. Rather odd, in a way. You'd have thought she'd have been keen to field every call, in case it was another big offer for her pictures.'

'Maybe it's just you she isn't picking up on. She'll get your name on that little screen, won't she? Sorry, I'm still a bit vague about how these things work.'

'Yes. If she's keyed in my number to her contacts, she should know it's me ringing. Do you really think that? But I've done my best for her. Ringing her about George Marsden. If it hadn't been for me, she wouldn't have been in the High Street seconds after the bomb went off.'

'Maybe that's what she's blaming you for. She could have been killed. And her big story never happened, did it?'

'About the bombing, no. She did try to get another crack at George Marsden after the memorial service, but it all went haywire. He was making so much noise that all the other reporters came crowding round. They didn't realize it was meant to be another of Joan's exclusives.'

'Hmm. In the end, I don't think he had much to say, even if

he does have a tendency to say it at the top of his voice. Right then, umbrellas at the ready. Glastonbury Lake Village Museum it is.'

'I feel as though I should have brought my wellingtons.'

As they set out through the drizzle, Hilary's eyes were going ahead towards the High Street. It seemed odd to find it busy with morning traffic, with shoppers and sightseers on the pavement. The bomb-damaged houses ahead had been sheathed in green tarpaulins. Scaffolding gave access to workmen busy on repairs.

'It's good to see things getting back to normal,' Veronica remarked. 'Though I dare say there will be wounds that can't be repaired that easily.'

'It's shaken me,' Hilary admitted. 'Last night, coming back up that street past the abbey grounds, I let myself get properly scared when I heard those footsteps behind us. And the assailant I feared turned out to be Sister Mary Magdalene, of all people. I must be getting neurotic in my old age.'

For all her laughter, she could feel again how that sound in the thickening dusk had made her skin crawl. She was reminded, not for the first time, that the shocking events of the week had affected her more deeply than she liked to admit.

In daylight, even on a dull damp morning, it was a pleasure to look down the road to the welcoming gateway of the abbey's main entrance. She tried to picture the similar grey stone arch which led to the retreat house on the far side of the grounds, through which Sister Mary Magdalene had emerged last night.

It was a pity they hadn't known about Abbey House before. As Sister Mary Magdalene said, the retreat house might have been a good place to stay, with access to the Abbey ruins after hours. She could have done with spending more time wandering round the remains of the magnificent medieval abbey, and imagining that older wattle church, dating back even earlier than the Saxons, and all the changing churches of the centuries which followed it.

Her daydreams were broken by Veronica's cry. 'What's happening? Hilary! Something's wrong.'

They had reached the market place, not far from the museum. Hilary followed Veronica's eyes back down the road that led to the abbey. Only a short way down it, there was a sudden flux of people out of the gateway on to the pavement. From their body language, it was evident that something dramatic had happened. Hilary's mind snapped back to the reality of the present.

'That's the entrance to the abbey!'

Even as they watched, more people were being shepherded out to form a sizeable crowd on the street. She could make out the dark bulk of a uniformed police officer. She had hardly spotted him before the air was rent by the wail of emergency sirens. Two police cars tore down the High Street and rounded the corner by the market place. Seconds later, an ambulance followed. The crowd at the entrance parted hastily to let them through. All three vehicles disappeared into the abbey grounds.

Hilary felt a cold sinking of her heart. 'Dear God! What now?'

Veronica was striding ahead, past the pillared market cross, to reach the fringes of the crowd on the pavement.

'What is it?' she asked the nearest person. 'What's happened? Is it another bomb?'

The harassed-looking man in the wet anorak shook his head. He glanced down at the two young girls at his side, who were looking up at him in scared enquiry. 'No. Nothing like that. Can't really tell you what it was. We were too far away. Sounds as if they found someone in that big church thing. Someone must have phoned the police. Next thing we know, they're herding us out of the gate. We've only been there twenty minutes. I hope they're going to give us our money back.'

'Daddy! Is it a murdered person?' the younger girl asked.

'I don't know, love. I didn't get a look at it. Don't you worry. The police will look after it now. And the ambulance. They'll take her to hospital and see if she's all right.'

'She?' Hilary asked sharply.

'Don't ask me. But that's what some of them who were nearer than us are saying.'

Hilary muscled her way through the crowd. She seized upon a woman of her own age. 'Did you see what the trouble was? They're saying it may have been a woman. Possibly dead. Is that true?'

The woman looked shaken. Lipstick showed incongruously bright pink on her pale face. 'I'm rather afraid it may be. She was lying inside the Galilee – that's the bit between the nave of the church and the Lady Chapel—'

'I know!' Hilary snapped. 'Sorry. Go on.'

'We were up by the chancel when someone screamed. We went running down the nave to see. And there she was. Well, I say she, but you can't be sure these days, But from where we were standing, it looked like it. She was half-hidden in the corner between the steps and the wall. Quite a slight figure, really. Black leather jacket, white shirt, black leggings. Well, one of the staff, security guard or something, came running. He took one look at her, then ordered the rest of us back and phoned the police. After that, they moved everybody out to the gate. And now, well, as you can see, the emergency services are here in force.'

'Would you say she was a young woman?'

'I didn't get a close look, of course, but yes, from her build, I had a feeling she was.'

Faces wheeled through Hilary's mind. Amina's blue eyes through the burka. Mel, edging away in the gift shop, looking scared. Even – her conscience smote her now – the insistent Eeyore-like face of Joan Townsend, as she pursued her story.

But Amina would have been wearing her burka.

'Did she have bright blonde hair?'

'As I say, we didn't get right into the Galilee. But no, not as far as I could see. Why, is it someone you know?'

'And a black leather jacket? Not a baggy brown cardigan?'

But Joan would have been wearing more than a cardigan on a wet day like this. A fear she had not expected was growing in Hilary's heart.

She fought her way back to Veronica. 'Not good news, I'm afraid. A young woman, by the sound of it. And by the signs, police and so on, I'd say she was probably dead.'

'Amina!'

'No burka. The woman I talked to, who was in the nave when they found her in the Galilee, didn't think that she had blonde hair. That rules two of them out. And you say that Joan wasn't answering her phone.'

'Oh, no! Wouldn't it be awful if it ended like this?'

'She's been pretty careless about the people she upset. I've given her short shrift in the past, but I'm beginning to have a bad feeling about this.'

'Or was it more than that? Was she a better journalist than we gave her credit for? What if she'd found out who really was behind that bombing?'

'I need to talk to a police officer. Like it or not, we may know more about what was going on than they do.'

TWENTY

I t was no good sidling up to the gate and making a polite enquiry. Hilary summoned up her nerve and marched up to the entrance, past the sign that said 'Abbey Closed', with a show of greater boldness than she felt. One half of the great wooden doors had been shut. The tall young policeman barring the way stiffened to alertness as she approached. She saw the flicker of nervousness in his eyes. Good, she thought. If I remind him of one of his more formidable teachers, so much the better.

'The abbey's closed, madam.'

'I can see that, you fool. It's not the abbey I want to see. It's the senior investigating officer inside.'

'I'm afraid I can't let any members of the public in.'

'Let's not beat about the bush. You have a young woman in there, probably dead. I may have vital information about who she is and why she died.'

The policeman's eyes widened.

'Are you sure? I mean, you can't have seen the body. Not up close.'

The body. So Joan was dead. She had known it must be so, because of the size of the police presence. In spite of her reservations about the young woman, Hilary felt a sharp pang of compassion.

'Are you going to let me talk to your superior officer, or do I have to report you for impeding a criminal investigation?'

The officer bent his head to speak into his radio. With a wary glance at Hilary and Veronica, he murmured, 'Right-oh, sir.' He lifted aside the plastic police tape that barred the entrance.

'Through there, if you wouldn't mind. He's coming to meet you.'

It felt strange to be walking up the deserted ramp to the ticket office and museum, which should have been thronged with visitors.

Unlike the Chalice Well gift shop, after Hilary's discovery of the bomb, the space here was empty. Two nervous-looking staff stood behind the ticket desk chatting in low voices. Of course, Hilary thought, the abbey had only just opened when they found the body. Hardly time for one of today's visitors to have done the deed or to be a significant witness. Whatever had happened must have been done overnight.

She threw a reassuringly confident smile at the man and woman guarding the desk.

'It's OK. We're on our way to see the officer in charge here.'

They were ushered through.

Among the wall displays and glass cabinets that told the abbey's history, two uniformed officers in fluorescent jackets, one male, one female, were earnestly conferring. They looked up sharply as Hilary and Veronica approached, but Hilary turned sharply right out on to the west grass before the ruins.

Instead of tourists in colourful clothes, today the green lawns out of which the pillared arches rose were busy with dark-uniformed police. Heads bent, they were scouring the expanse of mown grass within and around the once magnificent Abbey church. Another man, dark-suited, but not in uniform, came striding towards them. To Hilary's relief, it was Detective Inspector Fellows.

He stopped in evident surprise.

'You again!' But there was not the scornful condemnation that his detective sergeant would have shown.

'Yes, we turn up like a couple of bad pennies, don't we? But I'm glad it's you. You already know about the Chalice Well thing, even if they've moved the bigger boys in for the High Street bomb.'

'A big girl, as it happens. Detective Chief Superintendent Allenby. The constable at the gate said you had information. That you can identify the body.'

'Can *you*? Was there any evidence on her?'

He studied them for a while in silence. 'I think it's better if I ask the questions. Just tell me who you think she is, and why.'

Hilary glanced at Veronica. She drew a deep breath. 'Well, I know this may sound as if I'm trying to teach you your job, but there are three young women we've been particularly concerned about. Two of them you've met already. You interviewed them at the Chalice Well. The third one you may not know.'

'But we think we can rule out the first two,' Veronica went on. 'We came to see your sergeant last night because we were worried that one of them, Amina Haddad, had gone missing. She may have upset Rupert Honeydew. I know he acts like a fool, but he's an unstable character. We've seen a rather unpleasant side of him . . .'

'Excuse me, Mrs Taylor, but I thought you said you'd ruled Miss Haddad out.'

'Well, yes. She wears a full-length burka. You'd certainly have known if it was her.'

'So?'

Veronica shot a nervous look at Hilary. 'Then there was Mel Fenwick, from the Chalice Well gift shop. We thought she looked . . . frightened. We think she may be scared of Rupert Honeydew too. She was dancing in the streets with his crew.'

'But you've also ruled her out.'

'She has ash-blonde hair.' Veronica looked enquiringly at the inspector.

'Right.' Inspector Fellows was giving nothing away.

'So that leaves Joan Townsend.' Hilary took over. 'You may not have seen her, because she wasn't at the Chalice Well when we found the bomb there, though she reported on it afterwards. But she's got a major feature in one of the tabloids this morning. Pictures of Rupert Honeydew's lot dancing in the streets at night in animal masks. The whole tenor of the article is accusing Honeydew of practising black magic, and linking it to the bomb in the High Street. He might take unkindly to that. And Veronica's right. I've a feeling that underneath all the folklore flummery he can be a very dangerous man.'

'And Joan's not answering her phone this morning,' Veronica put in.

'This Joan Townsend. Can you describe her?'

Hilary thought. 'Early twenties. Medium height. Rather lank brown hair. Not fat, but maybe carrying a little too much weight. Hard to tell. She inclines to sloppy clothes, like a baggy brown cardigan she seems particularly fond of. But it was raining last night. What was the girl you found wearing?'

'I'm not sure that's information I want to reveal.'

'We were talking to people outside,' Veronica told him. 'Someone mentioned a black leather jacket, a white shirt and black leggings. I haven't seen Joan in those, but of course we don't know the full extent of her wardrobe.'

'I think I can put your minds at rest. Your description of Miss Townsend doesn't fit the woman we found.'

A small sigh escaped Hilary. She had not liked the young journalist, but she was more relieved than she had expected to find that she wasn't dead. Still, she reminded herself, another young woman was. Could it really be someone unrelated to the catastrophic events of this week?

'And no, the victim doesn't have blonde hair and there was no burka. Just as you say: white shirt, black leggings, black leather jacket and blue and gold sandals. I'm afraid, ladies, you've had a wasted journey. But thank you for your help.' A tired but polite smile creased his face. He turned to go.

But Veronica shot out a hand and caught his arm.

'Say that again! What was she wearing on her feet?'

'Blue and gold sandals. Didn't you tell me you'd heard that outside?'

'Not the sandals. Hilary, don't you remember?'

'No.' Hilary returned Veronica's excited stare blankly.

'That's what Amina was wearing under her burka. That's all we could see of her. Just her eyes and her feet. Rather stylish sandals, with alternate straps of blue and gold leather. I remember thinking how strange it was to cover herself up completely with the burka, to stop men having lascivious thoughts, and then to show such pretty footwear. Oh, what am I saying? That means . . . she's dead. Oh, poor Amina!'

Detective Inspector Fellows's face had taken on a grimmer expression.

'Would you mind? Mrs Masters, Mrs Taylor, could I ask you to follow me?'

Hilary's mind was a turmoil of thoughts as they walked across the wet grass. Amina dead. She had grown unaccountably fond of the unseen girl under the burka, with her Birmingham accent and her forthright defence of her chosen lifestyle. It was a more genuine pain than she had felt when she believed it was Joan who had died. Yet she couldn't resist a little crow of triumph that she and Veronica had actually solved a mystery which might have baffled the police for days. She slapped the thought away.

The walls of the nave and chancel had mostly been flattened when the abbey was sacked at the Reformation. Only two portions of the east end stood tall. But the Galilee at the west end was much better preserved. It was here that DI Fellows was leading them.

The Galilee, the outer porch where the unbaptized could listen to the first part of the communion service in the church. Appropriate, somehow, that the Muslim Amina had been found here. Or was it? As an adult convert, she might well have been baptized a Christian as a baby.

They were through the archway into the roofless stone-flagged space. There were two figures in the north-east corner. A wide flight of steps led up to the nave, but did not quite meet the northern wall. In the narrow space it left was a woman in white overalls, whom Hilary took to be a forensic medic. And Detective Sergeant Petersen. It was a small pleasure to Hilary even now to see the startled glare on the woman's face.

And something else. An inert form in black and white, lying in that shadowed gap.

At their approach, DS Petersen swiftly drew a green plastic cover over the body and stood to face them. The woman in overalls got to her feet and stood back.

'Just a detail, Olive.' DI Fellows lifted the sheet to uncover the victim's feet.

Hilary stared down at them. Such small neat feet, the toenails painted a frosty pink. And the sandals, straps of blue and gold leather arranged diagonally across the instep. She had to confess that she had never noticed Amina's feet, only those surprisingly blue eyes through the slit in the burka.

But Veronica gave a little cry of distress. 'It's her! They're the same. I'd recognize those sandals anywhere. Oh, poor Amina!'

'How did she die?' Hilary asked gruffly.

The detective inspector shook his head. 'I'm sorry, Mrs Masters, Mrs Taylor. I think you know I can't tell you that.'

Hilary was secretly glad that he had not lifted more than the foot of the sheet to show them the rest of the body and Amina's face.

'I need you to tell me everything you know about Amina Haddad. How you came to know her, anything you've learned about her. We'll need a formal identification, of course. That will mean tracing her relatives. But I'm inclined to believe you've got it right.'

They were walking across the grass in the slackening drizzle in the direction of the open-air café.

'There would have been no point in showing us her face,' Hilary said. 'We never saw it.'

'So I understand.'

Suddenly the ground heaved up in front of Hilary. She felt the world tilting. She was falling.

When she came to, she was being supported by the strong grip of DI Fellows under one elbow and Veronica's lighter hold on the other.

'Put your head down between your knees,' the DI said. 'I'm sorry. I should have prepared you better. I thought if you only saw her feet . . .'

'Idiot!' Hilary murmured, more to herself than him. 'I never faint.'

'We'll get you sitting down with the proverbial cup of strong sweet tea.'

'Make that coffee.'

They helped her across to one of the few sheltered tables of the café. As at the ticket office, the young man behind the counter stood looking disconsolate and scared. A solitary policeman stood guard.

Soon the promised cup of coffee was steaming in front of Hilary. She tried not to mind that it was heavily sugared. Her face felt strange, as though the skin was stretched too tightly across the bones. Only as the hot liquid coursed through her chilled body did she begin to relax.

'Sorry about that. I wouldn't have thought I'd make such a fool of myself over a dead body. I hardly knew the girl.'

The detective inspector's eyebrows twitched. 'I wouldn't say that. It was a short acquaintance, admittedly. But you cared enough about her to find out where she was staying, to take yourselves round there to warn her of what you perceived to be a danger, and then to report her disappearance to the police. Not to mention barging your way in here past my constable this morning.'

'One tries to do the right thing.'

'I can't tell you how grateful I am. We could have wasted days trying to find out who she was.'

Hilary was aware of a choking sound behind her. She turned her head to find Detective Sergeant Petersen glaring daggers.

It was the first cheering sight Hilary had seen for some time.

'What gets me,' Veronica said, 'is that she wasn't wearing her burka. Did the killer remove it after he murdered her, to hinder the identification? I mean, in most places, a burka is a form of concealing identity, but in Amina's case, she seems to have been the only woman in Glastonbury wearing one. If it hadn't been for her sandals . . . Or is there any possibility that she went out without it, because she didn't want anyone to know who she was? Nobody's seen her without it, not even her landlady.'

'Mmm. That's an interesting question.' The fingers of the detective inspector's right hand played a passage of music on the table top in the way that Hilary remembered. 'Removing her burka as a means of disguise.' He straightened up briskly. 'Now, ladies, if you wouldn't mind, I need everything you can tell me about her, from the top. Olive?'

Detective Sergeant Petersen sat down beside him and opened her notebook with an affronted flounce.

'That reminds me,' Hilary said suddenly. 'I take it you didn't find a handbag or wallet, or anything like that, or you'd have known who she was. But did you find her notebook? She never seemed to go anywhere without it, and she was scribbling down everything she saw.'

DI Fellows turned to his sergeant.

'No,' she said. 'She had nothing with her. Just that bit of Glastonbury Thorn clutched in her hand.'

The detective inspector drew in a sharp breath. Hilary guessed he had not meant to tell them that.

'It's all right,' she said swiftly. 'If you don't want that to be public knowledge, we can keep our mouths shut.'

DS Petersen scowled at her from under the dripping roof.

'I'd be grateful for that. It's the sort of thing the papers could turn into a sensational story. *Murder over Holy Thorn.*'

'You don't have to tell me. Coming on top of Joan Townsend's piece about black magic practices at midnight. It would confirm everything the general public believes about Glastonbury.'

'But the Thorn's good,' Veronica said. 'Flowering at Easter and Christmas. It's a sign of divine life. All the same, it has to mean something else here, doesn't it? Whether she picked it herself or somebody put it into her hand after she died.'

Hilary's mind flew back to that very first afternoon in Glastonbury. Climbing Wearyall Hill and seeing the Thorn tree desecrated by vandals. They had never discovered who did it, had they? Could it have anything to do with the bomb at the Chalice Well, the explosion in the High Street and Amina's murder? The improbable connection of these things whirled through her brain.

She was no nearer to finding a solution when the interrogation was over and they had told DI Fellows all they knew about Amina.

TWENTY-ONE

As they approached the exit, they heard the sound of a woman's voice from a group of people by the ticket desk. 'You poor things! What a terrible thing to happen! A death in the abbey, and so soon after the bomb. I came as soon as I heard.'

'Do you suppose the police will want to keep the abbey closed for the whole day?' came a man's voice.

The two employees on the desk had been joined by another pair. One was a tall, worried-looking man, his bespectacled head stooped forward. The other, a short, dark-haired woman with a severe haircut, wearing a green raincoat.

The woman laid her hand on the arm of the man beside her. 'Paul, I know this is shocking, but we must let the police do what they must. They'll want to examine the body before they remove it for the post-mortem, and then they'll have to comb the site for evidence. It's bound to take some time.'

'We've a school party booked in for eleven. Do you think it's too late to put them off?'

The man ran his hand through his thinning hair. He was quite formally dressed in a pale grey suit. Pink-rimmed glasses balanced uncertainly on his nose. These two must, thought Hilary, represent a more senior level of management than the unhappy pair on the ticket desk.

'Ring them anyway. We must give the police all the help we can. Apart from that, all we can do is pray for the poor woman, and the person who did this.'

She turned her head as she heard Hilary and Veronica approach.

Hilary was startled to see that under the open raincoat, the woman wore a black dress with a familiar-looking silver cross interlaced with a Celtic pattern. She heard Veronica gasp beside her.

'Sonia Marsden!'

Hilary stared. She had last seen Sonia Marsden outside the memorial service at St John's, remonstrating with her angry husband, and before that, at the Archive of Avalon bookshop seconds before the bomb went off, and again at the Chalice Well bookshop. To her relief, the loud-mouthed George was not with Sonia this morning. For the first time, Hilary found herself looking at his wife as a person in her own right, and not merely someone trying to tone down his decibels.

Hearing her authoritative tones now, she realized that this was a woman whose real existence she had not guessed. One whose life was devoted to Glastonbury Abbey. Someone who cared about her employees and the woman whose corpse lay in the Galilee.

All four faces had swung to survey Hilary and Veronica as they approached from the abbey grounds.

'You don't look like CID,' Sonia Marsden said. 'The abbey's closed. How did you get in?'

'Through the front entrance,' Veronica answered. 'The constable let us through. As did your colleagues here. We had evidence to give to the investigating officer.'

Sonia Marsden's dark eyebrows rose. 'What evidence?'

Hilary intervened. 'I'm afraid that's a matter between us and the police. We've done our duty. Now we're on our way back to our hotel.'

'Not locals, then?' asked the man Sonia had called Paul.

'No.'

'But you know something about the murder?'

'If it *is* murder,' put in Sonia. 'Don't you think it's too much of a coincidence? Two acts of violence in as many days. What if this is the High Street bomber and the poor woman had a crisis of conscience? She might have come to the abbey to repent, but taken her own life. If only we could have got here earlier, to tell her there *is* forgiveness.'

Hilary felt a sudden cold hand descend on her heart. She had never truly allowed herself to believe that Amina could be the bomber. But she had only a fleeting knowledge of the woman beneath the burka. What if Sonia Marsden was right?

But why would a Muslim choose Glastonbury Abbey?

Sonia was looking at them curiously. 'Now that I come to think of it, I've seen you two before. In the gift shop of the Chalice Well when someone discovered that bomb in a knapsack. And in the High Street on Wednesday. I ran into you on the pavement at the very moment the second bomb went off. It was you, wasn't it?'

'Yes, as a matter of fact, it was.'

'And now here you are on the morning of another death.'

Hilary found herself unaccountably guilty before that dark level stare.

'I told you, they let us in after the body was found. We had some relevant information.'

'We helped them identify the body,' Veronica said, her voice still shocked and quiet.

Hilary wished she could have prevented her friend from saying that.

'Identify her? And you've only just arrived in Glastonbury! Who is she?'

All four of them were staring in avid curiosity.

Hilary gripped Veronica's elbow and urged her forward. 'I'm sure the police will reveal her name when there's been a formal identification. We didn't know her well enough to do that. Now, if you'll excuse us, I think the police would like us to leave. We've no further business here.'

They walked past Sonia's questioning gaze to the gateway. Hilary still felt more shaken than she cared to admit.

'Fancy that being Sonia Marsden, of all people,' Veronica said. 'It looks as if she's fairly senior Abbey staff.'

'I'm kicking myself now. Here was I, assuming she'd be just another bigot like her husband. But the way she looked at me, I felt that I was the guilty party. She sounded quite caring. Shocked, but wanting to pray for the victim. Even if Amina . . .'

'I never thought it might be suicide.'

'But why would she come to the abbey? No, don't let's think about that.'

They smiled their thanks at the policeman who raised the tape to let them out. Most of the crowd outside had gone.

'Where are all the visitors you threw out? Have they drafted in more officers to interview them, or did you simply let them go?'

The young policeman shrugged unhelpfully.

'It seems unlikely that any early visitors would have had much to report,' Veronica said as they walked up the street, 'except for the ones who actually found the body. But then, what do we know? If it *is* a murder and Amina had been recently killed, they might have seen someone coming away from the Galilee.' She shuddered.

'Somehow, that seems improbable. If you're going to kill someone at the abbey, would you wait until after opening time? Amina's been missing for more than twenty-four hours. She could have died any time.'

'But why the abbey? Did someone meet her here after hours? Or transport her body under cover of darkness? How did they get in? And why?'

'And that macabre detail of the Glastonbury Thorn in her hand.' Hilary frowned. 'There hasn't been a Thorn tree at the abbey for some time.'

'Does this really have anything to do with the bombs? Or is it just a coincidence?'

'Maybe somebody thought that killing her so soon after would conveniently link her death to the bomber. A golden opportunity to send the police down the wrong track.'

'But why would anyone want to kill the poor girl?'

'You were the one who was worried about her. Your three endangered girls. You thought she might have angered Rupert Honeydew.'

'Oh dear. That's an even more upsetting thought. That scary figure in the rags and the top hat, grinning as he suffocated her, or hit her over the head.'

'Steady on.'

But Hilary no longer knew what was believable and what was not.

'I suppose they'll get on to her family – if she has any. Break the news and get someone to formally identify the body. And they'll want to search her belongings at her digs and tell her landlady she won't be coming back. But I'm afraid it's down to me to tell her professor. Poor man. He'll be upset. I think he had a high opinion of her as a student.'

Hilary sat down on her bed and looked at her phone reluctantly.

'That's a whole other side of her life we know little about,' Veronica said. 'The reason for her death could just as well lie there as with anything that happened here in Glastonbury.'

'You mean, someone else may be playing tricks with disguise? Kill her and dump her body where there have already been other violent deaths. Drag in the Glastonbury Thorn as another red herring. And the real cause could be miles away in Bristol University.'

'The Thorn on Wearyall Hill looked pretty dead. It certainly didn't have blossoms. But it's not the only one, is it? There are others in the town. Like the one in St John's churchyard.'

'What would Amina have been doing in the churchyard at night? Or in the abbey, for that matter?'

'Assuming she *was* at the abbey when she was killed. She could have been murdered somewhere else and the body put there to be found in more dramatic and misleading circumstances.'

'Don't you think Glastonbury is just a bit too full of colourful stories for the credulous to grab hold of?'

'Some of the colourful stories are all too credible. Did you know that the last Abbot of Glastonbury, Richard Whiting, was hung, drawn and quartered on Glastonbury Tor?'

'Don't!'

'Sorry. I don't want you fainting as well. I could have kicked myself for keeling over like that.'

'You're not the hardbitten pedagogue you like to pretend you are. Talking of which, don't you think you ought to phone David this time? I know the murder of one young woman doesn't make the same headlines as a terrorist bomb, but you really don't want him to hear about this from anyone else. I'm going to phone my own kids, before it hits the headlines.'

Hilary made the difficult call to Professor Hadley first.

'I'm sorry to be the one to tell you this. But I expect the police will be wanting to talk to you before long. I wanted you to be prepared. You know I rang you because I was concerned about Amina Haddad . . .'

Her hand was trembling slightly as she laid the phone down on the duvet. Professor Hadley had seemed genuinely shocked and grieved.

She looked at her watch. It would still be the working day in Gaza. All the same, she ought not to delay.

It was a reassuring joy to hear David's voice.

She drew a deep breath and poured out her story, trying to keep it as factual as she could.

'But there was one strange thing this detective inspector let slip – at least, his sergeant did. When they found the body she was clutching a sprig of the Glastonbury Thorn.'

'Hilary. I don't like the sound of this. You're getting too close to too many bad events. I want you to leave Glastonbury immediately. Promise me.'

'I'll talk to Veronica. You're right. We've been here four days, anyway. There's nothing to keep us now.'

Veronica was busy making her peace with her three children. Hilary left messages for Bridget and Oliver.

'Right. Duty done. We can pack up our bags and go. All we have to decide is where. Home, or somewhere else?'

'I keep thinking of Joan. I rather wish we hadn't promised the inspector we'd keep quiet about the Glastonbury Thorn. Think how thrilled she'd be if we fed her a detail like that.'

'Veronica!'

'Yes, I know. We can't tell her.'

Hilary stomped her way back upstairs from the hotel reception desk.

'They're not playing ball, I'm afraid. They say we're supposed to give twenty-four hours notice of cancellation, and we've already outstayed the time for clearing our room. I don't suppose you can blame them, really. They've had quite a few people cancel since the bomb went off.'

'It doesn't matter,' Veronica said. 'It will hardly break the bank if we have to pay them for one more night, even though we go somewhere else.'

Hilary's phone rang. She gave a startled twitch. 'I hate it when it does that. It's all very well leaving it on to please the children. But then I have to remember what I'm supposed to do to take the call.'

'Hilary! Don't pretend to be such a dinosaur.'

She fished out the offending mobile and found the right key to press. 'Hello,' she barked.

'Mrs Masters? Detective Inspector Fellows. I'm sorry to bother you again, but there's something I forgot to say. You and Mrs Taylor have been very helpful with your information, but I wonder if I can ask if you are planning to stay around in Glastonbury? You seem to have picked up some remarkably pertinent facts in the short time you've been here. It's asking a lot, I know, and I can't keep you if you want to leave, but I'd be grateful if you stayed within reach for another day or two. We can't be sure where this investigation is heading yet. You've already given us some interesting ideas. It's just possible you may have something more to contribute which you haven't told us yet.'

'We gave you everything we could remember.'

'I'm sure you did. But I don't yet know if we've asked you the right questions. You're not planning to leave today, are you?'

'As it happens,' a grim smile twisted Hilary's lips, 'no. It looks as though we're staying one more night.'

Veronica's face registered surprise.

Hilary put the phone away. 'DI Fellows. He'd like us to stay around. If David or the children complain, I shall say we're co-operating with the police.'

TWENTY-TWO

'If we're not leaving straight away, there's one thing I'd like to do.'

'Which is?'

'Mel Fenwick.'

'Hilary!'

'I know, I know. But the more I think about it, the more sure I am she was frightened that day we saw her.'

'Hardly surprising. We'd just found an unexploded bomb at the place where she worked.'

'Yes, but I felt it was something more than that. We didn't know anything about her at the time, but now we know she was one of Rupert Honeydew's acolytes. Everything keeps coming back to him. And he was there at the Chalice Well that afternoon. He was in the shop. I mean, how often does he go there?'

'Quite a lot, by the sound of it. He thinks the water has spiritual powers.'

'Hmm, well. Still, I have a hunch that Mel knows more than she's saying.'

'Shouldn't we leave it to DI Fellows? Or the Detective Chief Superintendent who's investigating the big bomb.'

'Ye-es. I admit that last one is a bit of a puzzle. Why would he do that?'

'Why would he bomb the Chalice Well, for that matter?'

'He didn't. I found a bomb left in a knapsack. It didn't go off.'

'You think it wasn't meant to?'

'The police will know more about the answer to that.'

'And Mel might know more about it than she should? Is that what you're saying?'

'If she does, then the bomb that went off two days later must have scared the daylights out of her.'

'Hilary, you're not CID. You can't just go around interrogating people. We've already told DI Fellows we were worried about Mel. Leave him to follow it up.'

'If she's already frightened, then the sight of a police warrant card will be enough to terrify her. I rather fancied the soft touch.'

'Soft touch? You?'

'I've spent a lifetime dealing with recalcitrant schoolgirls. I can be a dragon when I need to be, but I can also show my softer side if I think it will get results.'

'Very well, then.' Veronica sighed and picked up her handbag. 'Has the rain stopped?'

A fitful sun glanced through the clouds and glistened on wet roofs and pavements. The two of them made their way in silence along the road to the Chalice Well. It was impossible not to be conscious of the bulk of Glastonbury Tor looming ahead of them. Its steep sides darkened as the sun went in.

Hilary made straight for the gift shop.

She halted in the doorway. It had been possible to stave off the horror of what had happened by focussing on her determination to clear up the puzzle which had dogged them since Monday. But the grey-haired woman chatting with Beth Harkness behind the counter was certainly not the young blonde Mel. Hilary felt a sinking of her spirits.

There was only one other couple in the shop, wandering along the display cases with little evident intention of buying anything. Hilary approached the counter and summoned a smile for the manageress.

'Yes, it's me again. Don't worry. I haven't found any more bombs in the garden.'

'I should hope not! That was terrible, what happened in the High Street. I go cold when I think it might have been us. If you hadn't found that knapsack . . .'

'Yes, well, never mind that. I was wondering if I could have another word with Mel.'

'Why? She didn't know any more about it than I did. We were here in the shop the whole time. Well, bar the odd trip to the cloakroom, of course, and half an hour off for lunch.'

'But she's not here this morning. Is it her day off?'

'No, that was Wednesday. Lucky she wasn't caught out in the High Street.'

'Hmm. So that's why she was out dancing in the streets that afternoon.'

'Only next day, that would be yesterday, she phoned in sick.'

'Did she, indeed? And she's not back today?'

'No. I've had to get Caroline here to put in some extra time.'

'Do you know when she'll be back?'

'She didn't say.'

Hilary tapped a rhythm on the counter. Her keen determination to solve the questions buzzing in her mind collapsed in frustration. She had been so sure that Mel Fenwick held at least a part of the answer to the week's events.

She was still sure. Anxiety was beginning to grow.

'Thank you.'

She was aware of Veronica beside her letting out a sigh of relief.

The grey-haired assistant Caroline spoke up for the first time.

'If you really need to see her, I can give you her address. She lives just round the corner from me. Here, I'll write it down for you.'

'Caroline!' Beth Harkness began to object. Then she shrugged one shoulder. 'Oh, well. I don't suppose there's any harm.'

Caroline pushed the slip of paper across the counter.

'I don't know what you want her for, but if it's to help with finding whoever did that in the High Street, good luck to you.'

'I've no idea if she can help or not, but it's worth a try.'

'Are you the police?'

'No, but they've asked us to help them.' Hilary smiled.

It was an older terraced house tucked away behind the High Street. Hilary rang the bell. A comfortable-looking woman in a flowered dress and cardigan answered the door.

'Is Mel in?' Hilary waved the box of chocolates in her hand. 'We heard she wasn't well. Is it possible we could see her?'

Mrs Fenwick looked them up and down. 'You're nothing to do with that Honeydew bloke, are you?'

'Definitely not.'

The woman peered along the street in either direction with a worried expression. Her voice dropped to a murmur.

'She isn't here.'

'Really? To tell you the truth, we're worried about her. We came to see if we could help.'

'Who are you, then?'

'Hilary Masters and Veronica Taylor. She may have spoken about us. We found the bomb at the Chalice Well.'

'That was you! I remember now. You were on the telly!'

Hilary tried to shut out the memory of that experience.

But the imprimatur of the BBC seemed enough to satisfy Mrs Fenwick.

'It's upset her that much, she didn't want to stay here. She's gone to her granddad's. He's always had a soft spot for her. She said she'd feel safe there.'

'Safe from what?'

'How do I know? All these bombs. Two in the same week. And that Honeydew fellow making her go dancing in the streets like it was May Day. It wasn't respectful. But she went. The first time, anyway. It's in the papers they were out again at midnight. Dressed up like animals and all. But not my Mel. She'd taken herself off by then. And I wasn't for telling that Honeydew fellow where she'd gone.'

'Was he here?' Hilary asked in alarm.

'About an hour ago. Demanding to know where she was. Poncey beggar!'

'And this grandfather?' Veronica asked. 'Is he your father? Can you tell us where he lives?'

Hilary held her breath. Could they strike lucky for the second time?

Mrs Fenwick paused for an excruciating time. 'Well, if it was you that found the bomb, there can't be any harm in it. His name's Ben Hardiman. He's out at Straightway Farm, just this side of Meare.'

'Thank you! Here.' Hilary thrust the chocolates at her. 'Since Mel isn't in, you'd better have these.'

TWENTY-THREE

'Y ou are going to tell Inspector Fellows, aren't you?'
Veronica's voice rose in anxiety. 'If you don't, I will.'
'Tell him what, exactly? We've already told him we
were worried about three young women. Mel was one of those.
We said we thought she was frightened. Probably of Rupert
Honeydew. What do we know more than that?'

'Where she is.'

'Hmm. Veronica, DI Fellows is a very busy man. So are the
rest of the team. An unexploded bomb at the Chalice Well. A
real explosion in the High Street, killing seven people. And now
Amina's murder, if that's what it is. Unless he thinks Mel Fenwick
is a prime suspect for all of that, what would he do? Can you
imagine the hatchet-faced DS Petersen sent out to Straightway
Farm to get Mel to open up and talk? No, I don't think it would
work, either.'

'So you're going to employ your own well-known skills of
empathy and a motherly shoulder to cry on.'

'No. You are.'

The road from Glastonbury ran straight towards Meare. Hilary
drove.

They were down on the Levels again. Meadowland stretched
away on either side of them, flat as a billiard table, and as green.
Here and there, the uncertain sun glinted on water channels, ruler
straight. Ribbons of oilseed rape gilded their banks.

'It's recovering,' Veronica said, wondering. 'The floods of last
winter seem to have gone.'

'Keep your eyes open for the turning. According to the OS
map it should be somewhere along here on the left.'

Veronica craned forward and wiped the mist that was beginning to form on the windscreen.

'Hang on. There's something ahead. Slow down while I read
the notice at the gate.'

The wire fence was broken by a gap. A metal five-barred gate hung somewhat drunkenly ajar. Its rungs were plastered with dead grass and weeds. Veronica strained to decipher the name board.

'It's still smeared with mud. It looks as though this was underwater in the floods. But I think . . . yes . . . it says "Straightway Farm".'

'Very appropriate. There's not much here for a road to bend around. No hills.'

She eased the car through the gateway. The track was unpaved. It led between low hedges to farm buildings glimpsed some distance ahead.

'Are we just going to drive up to the door?'

'I don't see why not. The outcome's likely to be the same, whether we arrive on foot or by car.'

The farmyard was deserted. It had a sodden look, that might not all be due to the recent rain. Hilary got out of the car and thought she could smell rotting hay.

'I hope to God we get a hot dry summer. The water's gone down, but the place is like a saturated sponge.'

They walked up to the front door of what looked like a mid-nineteenth-century farmhouse. Hilary looked in vain for a doorbell and in the end rapped loudly on the door.

An unwelcoming silence hung over the house.

'There's nobody in.' Veronica sounded almost as if she wanted it to be true.

Hilary knocked again. This time the noise provoked a storm of barking from the back of the house. Round the corner raced a black-and-white collie, shouting defiance at them. Veronica backed away round the car.

Hilary held out her hand, palm open. 'Good boy. Yes, you've got visitors. Any excuse for a good shout, eh? Where's your master?'

The collie sniffed her hand and wagged its back end. The barking subsided, but now and then the animal could not resist letting out another strangled yelp.

Hilary looked up from stroking its chin and stiffened. From the rear of the farmhouse came another, larger figure.

Ben Hardiman was dressed in clothes the colour of his muddied farmyard. His chin sprouted the beginnings of a curly beard. In his hands he held a long-barrelled gun.

'What are you doing on my land? Who are you?'

Hilary held up her hands placatingly, almost as she had to the dog.

'It's nothing to worry about, Mr Hardiman. We're not from DEFRA, or anything like that. This is a personal matter. We need to talk to Mel.'

The angry challenge of the farmer's eyes grew wary. 'Who? There's nobody of that name here.'

'Your granddaughter. Mel Fenwick.'

'You've come to the wrong place. She lives in Glastonbury.'

'But she's not there now. She's here. It's all right. Her mother gave us this address. Mel's not in trouble, but we do need to speak to her.'

Hilary crossed her fingers as she spoke. She had no idea how much trouble Mel might really be in.

'I told you, I'm on my own. Lord knows I've enough troubles, without some nosey parkers banging the door down.' He glanced down at the shotgun, as though unsure how it came to be in his hands. 'I'm a peaceable man, but the best thing you can do is to turn that car round and get back where you came from.'

Her luck was running out. It had been too good to hope that the help she had been offered in the gift shop and at Mel's home would follow her here. It was still exasperating to know that the frightened Mel was inside this house, needing help, and they would have to go away without speaking to her.

Reluctantly, they turned to go. Ben Hardiman lowered his gun.

Hilary was just opening the driver's door when a movement in the barn alongside stopped her. The collie ran forward, wagging its tail frantically. Around the corner of a stack of dank-smelling straw came a slight figure with ash-blonde hair.

'Mel!' Veronica cried. 'Are you all right?'

'Who are you? Oh, I remember. You were in the gift shop. You were the ones who found the . . . bomb.' Her voice shook. 'Did my mum really send you?'

'Yes, she did. Mel, I don't know why you've run away, but you need to know that Rupert Honeydew has been round to your house looking for you.'

The girl gave a violent shiver.

'Yes, he scares me too,' Hilary assured her. 'Look, can we go inside and talk about this? You've got yourself into something that could be very dangerous, haven't you? I don't know what you've done, or what's been done to you, but you need to talk to somebody.'

Mel bit her pale lips and nodded. 'Yes,' she whispered. 'It's terrible. I don't know what to do.'

They sat on the flowered settee in the front room of the farm-house, which looked as though it was rarely used. Copies of the classics in leather bindings stood in rows in a glass-fronted cabinet, but no newspapers or magazines littered the floor or furniture. The television was obviously in the big farmhouse kitchen behind.

The armchair Mel sat curled up in looked too big for her. She had dismissed her grandfather with a nod of her head. 'It's all right, Gramps. I want to talk to them.'

Now she sat chewing her lip and looking up at them from under pale-lashed eyelids. Her face had the bruised look of one who has not slept well.

'You said he'd been to the house?' Her voice was still no more than a whisper.

'Yes. I've only met Rupert Honeydew three times, but I'd say he could be a dangerous man.'

'I thought he was wonderful.' She twisted the cord that edged a cushion. 'He told us all about how his Goddess could heal people. My friend Fran's mum had cancer, and he gave her some of the water from the well, and they did a dance for her, up on the Tor, and she got better, just like that. At first I thought it was a bit of a laugh, all that dancing and stuff, and putting flowers in your hair. I only did it to back Fran up. But then . . . well . . . when he looks right into your eyes, it gives you a sort of shiver. He makes you feel, like . . . special. As though you were the only one in the dance who was important to him.'

She stared into the empty fireplace for a long time.

'But then,' Veronica suggested gently, 'the bomb at the well? Why would he do that? It was him, wasn't it?'

Mel raised wide, tear-bright eyes to them. 'It was me.'

'Mel!' The shocked exclamation escaped Veronica. 'Why?'

'Because he told me to. He said not enough people knew how

sacred the Chalice Well was. That it had the power to heal all England. Only nobody cared about that sort of thing nowadays. So we had to *do* something. Something that would get it in the papers and on TV. So nobody could say they'd never heard of it. And then he could tell people about his book. And there wouldn't just be hundreds of people coming to see the well and drink the water, there'd be thousands.'

'But you didn't make the bomb yourself, of course,' Hilary said.

'What, me? I couldn't tell one end of a Bunsen burner from another. I got an F in General Science. No, he brought the knapsack in under his costume and left it for me in the bushes. All I had to do was slip out in my lunch break and put it in place, so Rupert wouldn't be seen up there beforehand.'

'And you made sure no one saw you either.'

'That's right. It usually goes a bit quiet about lunchtime. Well, except for people picnicking on the lawns . . . But he said it wouldn't go off! Somebody would find it, and we'd still get the publicity. And you did.' She was almost pleading with Hilary.

'And then, two days later . . .' Hilary prompted.

At that, Mel burst into tears.

'I don't know anything about that! I swear to God it wasn't me! I wasn't anywhere near there. All those poor people!'

Veronica went to put her arms around the sobbing girl.

'There, Mel. I'm sure you didn't. Nobody believes that.'

'But was it him? Was it because of me? There wasn't all that much stuff in the papers and on telly about it. Just the local news and a few bits and pieces in the inside pages. It wasn't like he meant it to be. Do you think . . . if the first one didn't work . . .? And now I'm the only one who can tell them it was him who made the first bomb. Only I'd have to tell them I put it under the lid of the well. They'll blame me for the one in the High Street. I know they will.'

Sobs racked her body.

'Mel. Trust us. No one but us, your mum and your grandfather know you're here. The best thing you can do is come clean to the police. If Rupert Honeydew *did* plant the bomb in the High Street, then you're in very real danger. You need protection. Look, stay here. Veronica and I will go straight away and tell a very nice policeman we know. He'll look after you. Nobody will blame you for the second bomb. I promise.'

She got to her feet.

'Now, you've done the sensible thing. Your grandfather isn't going to let anyone else in. Just stay here out of sight until Detective Inspector Fellows gets here. Can you remember that name?'

'Detective Inspector Fellows,' Mel gasped between sobs.

'That's right. I need to tell him this in person, but I don't think it'll be long before he's here. Chin up.'

She grasped the shaking girl's shoulder. 'Just tell your grandpa to keep that shotgun handy. He scared the living daylights out of us.'

The engine roared as Hilary made rather too swift a turn in the farmyard, scattering wisps of straw. They bumped their way up the unmade track towards the road.

'Shouldn't we phone DI Fellows to let him know we've found Mel? And to tell him that, of all the unlikely people in Glastonbury, she's the Chalice Well bomber?' Veronica was delving in her handbag as she spoke.

'Never mind your mobile,' Hilary said. 'I've never liked those things. This is something I need to explain face to face. If he gets the wrong idea and the police come charging round here with sirens blaring, they could send her and her grandpa into a flat panic.'

'Oh, well.' Veronica still sounded doubtful. 'I suppose it's only a few miles.'

Hilary drew up at the lopsided gate that gave access to the road. Some distance in the Glastonbury direction, a car was approaching at speed. She nosed forward, wondering if she had time to swing across the road before it reached them. But it took a moment to ease round the crooked gate. She braked.

She had expected the silver car to shoot past them, on towards Meare. She was momentarily confused when it slowed as it approached the entrance to Straightway Farm, then stopped. For all his apparent hurry, the driver must have halted to allow her to cross the road. She raised her hand in cheery acknowledge-ment and put her foot on the accelerator.

'Hilary!' Veronica hissed beside her. 'It's Rupert Honeydew!'

Startled, Hilary took her eyes off the road ahead and swivelled to peer through the side window. The first thing that registered was that the driver must be unnaturally tall. His head seemed grotesquely near the roof of the car. The long, moon-shaped face wore no Guizer's marks of soot. There was no battered top hat. But he was unmistakable. This was the undisguised Rupert Honeydew they had met on Glastonbury Tor.

She had slammed on the brake again without realizing she was doing it. Her car was slewed across the road a hand's breadth from Honeydew's bonnet. The two glared at each other.

'Give me that!' She snatched Veronica's phone. There was a frantic moment when she fumbled in her own bag for the card with DI Fellows' number.

'Thank God for mobile phones!'

'Hilary! You hypocrite!'

But Hilary was tapping in the digits undeterred.

It was a reassurance to hear DI Fellows' voice. He, at least, didn't keep his phone switched off.

'It's Hilary Masters. We're at the entrance to Straightway Farm. That's halfway between Glastonbury and Meare. We've just found out that Mel Fenwick from the Chalice Well is the one who planted the bomb there. At the bidding of Rupert Honeydew. Go easy with her. She's terrified. She's at the farm and Honeydew's here at the gate. His car is practically scraping the paint off mine. He can't get in because my car is blocking his way. Do you think you could send reinforcements?'

Whatever DI Robert Fellows felt about this bizarre message, he reacted with commendable speed. She heard him shout an order across the room. Then he was back to her.

'Get yourselves out of there. If Honeydew is the bomber, there's no saying what he'll do. We'll be with you in minutes.'

'Mel's at the end of this track, with her granddad, his shotgun and a collie dog. Our car is the only thing stopping Honeydew.'

'We'll be there. We've got seven dead already. I don't want you to be the next. Stop playing the heroine. Go!'

The call was abruptly cut off.

Rupert Honeydew was opening the door of his car. A long leg appeared on the roadway. Hilary found she was shaking.

'Hilary!' whispered Veronica. 'What do we do?'

Hilary tried to put the car into gear, and stalled. She swore. At the second attempt, the clutch engaged. The car moved jerkily forward, almost into the path of an oncoming car. A horn blared at her and the driver yelled through the open window. Then the road was clear. She swung right towards Glastonbury.

Part of her mind was protesting that she was betraying Mel and her grandfather. Through her rear-view mirror she could see Rupert Honeydew getting back into his car. He was reversing, to take a wider turn into the gateway. Surely he wouldn't risk doing anything to Mel now that he had been seen approaching the farm?

She thought of the unexpected hatred she had seen in his eyes on Glastonbury Tor. Rupert Honeydew was the bomber. She had no idea what he might do next.

She had barely brought her mind back to the road ahead when she was aware of a column of cars racing towards them. Police cars, sirens wailing, lights flashing. An unmarked car she hoped was DI Fellows and the redoubtable DS Petersen. She found herself relishing the idea of the sergeant clapping handcuffs on Rupert Honeydew. She drew over to the verge and glided to a stop.

'Thank the Lord!' she said. 'They were quick.'

They were too far away to make out what was happening behind them at the gate. There was a knot of vehicles there. Hilary lowered the car window. There was no sound of sirens now. If a car was making its way down the track to the farm, it was doing it without fanfare.

'We ought to go back,' she said. 'Who knows what Mel may do if she feels cornered. Let alone her grandpa with that gun.'

'Hilary, it's out of our hands now. Mel's a criminal, however sorry we may feel for her.'

'The Chalice Well bomb didn't go off.'

'We've only her word for it that she had nothing to do with the one that did.'

'I believed her. I thought you did.'

'All I know for sure is that she's terrified. Of Rupert Honeydew. Of what she might be blamed for. Or of what she's done?'

'It's too late, anyway. Fellows will be there by now.'

She sat there for a long while. Then she sighed, wound up the window and drove on.

TWENTY-FOUR

Detective Chief Superintendent Janet Allenby had dyed blonde hair that did not quite cover the grey roots. Not for her a screened-off cubicle in the church hall. She had taken over a smaller room at the back of the building. She steepled her hands and looked at Veronica and Hilary with steely eyes.

'I suppose you think I should commend you for leading us to Melanie Fenwick and Rupert Honeydew. But may I remind you that this is not a game. We are dealing with some ruthless people here. People who have not hesitated to kill.'

'Not Mel,' Hilary objected. 'I'm sure she believed him when he told her that the Chalice Well bomb wouldn't go off. And it didn't.'

'But the second one in the High Street did. Whether she planted it or not, Rupert Honeydew is the one you should have feared. He now knows that it was you who turned him in.'

'But you've got him in custody?' Veronica's cry of surprise was close to a question.

'For the moment, yes. But I'll be honest with you. All we have at present is Melanie Fenwick's evidence against him. And that only relates to the Chalice Well. Hearsay, his lawyers will argue. And anything else is pure speculation. If we can't find any stronger proof, we may have to let him go.'

'But you're searching his house?' Hilary demanded. 'You'll find evidence there, won't you? You can't go around assembling bombs without leaving traces. And what about the terrorism laws? You can stretch a point with those, can't you?'

'Mr Honeydew strikes me as a clever man. It would not surprise me if the evidence is somewhere else. I don't want to alarm you, but I would still recommend that you leave this town in the next twenty-four hours.'

'We plan to, anyway. But are you saying that if he can't be

proved to be responsible for the High Street bomb you're unable to protect us from someone you know to be a killer?'

'That's just the point, Mrs Masters. We *don't* know he's the High Street bomber. Even Miss Fenwick couldn't testify to that. She just assumes he is, because of the first bomb. All any of us has is a gut feeling. While that remains the case, all our efforts have to go into finding who *did* bomb the Spiritual Sphere. Yes, we'll keep a discreet watch on Mr Honeydew, but we can't afford you twenty-four-hour protection. I think it's best if you quietly disappear and don't tell anyone where you're going. Except us, of course. It would have been a great deal better if you had left it to DI Fellows to question Miss Fenwick at Straightway Farm.'

She sat back in her chair, indicating that the interview was over.

Veronica and Hilary threaded their way through the hall. It was as active as ever, with officers busy at computers, wall charts and telephones. But Hilary detected a feeling of weariness. They had been working flat out for much of the week.

Out on the street, Hilary grumbled, 'What beats me is how Rupert Honeydew knew where we were. I'm sure he wasn't following us. We'd been at the farm quite some time before he turned up. So how did he know where Mel was hiding? Her mother certainly didn't tell him, by the sound of it. She seemed more likely to send him away with a flea in his ear.'

'It might have been one of Mel's friends. That Fran she mentioned. The one whose mother's cancer went into remission after she drank the Chalice Well water and they danced for her. If she was besotted with him, she might have told him that Mel was close to her grandfather and pointed him to the farm.'

Hilary shook off a shiver. 'That DCS is right. I don't like the thought of Honeydew out on the streets again. He has to be the High Street bomber, evidence or not. And even if he isn't, he glared enough hatred at us to curdle milk.'

They found themselves walking back along the High Street, which was gradually coming back to something like normality, in a more subdued way. Tarpaulins still shrouded the most damaged buildings.

'We seem to have missed lunch, what with all the excitement,' Veronica remarked.

'I could murder a sandwich.'

'We could go back to the Copper Kettle.' Veronica paused as she saw Hilary's face. 'Or perhaps not. Too close to where the bomb went off.'

'You could say that. Every time I look at the damage I think about that poor boy Baz. Whether he's died. Whether he's come round enough to be questioned. Whether he did have anything to do with the bomb. Sonia Marsden's shaken my faith in Amina. Could I be wrong about Baz too?'

'If they've arrested Rupert Honeydew, it should mean the police think Baz is innocent, shouldn't it?'

'They've nothing to connect Honeydew with the big bomb. And since we don't know why they suspected Baz in the first place, I can't answer that.'

They found a pleasantly historical-looking hostelry which offered comfortable easy chairs in the bar. Hilary ordered a plate of barbecued chicken sandwiches with lime pickle and a pot of Earl Grey tea.

'Will you excuse me a moment while I make a phone call?' Veronica asked.

'Go ahead.'

While Veronica was gone, Hilary sank back into the upholstery, feeling the energy drain out of her.

Her companion was quickly back.

'Everything OK?' Hilary asked.

'Yes, thanks.'

'I hope they go easy on Mel. It can't have been easy to confess what she did. Little idiot!'

'She should have spoken up straight away. After the High Street bomb went off.'

'You've got more judgemental over your three chicks.'

'Not Amina. I don't buy the idea that she bombed the High Street and then committed suicide in the abbey.'

There was an awkward silence. Hilary put down her half-eaten sandwich.

'Where does *she* fit into all this?'

'I've no idea. All we know is that we last saw her following Rupert Honeydew to Glastonbury Tor. Maybe she got too close.

Found out things she wasn't meant to. Busily scribbling them down in the little notebook of hers.'

'But what became of the burka? We still don't know whether the killer removed it, or whether she went out later without it.'

'We're probably never likely to.'

'Don't be such a pessimist, Veronica. If the police solve the bombings, it's pretty sure to lead them on to Amina's murderer. I can't believe they're not related.'

Veronica sipped her tea. 'It's out of our hands now. Which reminds me, we haven't decided where we're going to stay tomorrow night.'

'Do we need to? We're free agents. We can just take off and stop wherever we fancy. Come to think of it, that might be better. Forgive me if I sound paranoid, but the Detective Chief Superintendent might be better pleased if we didn't leave any clues.'

Veronica's shoulders twitched in distaste. 'I wish I could be sure that what we did wasn't enough to bring down Rupert Honeydew's revenge on us. It all sounds a bit melodramatic, but . . .'

'But he's a melodramatic character. With a streak of nastiness underneath. And if it hadn't been for us, Mel might not have shopped him.'

They finished their sandwiches in silence. Hilary was just pouring herself a second cup of tea when the door of the bar swung violently open and a dishevelled figure burst on the scene. She threw her arms around Veronica and hugged her.

'I can't thank you enough! I've sold the story! That's a second exclusive in a week!'

The back of the brown cardigan and the mousy hair told Hilary that this whirlwind was Joan Townsend. Only this morning, she had feared that it might be Joan who was dead. It was odd to remember that pang of compassion now. The reporter was very much alive.

Hilary watched them both blankly. Veronica emerged from the embrace, her face oddly flushed.

'It was only a little thing, but I thought it might help.'

'Veronica Taylor,' Hilary demanded, 'what have you done?'

'Well, it's bound to come out soon, isn't it? I just thought Joan might get ahead of the pack.'

'*What* is bound to come out?'

'That Rupert Honeydew's been arrested.'

Joan swung round, her eyes shining. 'It all fits in with my story about black magic on the Tor. Rupert Honeydew! I mean, what editor could resist a character like that! Veronica, I'm going to buy you the biggest bouquet of flowers you ever saw. You've no idea what they're paying me!'

'I'm glad it worked out,' Veronica said primly. 'Well done.'

Joan's eyes narrowed. 'Is it true that the body they found in the abbey is that Muslim girl?'

Veronica drew a breath, then caught Hilary's eyes and hesitated. 'I'm afraid I can't tell you about that.'

'Never mind. I'll find out soon.'

The young journalist swept out of the room on a cloud of euphoria.

'Veronica. I can't believe you did that,' Hilary said.

The blush had not quite receded from Veronica's cheeks. 'It's been such a dreadful week. I wanted something good to come out of it. You can see how delighted she is.'

'Little ghoul. But, in spite of myself, I'm glad she's still alive. Still, I shudder to think what DI Fellows is going to say about this. Let alone his Chief Superintendent. They're bound to know it was us. Well, you.'

'Don't begrudge Joan her moment of glory, Hilary. She's had enough disappointments.'

'Hmm! If the police have decided *not* to release Honeydew's name, there's going to be hell to pay. It's just as well we're leaving tomorrow.'

TWENTY-FIVE

They negotiated the narrow stretch of the High Street where scaffolding allowed builders to work on the shattered shop front. For some distance around it, the pavement and the surface of the road had been pockmarked by the force of the flying debris. Hilary recalled lying face down in the midst of that storm. It could have been so much worse. She or Veronica might have been one of those seven dead, or gravely injured, like Baz.

She was brought back to the present by Veronica saying, rather doubtfully, 'Do you still want to see the Glastonbury Lake Village Museum? We're almost there. We were on our way there this morning, you remember. Only . . . poor Amina!'

'I don't know about you, but I've rather gone off sightseeing. I thought I might drop into the church and say a prayer for her.'

They walked on in silence for a little way. They were approaching the churchyard of St John the Baptist. It was quiet this afternoon, not like the crowded memorial service.

'That sprig of Thorn in her hand, what do you think that was all about?'

'I've no idea,' Hilary said. 'Did she pick it herself, or did someone put it into her hand after she was dead? Either way, it must have significance, either for her, or for them.'

'There are a lot of legends around the Thorn. It's the sort of thing that would have appealed to Amina, all that folklore tradition.'

'Or was the killer making some sort of statement?'

'Whichever it was, they probably picked it from the tree in St John's churchyard. I rather fancy having a look at it myself.'

'Don't you think Inspector Fellows will have had the same idea already? I doubt that you'll be able to get anywhere near the Thorn. They'll be looking for evidence. Footprints, or whatever. Maybe a thread of clothing caught on a thorn.'

'You're right. Damn.'

As they drew level, they saw what the tall Celtic cross war memorial had hidden from them until now. Blue-and-white police tape lined the path up to the church door. On either side of it, police officers in regulation overalls were combing the grass between the few remaining gravestones. Hilary and Veronica stopped to look.

'The Thorn tree's set rather back from the road, behind that bigger tree,' Veronica mused. 'It would have been in shadow at night.'

'So what was Amina doing here after dark? It must have been at night, mustn't it? Or if she wasn't killed here, it must have been in the abbey grounds. How did she get in? And why?'

'Maybe she had an assignment to meet someone,' Veronica suggested.

'Or she was stalking someone, and got caught.'

'That would explain the lack of a burka, wouldn't it? She must have thought that if anyone saw her, it would be all too obvious who she was, dressed like that. But a young woman in black jacket and leggings . . . She could have been anybody.' She paused. 'But what about her religious scruples?'

'She was an intelligent young lady,' Hilary answered. 'She made a conscious decision to adopt strict Islamic dress. She could just as well have made the decision to abandon it for one night. She wouldn't have expected anyone to see her, if it was really late.'

'But who was she meeting . . . or following?'

'If they've been clever enough, we may never know.'

They walked up the churchyard path, between the lines of tape. To their right, there was a curious labyrinth marked out by stones in the grass. Hilary stopped to study it.

'It's meant as a means of meditation. Walking the labyrinth. But I can't help being reminded that the path around the Tor is also supposed to be a maze.'

The nearest two police officers lifted their heads from their search and watched them enter the church.

In the south transept of the spacious interior, tea-lights burned on a stand in memory of the dead. Hilary walked slowly forward and lit another. Her mind silently framed a prayer for Amina.

She sat in a pew trying to calm her thoughts. Veronica wandered a little further away, looking thoughtfully up at the stained-glass windows and carvings. Then she chose another pew and did the same.

Hilary's mind told over all the troubled people she had encountered this week. Mel and Beth at the gift shop. What was happening to Mel now? Was she in custody? Sonia and George Marsden. She had taken a dislike to them, but she had seen a different face to Sonia today. And what had George actually done? Just ranted because the world was not as he wanted it to be. Joan Townsend, desperate for success. Rupert Honeydew. He was harder to pray for. She still remembered the malignant look in his eyes.

Then the lives shattered by the bomb. The injured. The grieving relatives of the dead. Those who had, at least temporarily, lost their homes. Baz. Why *were* the police mounting a guard over him? What was it she didn't know?

And now Amina. Clever, righteous Amina, defying the norms of the society around her for her faith. But still engaged in the world of academic research and pursuing with enthusiasm the project she had set her heart on . . . until now. Just when and how had her life ended? It had to be Wednesday night. She had been missing for more than twenty-four hours before Hilary and Veronica had called at her digs. The night Rupert Honeydew and his masked crew had wound their way through the streets under the full moon. Hilary and Veronica had followed them. They had seen no sign of Amina then, but they had been looking for a woman in a burka. Amina could have slipped by them in her leather jacket and they would never have guessed.

Or had she been watching the dance from here, on the raised graveyard of St John the Baptist? Hidden by that spreading tree? Only a few steps away from the Glastonbury Thorn.

She shuddered. Had someone seen her, and had reason to fear her presence? It would only have taken a few seconds for one of those masked men – Hilary was almost sure they *had* been men – to leap through those sculpted pillars at the gate and deal with her. Had Amina retreated in fear, grasping the Thorn in the last moments of her life?

Hilary sighed. But what had happened in the intervening day and night? Why had a second morning dawned before Amina's body had been found in the corner of the Galilee of the abbey church?

She got up. There was no way she was going to find the answers to these questions. She would have to leave it to the police. Only when she turned to go, and Veronica silently rose from her pew to join her, did they see that a policewoman was watching them from the back of the church.

'There's nothing left for us to do,' Veronica said. 'I'm beginning to think we should have left when we told our families we would.'

'Inspector Fellows asked us to stay around. He seems to think we might still have information he needs. I wish to God we did, but I can't imagine what it is.'

'I have to confess, I'm feeling a bit uneasy. We don't know why Amina died, but it's a reasonable guess that she found out something which would identify the High Street bomber.'

'But we know who it is now. Rupert Honeydew. And the police have got him behind bars, or at least in the interview room. For a minimum of twenty-four hours.'

'But he may not be working alone,' Veronica objected. 'Think of all those people who follow him in his dances. From what Mel said, he has this power over them. I can believe it. Those eyes. They frightened me, but I imagine he can switch on the charm too. I keep remembering all that crew who were dancing in the streets at midnight. Especially the men in animal masks. There's something scary about masks. Like the Venice carnival. It makes people feel they have a licence to behave transgressively because no one knows who they are.'

'It's the same in school,' Hilary commented. 'Kids can look really startled when you call them by name. If you don't know who they are, they think they can get away with murder . . . Sorry!'

'That's exactly what I mean. And if they take those masks off, we've no idea who they are. They could come up to us and we'd never know we were in danger.'

'Why should we be?'

'You said yourself, DI Fellows still believes we have something more we could tell him. Something which could identify the murderer.'

'You're not making me feel any better about today.'

'I'm just being realistic.'

They crossed the market place.

'It looks as if they've opened up the abbey again,' Hilary said, looking down the street at the people going in and out of the gateway.

'I dare say Sonia Marsden will be relieved.'

Their hotel was only a short distance ahead. For a moment, Hilary thought of turning aside and paying another visit to the abbey. It might be better than sitting aimlessly in one of the hotel rooms. Then she thought of being shown Amina's shrouded body in the Galilee and changed her mind.

Glastonbury Abbey had suffered violence, fire and murder

before now. She must believe that it would emerge, serene and holy, after this.

They entered the hotel's wide lobby and were heading for the stairs when a figure shot out of the lounge bar alongside them. A young woman with a swinging curtain of fair hair.

'*There* you are, Mum! Where have you *been*?'

Veronica turned with a startled gasp.

'Morag! Whatever are you doing here?'

'What am *I* doing here? That's rich! You were supposed to be out of Glastonbury today, and what is it?' She pointed to the clock over the reception desk. 'Four o'clock!'

'Keep your voice down, dear. You're making a spectacle of us. Why don't we just sit down in the bar? Would you like some tea?'

'I've drunk enough tea to launch Noah's Ark. I'd love something stronger, but I've got to drive back to London tonight.'

Morag flung herself down on one of the settees. Hilary hesitated, then joined her. Veronica looked as if she could do with some support.

'What brought you racing down here?' she asked kindly. 'The bomb was two days ago.'

'And now I get this phone call from Mum telling me you've found another dead body. You two have got yourselves into this up to your necks. I made her promise you'd leave Glastonbury today. This morning. But I know what she's like. Just because she doesn't argue with me doesn't mean she's going to do what I say.'

'Morag,' said Veronica mildly, 'I thought *I* was the parent.'

'Then start acting responsibly for once. Anyway, round about lunch time I got this really bad feeling. So I rang this hotel. I asked if you'd checked out, and of course they said you hadn't. I mean, Mum, *really*! So I phoned the others, and Bob's in Spain, and Cathy hasn't got wheels, so I'm the one who has to jump into the car and dash down here to sort things out. It's not fair!' She drew a shuddering gasp and collapsed into tears.

Hilary placed a hand on her shoulder. 'There! I think you need something a lot stronger than tea. It's the weekend tomorrow, so you can stay the night. We'll pay. And we really are leaving tomorrow.'

'I know you think we're being irresponsible,' Veronica

explained. 'But there's this rather nice Detective Inspector in charge of the Chalice Well bomb case and now Amina Haddad's murder. Believe it or not, we really *have* been able to help him. He asked if we'd mind staying around a little longer.' She held up her hand as Morag started to protest. 'And if it makes you feel any better, the prime suspect for the Chalice Well bomb, and probably the High Street one too, is under arrest. And, if I say it myself, Hilary and I did have something to do with that.' She smiled at Hilary for confirmation.

'Hmm,' was all that Hilary could say. It did not address the fears they had felt, coming back along the High Street past the bomb damage and the Thorn tree in St John's churchyard, that Rupert Honeydew had followers who were not in custody. Privately, she was beginning to agree with Morag. She would be glad to be out of this town.

'I've also done my bit for the cause.' Veronica smiled. 'Journalism. Hilary doesn't approve of this, but we've met this rather sad little reporter who'd like to make the big time. I don't know if you've seen it, but she did get an exclusive on this strange group who were doing a healing dance, or something, in the High Street at midnight.'

Morag sat up, the tears on her cheeks forgotten. 'Yes, I saw that! All those animal masks, and women with wreaths of flowers in their hair looking spaced out. Right in the street where the bomb went off. Do you think it's really black magic? You said healing. Did you give her that story?'

'Oh, no. That wasn't us. I mean, we were there . . .'

'They passed right under our bedroom window,' Hilary put in. 'It was hardly a secret.'

'No. But this morning . . .' Veronica shot an apologetic look at Hilary. 'I'm afraid . . . After we came away from seeing the arrest . . . Yes, that's a long story. I'll explain later . . . I phoned Joan – that's this journalist – and told her the name of the man they'd arrested. Hilary's cross with me, but I thought the name would get out anyway. And if Joan could get her story in first, it would be another scoop for her.'

Morag was leaning forward, her face shining now. 'And nobody else knows this? No member of the public, I mean. Mum, you've got to tell me!'

Hilary saw the expression of shock and dismay in Veronica's face. Had she forgotten that her own daughter was studying journalism? Of course she hadn't. That was why she had thought Morag would sympathize with Joan. But had it really not occurred to her that Morag, too, would want a major breakthrough to add to her portfolio when she came to look for a job?

She held her breath, willing Veronica to say nothing. She watched her friend wrestling with the dilemma.

'Well, I suppose it will be in the first edition of the papers on *Newsnight* this evening.'

'Veronica!'

The other woman turned pleading eyes up to her. 'How do we know the police won't release the name themselves?' She turned to Morag. 'If you must know, his name is Rupert Honeydew, and he's the local eccentric who led that dance.'

Morag was already reaching for her phone.

Back in their room, Hilary rounded on Veronica. 'Why did I let you do that? First you release information to Joan that the police may have wanted to keep to themselves. Then you go and break her exclusive by telling Morag as well. She's not going to take kindly to that.'

'But what was I to do? Give a young woman I've only met this week precedence over my own daughter? You heard her say how hard it is for youngsters to get jobs in journalism these days. This will be one foot on the ladder for her.'

Hilary shook her head. 'Inspector Fellows is not going to be pleased. To say nothing of his Chief Superintendent.'

'Well, it's done now.' Veronica sank down on to her bed and picked up her hairbrush. 'I wish the whole thing would just go away.'

'I think *we* should go away,' Hilary said. 'We've done all we can. I doubt very much whether we really have anything more we can tell Fellows.'

She hung her jacket in the wardrobe and turned to comb her hair.

'At least you had the sense not to tell Morag the identity of the body at the abbey. That's *really* going to be a sensation when it gets out. *Islamist Found Dead in Murder Abbey*, or some such nonsense.'

She heard Veronica's hairbrush drop to the floor.

'But somebody *does* know, besides us. Don't you remember? Before she left, Joan said, "Is it true that the body they found in the abbey is that Muslim girl?" How did she know that?'

TWENTY-SIX

With only the briefest of taps to warn them, the bedroom door was flung open. Morag burst in. She was a slender girl, but the fury with which she was bristling seemed to fill the room.

'That's it! I've never been made to feel such a fool in all my life!'

Veronica rose from the bed in alarm. 'What's up, dear? What's happened?'

Morag's eyes glittered with angry tears. 'You! Your supposedly exclusive information. I rang the *Mail* to tell them I'd got a big story. The identity of the Glastonbury bomber. And the woman actually *laughed* at me! She said, "Have you looked at your phone lately? It's all over Facebook and it's gone viral on Twitter."'

She flung the offending mobile down on Veronica's bed. The brightly lit screen, four times as large as Hilary's, was full of messages. Hilary looked at it doubtfully, but Veronica picked it up and scrolled down through more of them.

'Oh, Morag! I'm so sorry. I thought I was helping you.'

'I should have known there's no such thing as a scoop nowadays. That kind of thing went out with black-and-white television. Who needs newspapers when you can tell the whole world in five minutes on social media? All I've done is make an absolute idiot of myself.'

'*Oh* dear,' said Hilary with gloomy emphasis. 'You know what that means, Veronica? Poor old Joan won't have scooped the pack with this one, either. She was on a high this afternoon. Now it's all going to come crashing down around her ears. Just when she really believed she was getting somewhere. At least you won't have to face her fury for telling Morag as well.'

'But she said they paid her money. Lots of it. Will she have to give it back?'

'I shouldn't think so. They knew the risk. The police could have released the name to the press at any time. For all we know, they may have done so.'

'Still, she was the only one to report on that midnight dance. The really creepy one. She's still got that.'

'And why do you think that is? Why wasn't that all over Facebook and that Twitter thing? It was hardly a secret. I'll tell you why. Or what I think. The good people of Glastonbury know better than to get on the wrong side of Rupert Honeydew. They'll have decided to look the other way. Safer to pass him off as a harmless eccentric.'

'Like the smugglers' song?' Veronica suggested. '*Watch the wall, my darling, while the gentlemen go by.*'

'Something like that. But not Joan. Oh, no. She has to splash the story across the national newspapers. Well, one of the tabloids, at least. Salacious stuff about black magic. And you can bet the story she's sold about Honeydew's arrest is going to be linked to satanic practices, or some such nonsense.'

'Do we know it's nonsense?' Veronica asked.

Morag's expression of indignation had faded. She was listening with avid interest.

'Black arts or not, Rupert Honeydew is a dangerous man. Joan's a local too. But she was the one to put her head above the parapet and write about it in the national press. I'd like to think it was bravery. Putting ethical journalism above her own self-interest. But I'm very much afraid the wretched girl is so insensitive to what's going on around her that she can't see that, by indulging her lurid imagination to further her career, she's walking into a whole lot of danger.'

'But the dance was two nights ago. And she's not the one who's dead.'

'You're forgetting. It was too late to make Thursday's paper. That's why they printed her story today.'

Veronica's eyes widened. 'Is that really true? Is it only Friday? So much has happened today, it seems a lifetime ago.'

'The girl exasperates me, I admit, but I had something of a change of heart when I thought she was dead in the abbey. Now I'm wondering whether we shouldn't warn her.'

'Would the police help? Probably not. They'd say Rupert Honeydew's in custody.'

'But that hasn't made us feel completely safe ourselves.'

Veronica shot her a warning look, and nodded meaningfully at Morag.

'Don't mind me!' the girl protested. 'I've driven all the way from London to tell you to clear out of here. Of course I think you're involving yourself in something dangerous. It's what all of us have been saying all along. Ever since that bomb went off.' She swung round on Hilary. 'Your children too. I've talked to Bridget. And that wasn't the start of it, was it? Neither of you thought fit to tell us you'd found another bomb on Monday.'

'Yes, dear, we understand,' Veronica tried to soothe her. 'We've agreed to stay here today, in case Inspector Fellows needs us, but we're definitely checking out tomorrow. Of course, if you feel uncomfortable about staying the night here . . .'

'Mum! Don't patronise me. I'm trying to look after you.'

Hilary saw the expression change on Veronica's face. It should have been Andrew who was concerned for her safety, but now it had to be her teenage children.

'Let's go down to the bar,' she said, 'and relax over a glass of something before dinner.'

The television was on in the bar. Normally Hilary would have ignored it, but the three of them turned their chairs to watch the news headlines.

'The police have confirmed that they are holding a local man for questioning in connection with the terrorist bomb attack in Glastonbury. They have not released the name, but he is thought to be a folklore expert. His motive for the atrocity is not clear. Meanwhile, Basil Avropoulos, a student who was badly injured in the blast, has been moved to a hospital nearer his family home in Staines. It is understood that he is no longer a suspect for the bombing.'

'Thank God for that!' Hilary exclaimed. 'I've been terrified all along it was him. I know David would tell me I had to save his life, anyway, but . . . well, it's a relief. As for the real suspect, they didn't actually give the name, but they might just as well have shouted "Rupert Honeydew" across the air waves.'

'Ssh!' Veronica ordered.

The newscaster was still reporting.

'There has been a further development. The body of a young woman was found in the ruins of Glastonbury Abbey this morning. It is not known whether her death is connected in any way to this week's bombs. The police say they are treating the death as suspicious, but have not released any further details.'

'That's what you meant!' Morag swung round on her mother. 'You were talking about that journalist – Joan, was it? – and you said, "*She's* not the one who's dead." You knew about this, didn't you? You know who it is.'

Veronica set her lips in a prim line. 'I can't discuss it, I'm afraid. I've already told you more than I should. But Rupert Honeydew is a very public character. This one . . . isn't. I'm sorry, Morag.'

The journalism undergraduate glared at her mother. 'Does Joan know who she is?'

Veronica hesitated. 'I don't know how she could do, but she said something that makes me believe she may have guessed.'

Morag's fork hovered over the last bit of lemon sole on her plate. 'This body in the abbey. The one you won't tell me about. How did it get there? You've said it was found almost as soon as the abbey opened. So we're guessing it must have been there before that. Sometime between closing time last night and . . . when do they let people in?'

'Nine a.m.'

'So what was she doing there at night?'

'We have no idea.'

'I'm sorry we can't identify her for you,' Hilary said. 'But we do know she was missing from her digs since Wednesday evening.'

'And today's Friday. But she can't have been in the abbey all that time, can she? I mean, somebody was bound to notice a dead body.'

'Exactly. So was she killed elsewhere, and her body planted in the abbey last night? Or did she go into the abbey grounds to meet someone after dark?'

'How would she get in?'

'Good question. Along Magdalene Street – that's where the entrance is – there's a railing and a hedge in front of the Abbot's Kitchen. After that, it's a stone wall, the same as it is on the other side of the grounds. Elsewhere, I fancy there are houses backing on to it. At a pinch, she might have been able to climb over the wall . . . if she was still alive.'

'But could you heave a dead body over it?'

'Difficult, but in places not impossible. It depends how strong the killer was, or how tall,' Hilary said.

'Unless,' Veronica suggested, 'somebody had a key to get in.'

The three of them looked at each other in conjecture.

Hilary sighed. 'That opens up a whole other can of worms. Who could that be?'

'You'd have to start with the abbey staff, wouldn't you? Some of them must have keys to open up in the morning,' Morag said.

'Sonia!' Veronica cried. 'Sonia Marsden! I don't know what her job is at the abbey, but she looked to be pretty senior. She might have a key.'

'I began to change my mind about her this morning,' Hilary said slowly. 'Seeing her on her own ground, she sounded – I don't know – intelligent, compassionate. But this means we can't rule George Marsden out after all. I'd got him down as a loud-mouthed fool, who ranted against anybody and everybody, but who was essentially harmless. But what if he's not? What if he got hold of the keys and drove up to the entrance at night? In the small hours of the morning, when everything was quiet, and smuggled the body in that way?'

'But why would he do that?' Morag objected. 'Wouldn't it throw suspicion on himself, or Sonia at least, for just the reason you've suggested? He had the opportunity.'

'Hmm!' Hilary said. 'Perhaps he was making some sort of statement.'

'You're forgetting,' Hilary said to Veronica, 'there's another way in.'

Hilary looked at her blankly.

'Don't you remember? That night we were walking back from . . .' She stopped abruptly and glanced at Morag. 'Along the side of the abbey grounds,' she corrected herself, 'and we met Sister Mary Magdalene.'

'I remember well enough,' Hilary grunted. 'I had this horrible feeling of footsteps following us in the dusk. Only it was just this teacher nun we'd met,' she explained to Morag.

'But it was what she said,' Veronica persisted. 'About the abbey retreat house. Guests on courses there get access to a gate that lets them into the abbey grounds outside the normal opening times.'

'Oh, great,' Morag said. 'A spiritual retreat house. Just the place you'd find a murderer with a body to dispose of.'

'Sorry,' Veronica said. 'It was just an idea.'

But Hilary had a surreal memory of Sister Mary Magdalene emerging out of the fog of dust from the explosion, her clothes spattered with blood.

TWENTY-SEVEN

They were coming out of the dining room on their way to take coffee in the lounge when a figure rose out of an armchair to greet them. Detective Inspector Fellows held out a hand.

'Mrs Taylor, Mrs Masters, good evening. And this is . . .?'

'My daughter Morag.'

'Pleased to meet you. I'm Detective Inspector Fellows and this is my sergeant, DS Petersen.'

The detective sergeant had done no more than move to the edge of her seat in acknowledgement. Her face was set in a sullen expression. It struck Hilary that both detectives looked tired. She wondered what hours they had been working through this tumultuous week.

'Your mother and Mrs Masters have been very observant,' DI Fellows was explaining to Morag. 'They've provided us with some significant information for our investigation.'

Veronica gave Morag a rather smug smile.

'I was wondering,' DI Fellows went on, this time turning to Hilary and Veronica, 'if there was anywhere private we could talk. I didn't want to drag you out to the incident room at this time of night.'

Hilary cast her eyes around the lamplit lounge. 'There's the conservatory. Nobody seems to be using it at the moment. If anyone comes, I shall resort to schoolmarm mode and glare daggers at them.'

Fellows followed her eyes to the glass-walled extension built out from one side of the lounge. Potted palm trees made deeper shadows in the dusky interior.

'Fine,' he said. He waved the two women towards it. Detective Sergeant Petersen rose from her settee. Hilary saw the inspector look at Morag doubtfully. She intervened.

'Morag, dear, would you wait here and tell them we're taking coffee in the conservatory? You'll be all right on your own, won't you?' Summoning up her sweetest smile. 'I don't suppose we'll be long.'

She saw the expression of frustrated indignation in the student's eyes. How Morag would have loved to sit in on a real-life interview between a Detective Inspector and his informants on a murder case – especially when one of those informants was her own mother. But if Hilary had read DI Fellows' manner correctly, he had not wanted what he had to say to go any further.

When she joined the others, she found that Veronica had switched on a standing lamp which shed a pool of light over one end of the conservatory. Hilary noticed for the first time that DS Petersen had a bulky package on the cane chair beside her. Her hand was resting protectively over it.

'Now,' said Inspector Fellows, with the air of one making light conversation, 'how has your time here been? One unexploded bomb, one serious explosion, and a murder, all in the course of one week. I hope it hasn't been too devastating for you.'

Their reply was silenced by the arrival of the chinless waiter with their coffee. Hilary ordered more for the detectives, but DI Fellows held up his hand to stop her. 'No thanks. When we found you were having dinner we filled in the time with a cup. Rather better than what we brew up in the church hall.'

He waited until Veronica had poured the coffee. Hilary began to sense that beneath his suave politeness was a weary and frustrated man hoping, a little desperately, for a ray of light in the darkness of this week.

Veronica had barely set the coffee pot down when he began.

'You saw Amina Haddad in her burka, right? You talked to her at close quarters.'

'At the abbey, yes. I mean the first time we were there. Tuesday morning.' She glanced at DS Petersen and was sure the sergeant was remembering how she had berated Hilary and Veronica for interfering with the case. Petersen had been following Amina then. Clearly she had suspected the research student of planting the Chalice Well bomb.

'We have something to show you.' He too looked at Petersen.

Almost reluctantly, she withdrew her square-fingered hand from the parcel beside her. It was a clear plastic evidence bag, neatly labelled. The contents were blue. A bulky package of sky-blue cloth. Hilary drew in a sharp little breath.

'Yes, we believe it's Miss Haddad's burka.'

'Where did you find it?' Veronica gasped. 'Did she leave it behind at her lodgings?'

As so often, the DI ignored her question. 'Turn it over, would you, Olive?'

The other side of the bag revealed the intricate smocking that had covered Amina's forehead and surrounded the slit for her eyes.

Such surprisingly blue eyes, Hilary remembered.

'Can you say if this corresponds with the one Miss Haddad was wearing when you spoke to her?'

'So it wasn't at her digs,' Veronica exclaimed.

An expression of surprised annoyance crossed the inspector's face. 'I should not have underrated your intelligence. No, we found this elsewhere. Either she hid it, meaning to retrieve it later, or the killer put it there.'

Where? Hilary longed to ask, but did not.

'Yes,' she said instead. 'I'm not sure I could swear to it. I haven't seen a lot of burkas at close quarters, so I don't know how much they differ, but the cloth, the colour, the pattern of the smocking, as far I can remember, it's the same.'

'That goes for me too,' Veronica said.

'Well done, ladies.' DI Fellows smiled with relief. 'I'm afraid embroidery wasn't a strong point of the officers who interviewed her.'

DS Petersen wrote something in her notebook and put the package aside, somewhat possessively, Hilary thought.

'Now,' the inspector said more briskly, as though turning to another subject, 'you two ladies were in the High Street at midnight on Wednesday, following Rupert Honeydew and his crew.'

'They woke me up,' Hilary said. 'Right underneath our window. Despite the double glazing.'

'I won't comment on why you chose to get dressed and follow them, but the fact is that you were there. You saw them stop at the police tape.'

'Yes. There was a rather alarmed-looking officer holding the fort. He was joined pretty quickly by a policewoman in one of those fluorescent jackets. I rather thought Honeydew might just push the tape aside and lead the dance right through. Your officers looked as though they were radioing for help.'

'Yes, yes. We've got their statements. And you were fairly close when this happened? You seem to have taken in all the details.'

'Not at first. They'd passed our hotel some time before we'd put our clothes on and got down to the street. But once they'd stopped, yes, we caught them up.'

'So you passed St John's church?'

Something prickled alarm in Hilary's mind. The Church of St John the Baptist, with its labyrinth in the grass and the Holy Thorn tree.

'Yes.'

'And you know what Miss Haddad was wearing when she was found in the abbey two days later.'

'Black leather jacket, white shirt, black leggings, and those pretty sandals,' Veronica confirmed.

'You've already told us that you didn't see Miss Haddad in her burka that Wednesday night, although she'd been wearing it when she followed the same dancers to Glastonbury Tor that afternoon.'

'Not quite the same,' Veronica corrected him. 'There were no men in animal masks the first time.'

'Just so. But you told us you hadn't seen Miss Haddad that night.'

'I see what you're getting at,' Hilary said. 'We were assuming she would be wearing her burka. But she might not have been. You want to know whether we saw a girl in a black leather jacket whom we wouldn't have recognized as Amina.'

'Precisely.'

Hilary studied the glass-topped cane table with the coffee cups. So much had happened that it was hard to cast her mind back that far.

'I remember noticing that there were surprisingly few people out on the street watching like us. I saw a few curtains twitch. But I had the impression the folk of Glastonbury felt this was not a show for tourists and he was better left to get on with whatever it was he was doing. So no, there weren't many bystanders, and I don't remember a girl dressed in black and white. I could be mistaken, though. What I definitely remember is that idiot Joan Townsend letting off flash bulbs in his face to get her pictures for the papers. I'm surprised *she's* not the one who was found dead.'

'You asked just now if we'd passed St John's,' Veronica said thoughtfully. 'There's a pretty big tree at the front of the church-yard. She could have been standing in its shadow and we wouldn't have seen her. And that's where the Glastonbury Thorn is, isn't it? Just behind that tree. Your sergeant said Amina was clutching a sprig of it in her hand when you found her.'

The sergeant's face darkened with annoyance.

'Is that where you found the burka?' Veronica asked. 'In the churchyard?'

Again, that startled look in the inspector's eyes.

'Olive. Exhibit number two.'

The second evidence bag the sergeant was guarding was thinner. Inside was a white plastic carrier bag with a blue-and-black logo. Hilary peered closer and decided it was a stylized picture of a hammer. The lettering below it said *Arnold's*.

'It's from a local hardware shop,' Fellows explained. 'The burka was inside it . . . It's all right, Sergeant. I'm sure Mrs Masters and Mrs Taylor can be discreet . . . We found the burka in it.'

'But Amina . . .?' Veronica frowned.

'Yes, it's not the sort of shop you'd expect a single young woman living in digs to need. So did she put the burka in the bag herself, and hide it until she wanted to go back to her lodging? Or did someone else leave it there, perhaps to put us off the scent? We followed that up. The store owner remembered her. It's not often he gets a customer in a burka here. And I can see what you're thinking, Mrs Masters. Was she buying ingredients or equipment for a bomb? I can set your mind at rest on that score. She came in to buy a pot of petunias.'

Hilary relaxed. For a horrid moment she had wondered whether she had got Amina Haddad totally wrong.

'You haven't seen this bag before? That night, or earlier? Not that that would be conclusive evidence. There must be hundreds of them around. But it's certainly very possible that Amina put the bag there herself. She must have come out of her lodgings wearing her burka. It certainly wasn't among the possessions she left there. It could be that when she neared the High Street, she took it off so that no one would recognize her.'

'Why would she do that?' Veronica asked. 'She didn't mind being seen in it before.'

'I think I know the answer to that.' Hilary's eyes went enquiringly to the inspector. 'Only a few hours earlier, Amina had followed Rupert Honeydew and his acolytes up the Tor. She was writing notes about everything they did. From the look he gave us on Tuesday evening, when he thought we were intruding on him on the Tor, I'd say he didn't take kindly to that. Did he threaten her? Have you asked Mel Fenwick?'

'Have you ever thought of a career in CID? Yes, of course we've questioned Miss Fenwick about Rupert Honeydew and his antics. You're perfectly right. He threatened that if he caught Miss Haddad intruding on their ceremonies again, his men would not only strip off her burka, but a lot more besides.'

'So,' Veronica said slowly. 'She was in the churchyard, without her burka, thinking she was watching him secretly. So what went wrong?'

TWENTY-EIGHT

When the detectives had gone, Hilary and Veronica rejoined Morag in the hotel lounge.

Morag's eyes challenged them. 'Well, did you

manage to tell them anything they didn't know, after all that cloak and dagger stuff?'

The two women exchanged questioning glances. 'Not really,' Hilary said. 'Well, not much.'

'There was a little matter of embroidery,' Veronica smiled.

'Embroidery?'

'But they told *us* a great deal, at least Inspector Fellows did,' Veronica added.

'But you're not going to tell me.'

'I'm sorry, dear. We really can't. I think Inspector Fellows may have overstepped the mark as it is. At least, his sergeant thought so, by the look on her face.'

'I think he was hoping that something he said might prompt our memories,' Hilary said. 'I'm only sorry he didn't have much success.'

As Morag and Veronica drifted into family gossip, Hilary excused herself. 'I don't know about you, but it feels as though it's been a very long day. I think I'll have an early night.'

'I'll try not to disturb you.' Veronica smiled. 'We shan't be long ourselves.'

Alone in bed, Hilary felt the weight of sorrow for Amina that persisted beyond her night-time prayers. She felt angry with herself that, if she could not have prevented the student's death, at least she should have done more to convict Amina's killer. It must be Rupert Honeydew, mustn't it? He was undoubtedly the Chalice Well bomber, and it made no sense for anyone else to have planted the High Street bomb. She could not really believe that, for all his threats, he would have added to that by murdering Amina just because she had been so assiduously taking notes of his esoteric ceremonies. They had, after all, been very public dances in the streets. No, Amina must have stumbled upon something that linked him to the bombs. But what?

For a while longer she wrestled with the problem. Then sleep claimed her, before Veronica came upstairs.

Hilary woke suddenly, with a clarity of conviction that she had remembered something. She looked at the digits of the clock-radio beside her bed. Twelve-thirty.

What was it that had startled her out of sleep?

Then it came back to her. A statement of Veronica's, as she tried to soothe a tearful and angry Morag. *'There's this rather nice Detective Inspector in charge of the Chalice Well bomb and now Amina Haddad's murder.'*

It had just slipped out. After that, both Hilary and Veronica had been particularly careful not to give away the identity of the murder victim. Morag had been too upset to make any reaction at the time. But what if it had come back to her later, just as the memory had jolted Hilary awake?

Would her first instinct, like Joan Townsend's, be to ring a newspaper editor or a TV producer and break the story for a fee, and to give her a feather in her would-be journalist's cap? What had she been doing all the time Veronica and Hilary were talking to the two detectives?

Hilary was astonished at how much she hated the thought of seeing Amina's name plastered over the morning papers. For all her show of righteous indignation, she had not really minded all that much that Veronica had revealed Rupert Honeydew's arrest to her journalist daughter. Honeydew was a dangerous man, and a show-off extrovert as well. What did she care if his name made the headlines he deserved?

But Amina was different. Hilary was startled to realize how protective she felt about the odd, defensive young woman behind the veil. And she could imagine the headlines that would follow news of her death in a town that had just suffered a bombing outrage. Words like ISLAMIST and TERRORIST. They would end up making her sound like the perpetrator, not a victim.

Had Morag remembered the name? Had she acted yet?

Before she knew what she was doing, Hilary had swung her legs out of bed. She hadn't thought to bring a dressing gown for an en-suite room, but she snatched up a thick Arran sweater and pulled it on over her nightdress. Quietly she eased the bedroom door open.

The corridor was softly lit at night, but a stronger, colder ray streamed down its length from a window at the end. It was only two nights after Wednesday's full moon.

Hilary shook away a sudden thought of the men in animal masks and the hatred in Rupert Honeydew's eyes. She was safe in the Bowes Hotel, behind locked doors.

Morag's room was number six, further down the corridor and on the opposite side. Hilary padded towards it.

Halfway there, she found herself waking out of the trance-like compulsion that had driven her to advance on the student's door and demand that she did not break the police silence over the name of yesterday morning's murder victim.

She had been about to make a colossal fool of herself. There was not the slightest evidence that Morag had noticed the name her mother had inadvertently let slip. She had still been sore that the inside information about Rupert Honeydew's arrest was now all over the web and that the two women would tell her nothing further. There had been no indication that she now had another privileged story.

Hilary scolded herself that she really would have done better to stay in bed.

As common sense returned, she settled the sweater closer about her. The night was cold for May.

Something else was niggling at her mind. She shook her head, trying to free the thought. It would not come. She walked slowly beyond the glow of the wall lamps into the whiter moonlight at the end of the corridor.

There was a window there, on the side of the hotel, and a couple of basket chairs. Hilary sank into one of them and looked out. She gave a start. She was gazing straight along the path of the moon's rays to Glastonbury Tor. Even by daylight, it was an arresting sight. That conical hill rising straight up out of the Levels, with the finger of St Michael's tower pointing to the heavens. Now, with the almost-full moon rising behind it, the Tor had the Otherworld feeling that had held its grip on the human imagination for millennia.

She sat very still, gazing at it.

What was it, besides Veronica's careless dropping of Amina's name, that Hilary could almost remember?

She thought through all the questions the detective inspector had asked them. Amina's burka? No, they had been pretty clear about that. Rupert Honeydew's malevolence? But the inspector had known about that since Hilary's urgent phone call after that frightening encounter at the gate of Straightway Farm. There could be no doubt, surely, that the man Amina had called the Guizer was responsible for all three crimes?

What else then? Detective Inspector Fellows had wanted to hear if they had seen Amina on Wednesday night, not wearing her burka, but in the clothes Hilary had glimpsed in the Galilee of the abbey before the pathologist had shrouded her body.

If Amina had been watching from St John's churchyard, would Hilary have seen her? She racked her memory for a glimpse of a white shirt among the shadows. Nothing came. Amina might have been there, but Hilary had no recollection of having seen her, or anyone who could have been her.

And now a new doubt was growing. What would have brought her there, anyway? Hilary and Veronica had been roused by the music and drums under their window. But Amina's lodgings were at the other end of town, on the far side of the Abbey's extensive grounds. How would she have known there was to be a second dance at midnight?

Perhaps something had been said up on the Tor that afternoon before they chased her away. That must be it. Otherwise . . .

The detectives had found evidence to link Amina to the bag from the hardware shop in which her burka had been found. But he had said himself there must be many other such bags. What if Amina had not put it there herself? What if someone else had placed it, to make it seem that this was where Amina had died?

Was there a way from St John's churchyard into the abbey grounds? Hilary tried to remember the street map of Glastonbury. No, of course not. The church was on the wrong side of the High Street.

She sighed, beginning to think of the warm bed she had left.

Something was still niggling at her.

Detective Sergeant Olive Petersen had shown them two evidence bags. One contained the burka, the other, the plastic carrier bag. Hilary frowned harder. Was this what she was trying to remember? Had she seen a bag like that somewhere else? And if she had, would it change anything? Rupert Honeydew was already in custody. Nothing she recalled could alter the fact that he must have planted the High Street bomb that had killed so many people, as well as the unexploded one she had found at the Chalice Well. Whenever and wherever he had done it, surely he must be responsible for Amina's murder too?

She got up, took a last look at the sentinel tower on the moonlit Tor and headed back to bed.

TWENTY-NINE

Morag was already seated at the breakfast table. She brandished the morning newspaper at them. Her face was ablaze with indignation.

'Have you seen this?'

'Of course we haven't, dear,' said Veronica, sitting down. 'We've only just got here.'

Morag thrust it across the table. Hilary leaned sideways to see better.

Two major stories divided the front page. On the left, what was clearly another of Joan's photographs showed the flash-lit faces of Rupert Honeydew and two of his dancers, close up. One was in a donkey's mask, with long ears, the other was a pale-faced girl wearing a rather crooked wreath of flowers. The headline read: SATANIST ARRESTED FOR DEATH BOMB. But it was the right-hand story that made Hilary's throat constrict. MUSLIM WOMAN FOUND DEAD IN GLASTONBURY ABBEY. The picture this time was not of Amina in her burka, nor of her body lying in the ruins. It was a close-up of a hand clutching what Hilary knew could only be a sprig of Glastonbury Thorn.

The initial shock was overtaken by a sense of mild relief. The story was not as lurid as it could have been. 'MUSLIM' was less incendiary than 'ISLAMIST'. Amina was portrayed as a mysterious victim, rather than as a suspected terrorist. She must be grateful for small mercies. But how was it possible that someone had photographed her hand holding the Thorn?

'You knew this, didn't you?' Morag demanded, pointing to this second story. 'You knew her identity and you wouldn't tell me.'

Another wave of relief. Clearly, Morag had not remembered

that careless slip Veronica had made. It had not been she who had sold Amina's story to the press.

'I don't know who did this,' she said. 'As far as I know, we were the only people besides the police who knew who the body in the abbey was.'

'There's her landlady and her husband,' Veronica said reflectively. 'They knew Amina was missing. The police went to visit them, after we did. When they heard about the body, they must have guessed.'

'True enough. But it wasn't them who took this photograph.'

The three of them stared at the picture. Just a hand, with a glimpse of white cuff, and the sprig of fabled Thorn. It was more compelling than a full-length picture of the body would have been.

'Could it have been Joan?' Veronica wondered. 'There was that curious question she asked us: *"Is it true that the body they found in the abbey is that Muslim girl?"* How did she know that?'

Hilary scanned the article and turned to an inside page for more. 'There's somebody else's byline. No mention of Joan's name as the informant. And she was always desperate to get her name in the nationals. Besides . . . look at that!' She thumped her hand down on the article alongside it, making the cups jump. 'Her name's there clear enough on the other photo. And that ridiculous headline. Whatever else Rupert Honeydew may be, he's not a Satanist.'

'Are you sure?'

'I thought he was just a clown at first. Or one of those New Age types, on about his Goddess and the healing powers of the water. But unless he's a very good actor, I think he really did believe all that. Mel's story about why he planted the bomb at the Chalice Well made a kind of sense.'

'He scared me, though. Those eyes.'

'Yes. My head tells me he has to be the High Street bomber. I mean, are you going to have two bomb-makers in the town in one week? But I still feel there's something not quite right about it. An unexploded bomb is one thing, but this one went off.'

The horror of that afternoon seared itself on her imagination.

'Perhaps it wasn't meant to, like the first one,' Morag suggested.

'It must be a pretty scary thing, putting a bomb together. Especially if you've never done anything like that before. I know you can find all sorts of instructions on the internet, but actually doing it is something else. It could so easily go wrong. Either the bomb doesn't go off. Or it goes off when you didn't mean it to.'

'Hmm.'

'Do you really think he didn't do it?' Veronica asked Hilary.

'Let's say there's room for doubt. You notice our detective inspector was careful to warn us they might not be able to hold Rupert Honeydew indefinitely, if they couldn't link him to the High Street bomb.'

'Aren't there anti-terrorist laws to deal with that situation?' Morag asked.

'Yes, but if Hilary's hunch is right,' Veronica said slowly, 'then that means that, however unlikely it sounds, there must be a second bomber. And this one's not locked up.'

The three of them sat taking in that thought.

'Well, it's out of our hands,' Veronica said finally. 'We've done all we can to help.'

'And you're getting out of this place today,' Morag said firmly. 'That's definite.'

'Yes, dear,' Veronica replied.

Hilary thought the meekness in her voice was not entirely genuine.

Hilary wheeled her case across the hotel car park. Veronica was already there, bidding farewell to Morag.

'You really must stop worrying about us,' Hilary heard her saying. 'We're perfectly capable of looking after ourselves.'

'Mum, there's at least one killer in this town. And you two have got a lot closer to him than you had any right to be. I shudder to think what could have happened.'

'But it didn't, did it? Rupert Honeydew is safely behind bars, and we did have a modest part to play in that. You ought to be congratulating us.'

'All I want is to see you pack those bags in your car and drive out of here.'

'There's nothing to stop us going today. We've told Inspector Fellows all we know. Here's Hilary now.'

Hilary heaved her own suitcase into the boot, alongside Veronica's. Morag was juggling her car keys from one hand to the other anxiously.

'You don't need to wait for us, dear,' Veronica said. 'You've got a long drive back to London.'

'I just want to make sure you go.'

'No problem,' Hilary said, getting into the driver's seat. 'We're off.'

She nosed the car out of the gate into the morning traffic. In the rear-view mirror she saw Morag follow them for a while, and then head off towards the motorway. She relaxed.

She swung the car into Magdalene Street and turned into the abbey car park.

'Hilary!' Veronica exclaimed. 'I thought we were supposed to be leaving.'

'We are. There are just a few loose ends I want to tie up first.'

They paid their money at the ticket desk. Hilary repressed a shudder, remembering how the last time they had come through here it was to view Amina's body.

Today the scene was totally different. The abbey grounds swarmed with Saturday crowds. A tall thin man in Anglo-Saxon costume, with an even taller hat, was leading a party of sightseers across the grass, talking enthusiastically about its history.

'We can trace Christianity at Glastonbury back to Roman times. Here, where you see this magnificent Lady Chapel, there was once a little church of wattle and daub. Then along came the Saxons in the seventh century. But by the time they got here, they had already become Christians. King Ine of Wessex built the first stone church here, at what is now the west end of the nave.' He had moved his group, without comment, past the flight of steps which led up from the Galilee where Amina's body had been found into the great monastic church. He flung his arm around him. 'St Dunstan, three hundred years later, enlarged it and added a tower. By the time of the Norman Conquest, Glastonbury was the richest abbey in England.'

Two thousand years, Hilary thought. All those centuries of reverence and pilgrimage. Conquest and yet continuity. Even Henry VIII's dissolution of the monasteries had not stopped people coming here to pray.

She pictured the sprig clutched in Amina's hand. What could it have meant to her?

But the Benedictine ruins, evocative though they were, were not what she had come to see.

Beyond the Abbot's Kitchen, the traffic was pouring along Magdalene Street.

Hilary went to peer over the hedge that rose above the railings. It was higher above the pavement than she expected.

'I suppose you *could* get a body over this at night,' she said. 'But it would be quite an effort to heave it up.'

Veronica walked across and examined the drop. 'That's quite a way to lift a corpse. You'd have to be pretty strong.'

'Or tall,' Hilary suggested. 'Still, it's shoulder height, even for Rupert Honeydew. And it would be a risk, even at the dead of night. There are houses opposite. Let's see what other possibilities there are.'

They skirted the abbey grounds along its wide perimeter. Hilary had been right about houses backing on to it. They turned the southern corner and went out past the fish ponds to where the Tor loomed surprisingly close. As they turned north again, Hilary recognized the grey stone wall that ran along the road out to the Tor. Long grass and wild flowers grew thickly between the trees. The drop to the road here would be considerable.

'He could hardly have dragged the body through the streets from the churchyard. He'd have had to use a car.'

At last they reached what Hilary had been looking for. The boundary swung sharply away from the road. A high wire fence angled outwards at the top, with strands of barbed wire. Through it, they glimpsed gardens and a fine old house.

'This must be it. Abbey House. The retreat house Sister Mary Magdalene told us about.' Hilary stepped closer through the undergrowth to survey it through the wire. 'She'd just come out of the front entrance when we were walking back from Amina's lodgings.'

'So somewhere along here there has to be a gate to the abbey grounds,' Veronica said. 'Remember, she said the retreat guests had access.'

They turned another corner. Suddenly the ruined abbey chancel was very close.

The wire surrounding Abbey House was fronted by a high yew hedge. At the far end, something gleamed pale against the dark foliage.

'And here it is!'

The gate was made of close-set planks of wood. The arched top rose higher than the yews. It looked quite new.

Hilary bent to examine the lock. 'See here. It looks as though they've cut a hole so that you can access it from either side.'

She stood back and studied it.

'I suppose it's possible,' she said after a while. 'You could drive up to the Abbey House and shift the body through the gardens to the abbey ruins from there. Less chance of being seen under street lights.'

'But how did he get it over? Unless he had a key.'

'Hmm. There must be things in the garden. Benches. Logs. He could have stood on something and heaved her over. Then put his foot in this hole in the gate and climbed over himself.'

Veronica looked round at the arched windows of the ruined chancel. At the far end of the nave stood the roofless walls of the Galilee.

'Wouldn't forensics have spotted if someone had dragged her across the grass from here?'

Hilary thought back to that slight figure under the plastic sheet.

'She wasn't very big. The killer could have carried her over his shoulder.'

'Unless he met her there in the Galilee, and killed her where she was found.'

'Twenty-four hours after she left her lodgings?'

'No, I suppose not. She has to have died sooner, hasn't she?'

'The police will know the time of death by now.'

They stood for while, baffled. Then Hilary said, 'Wait a moment.'

She retraced her steps around the wire fence. For the most part, the lawns around the ruins were kept meticulously mown, but here, close to the perimeter, the wild flowers had been allowed to grow tall under a scattering of trees. Hilary peered from side to side through this undergrowth. Suddenly she halted.

'Could that be . . .?'

She pointed to a small space where the hedge parsley had

been flattened, as though an animal had rolled in it, or trampled it down to make a bed. But Hilary could think of no animals that large in the middle of Glastonbury.

'Be what?' Veronica asked.

'Where the body lay on Thursday. There's no reason for anyone to come poking about here under these trees.'

'And it's just round the corner from that gate to the retreat house.'

Hilary stiffened. 'It keeps coming back to Abbey House.'

They both stared through the wire at the garden bright with rhododendrons, and the distant view of people sitting in contemplation on the outdoor seats.

'It would make it a whole lot simpler if someone had a key to that gate,' Hilary said.

'No!' cried Veronica, her eyes widening. 'Not Sister Mary Magdalene! Why ever would she?'

'Why, for that matter, would anyone want to kill Amina? Rupert Honeydew would have to be very twisted indeed to murder her for making notes about his folk dances.'

'Who else might have the key to that gate? Would Sonia Marsden? We know the retreat house people have access from the other side. Would someone on the abbey staff also have had a key?'

'Whoever it was, I have a dark feeling that the only motive to kill Amina must have been that she knew who planted Tuesday's bomb.'

Veronica stared down at the flattened flowers for a long while.

'Do you think the police search got this far? It's quite a distance from the Galilee where she was found. And Sonia Marsden's colleague seemed anxious to open up the abbey as soon as they could.'

'Sonia herself was telling him they must take as long as they needed to.'

Hilary got out her phone and looked at it reflectively. 'Should I call Inspector Fellows and tell him about this?'

'He'll think you're trying to teach him his job. The police have probably examined all the exits. They must have found this gate.'

'But we've come back around the corner from the gate. If they didn't search the whole perimeter, they might not have looked this far. It's not as if you could scale the fence here.' She looked up at the wire.

She pressed the key to switch on her mobile. The little screen stayed blank.

'Bother! I didn't put the wretched thing on charge.'

'Use mine.' Veronica fished in her shoulder bag. 'No, sorry. I seem to have left mine in the car.'

'Never mind,' Hilary said. 'It was probably teaching your grandmother to suck eggs. I think we've finished our usefulness here. But I'm glad I've got a clearer picture now of what happened, even if I'm only guessing why. And I've still no idea who.'

They started to walk back across the grass to the car park.

'You know,' Hilary said, 'something was bugging me in the night. Something the inspector asked us. That carrier bag from the hardware shop. Had we seen one like it?'

'The one they found her burka in? But we hadn't.'

'I'm not entirely sure of that now. Something at the back of my mind tells me that I have.'

THIRTY

The crowds of sightseers were becoming thicker again as they neared the heart of the abbey. It looked like an ordinary Saturday morning in early summer. Picturesque ruins, guides in period costume, romantic legends about King Arthur's final resting place and stories about the Grail and the tree that had once provided the crown of thorns. It seemed almost impossible to believe that twenty-four hours earlier the body of a young woman had lain just there, in the roofless Galilee, between the Lady Chapel and the abbey church's nave. Hilary felt the wave of grief return.

'Did Rupert Honeydew kill her?' she said aloud. 'Had she found out more than she should about the High Street bomb?'

'I thought you decided over breakfast that he wasn't responsible for both bombs. That there must have been somebody else.'

'Hmm. All I was saying was that there are pieces of the puzzle which don't match up.'

As they neared the exit they heard raised voices. A man was shouting something as yet incomprehensible.

'Oh, no,' Hilary said. 'Not him again!'

'Who?'

'George Marsden.'

They were now near enough to the gatehouse to hear the tirade going on inside.

'It comes to something when you find a heathen body in a Christian church! What was she doing there, I'd like to know?'

'George, calm down. The woman is dead, God rest her soul. We should be praying for her.' Sonia Marsden was doing her best to quiet him.

'Don't you "*Calm down*" me!' he roared. 'I'm a God-fearing Englishman, and this is one of the most sacred places in the whole country. It's a wonder they even let Muslims inside, let alone have one dying here. It's not decent. They should get back where they come from and their own mumbo-jumbo temples.'

'George!' Sonia Marsden's voice was becoming steely. 'Go home.'

Veronica and Hilary tried to edge past. George Marsden saw them and wheeled round.

'You two again! My wife tells me you were inside the abbey yesterday, when she wasn't allowed past the entrance. And now you're back again. First that bomb at the Chalice Well, then you were in the High Street when the big one went off, and now you're here, right where a murder happens. How come it's not you who are the ones under arrest?'

Hilary was uncomfortably aware of the queue at the ticket desk stopping, of faces turning towards them in shocked curiosity. She felt herself going red and was all the more exasperated because of it.

'If you think we had anything to do with it, you'll believe anything.'

She forged past the Marsdens and the staring crowd of sightseers.

The breeze blew cool on her face in the courtyard outside.

She had almost forgotten why they had come back to the abbey this morning and what they had found.

Veronica picked up her mobile from the front shelf of the car. 'Do you still want to phone the inspector?'

Hilary hesitated. 'Leave it for the moment. I feel I'm on the verge of remembering something. Something really important. When I know what it is, I'll certainly be phoning him. Meanwhile, it's time we set our children's minds at rest and headed out of here. Do you want to drive?'

'So that you can concentrate on getting those little grey cells to work?'

'Something like that.'

Veronica drove the car out of town. Between the residential streets and the pastures of the Levels, they passed a small industrial estate. Hilary let her eye run idly over the store fronts. She leaned forward suddenly.

'Pull over!'

'Where?'

'Here. That DIY store.'

Veronica steered into the large car park and came to a stop.

'Why? Are you planning on a bit of interior decorating before David gets back?'

Hilary pointed to the name in large blue letters over the entrance.

'Ring any bells?'

'Arnold's?' Veronica shook her head. 'You've lost me.'

'That plastic carrier bag. The one Fellows and Petersen showed us. The one Amina's burka was found in. It came from here. Don't you remember? A logo of a hammer and the name Arnold's.'

'I remember the logo. I'd forgotten about the name. But I thought they'd decided there was nothing suspicious about it. I could see how the cogs must have been going round in their minds. Hardware shop. Muslim. Homemade bomb. But when they came here they found they'd made fools of themselves. She was buying flowers.'

'If that was the whole story, why did they show us that bag and ask if it jogged any memories?'

Veronica drew her teeth over her lower lip as she thought about this. 'Ah!' she said, as the realization dawned. 'Amina may have been buying flowers, but what if she wasn't the one who left that burka in the churchyard? What if somebody else had been shopping here at the same time? And that person's shopping had . . .?' Her eyes grew wide.

'Let's get out and have a look around. I'm becoming more convinced by the minute that this bag may be a whole lot more important than it looked. I *know* I've seen another one like it. I just can't remember where.'

'Even if you did,' Veronica said doubtfully, 'there can't be many places in Glastonbury like this. There must be a score of shops where you can buy joss sticks, but you'd be hard pushed to find a paint roller. Lots of local people must come here.'

'Humour me.'

Outside the store, as well as the usual stack of shopping carts, was an array of plants at bargain prices. Hilary stooped to look down at a tray of purple and white petunias. Was it something like this Amina had bought to soften the heart of her landlady? Something wrenched inside her at the thought of this girl who would never watch them bloom.

She straightened her shoulders and walked inside.

The place was vast, but there were very few people in it. A handful of morning shoppers. A woman at the till. In the further reaches, a couple of men in blue aprons among the high-stacked shelves.

Hilary wandered in the direction of the electrical department. She studied the racks with a rather hopeless air. What did she know about the equipment required to make a bomb? Next to nothing. It was all very well to say that you could find the instructions nowadays on the internet, but the thought of actually doing that made her blood run cold. It was not just the horror of what the bomb was meant to achieve, it was almost inconceivable to imagine herself assembling it. Had the bomber worked alone? Had their hands trembled as they connected wires, tightened screws, set the timer? Did they really understand that what they were constructing in a small back room would bring down a house in the High Street, kill seven people, and injure many more?

She tried to reconcile this calculating manufacture with Rupert Honeydew, prancing through the streets in his top hat and enthusing to anyone he could buttonhole about the healing powers of his Goddess. Or George Marsden, with all his brag and bluster about being a Christian Englishman. Did he even know how to use the internet? His wife Sonia, though . . . No, they had seen another side of her. She sighed. Let the police work that one out. They had already questioned the Marsdens, but let them go.

Into her mind came a more unexpected picture. Of Sister Mary Magdalene overtaking them in the shadows outside the abbey walls. Of the gate to the abbey grounds from the retreat house. Of the flattened hedge parsley under the fence. She shook her head vigorously. She was becoming ridiculous.

She walked up to the woman at the checkout. The other tills seemed to be unstaffed.

'Excuse me. Where you here when the police came asking questions about a customer in a burka? One of those Muslim gowns that cover a woman from top to toe.'

'You'll need to ask Mr Arnold about that.' The woman nodded her head towards the gardening section of the shop. 'That's him in the blue overall.'

Hilary marched towards him, feeling her confidence draining away with every step. What did she hope to achieve that Inspector Fellows and his sergeant hadn't already done?

Veronica trailed behind her.

The large man with greying sandy hair turned at their approach. He wore a name badge on his blue apron which said simply JOHN.

'Are you Mr Arnold? The owner?'

'That's me. How can I help you?'

Hilary explained about the police search. 'I know you remembered the woman in a burka. And that she bought a pot of flowers.'

'That's right. Well, you could have knocked me down with a feather duster. We get all sorts in Glastonbury, but you don't expect to see one of those. We're not like Birmingham or Wolverhampton, or one of those places up north. Of course I remembered her. She asked me what she'd need to grow a sprig of Glastonbury Thorn.'

'The inspector didn't tell us that.'

'Of course, I told her it wasn't as simple as that. You have to graft a slip of it on to ordinary hawthorn stock. In the end, she said she'd just take a pot of flowers. A farewell present for her landlady, she said.'

A farewell present. The words echoed in Hilary's mind. For a chilling moment, she thought about suicide videos. Amina? Surely not? She hadn't blown herself up. Hilary pushed the thought away vigorously. She pulled herself back to the question which was bugging her.

'But I expect they asked about other things too. Other customers who might have bought the sort of things you could use to make a bomb?'

'Who are you, then? Are you more police?'

'No, nothing like that. But we knew Amina . . . the woman in the burka. And we were caught up in the High Street bombing. I helped a man with his leg nearly blown off. I'd like to know who did it.'

'So would we all. I'd string them up from the nearest lamp post if I had the chance.'

'So did you remember anyone else? Someone who might have bought that sort of thing?'

John Arnold shook his head. 'I'm either in the back office or helping out here in the gardening section. Growing things is what I like best. If I had my time over, I'd be a nurseryman. Now I just sell people plants other people have grown. Still, I like to talk to the customers, make sure they get what they really want and they know how to look after them. Ellie was on the till.' He nodded to the woman at the checkout. 'But you can see for yourself, we've gone over to do-it-yourself tills for two of the checkouts. Customers just scan what they've bought and the machine tells them how to pay.'

Hilary repressed a shudder. 'Wretched things. They're going over to those in supermarkets and the banks are even worse. You can hardly speak to a human being nowadays.'

'It saves on the wages bill. Keeps us solvent.'

'So no one saw anything that could have been suspicious being bought?'

'Sorry, no. They asked to check our till receipts, of course. They did get excited at one point, but if the customer went through the self-service till and paid in cash, that wouldn't get them any further, would it?'

'No,' Hilary sighed. 'I suppose not. Well, thank you for your time.'

'No luck?' Veronica asked as Hilary joined her.

'Our bomber could have bought the whole caboodle here, and it appears nobody could trace them. Except . . .' She walked through one of the self-service checkouts and picked up a plastic bag, 'through one of these. And even then, it would be a long shot. Not the sort of evidence that would stand up in court.'

They walked back to Hilary's car. Veronica stood beside the driver's door.

'So you still don't want to phone the inspector?'

'Don't hurry me. It will come back. I know it will.'

She stood, feeling the smooth plastic of the bag in her hand. She looked down at the logo. The stylized shapes, which seemed just an abstract design if you stared straight at them, but which resolved themselves into a hammer as you started to look away.

Where else had she seen that design?

THIRTY-ONE

Hilary was just about to get into the car, still puzzled over the bag, when her thoughts were interrupted by Veronica. 'Would you mind hanging on a moment? There's one more call I need to make.'

Through the open door, fragments of conversation drifted to Hilary.

'Yes, it's me, Veronica . . . I just wanted to say how pleased you must be with today's front page.'

Hilary sat up straight, the plastic carrier bag forgotten. Joan Townsend? Veronica was actually ringing Joan to congratulate her?

'They've given you credit for another photograph, if not for the whole article. That's good, isn't it? You must be so glad you managed to rescue the memory card after Rupert Honeydew smashed your camera.'

Hilary had a memory of Joan grovelling in the darkened roadway, under the shadows of the Guizer and his dancers.

Veronica was pressing on. 'But the second article. The one about the Muslim girl whose body was found in the abbey. That was you too, wasn't it? I know it didn't have your name on it, either the text or the photo. But I think you knew, didn't you? Did you take that photo? The hand holding the Thorn? It wasn't the real thing, was it?'

There was a long silence while Veronica listened. Then: 'Well, actually, we're on our way out of Glastonbury. We're going home. We're outside Arnold's DIY shop at the moment . . . Yes, well, I suppose I could.' She looked at her watch. 'Shall we say ten forty-five? . . . Yes, I think I can find it.'

She snapped the phone shut and climbed in beside Hilary.

'That was Joan.'

'So I gathered.'

'Don't look so disapproving. I know she hasn't behaved entirely admirably, but it was after meeting Morag. You saw how she reacted, even though she'd really driven down here because she was concerned about me getting involved. She still couldn't resist the lure of a good story. I tried to imagine her in Joan's place. Her big chance. First, an unexploded bomb. Then a real one. And finally a murder. And in between, all the shenanigans Rupert Honeydew was getting up to. It must have seemed like manna from heaven.'

'Not to the people who got killed or injured.'

'Oh, Hilary! You know I didn't mean that! But it's the flip side of "No news is good news". When something happens to hit the headlines, it's very likely to be tragedy for some people. A journalist can't help that. They don't make the news, but they have to report it.'

'If you say so.'

'But, as it happens, there was a bit of ferreting out of my own I wanted to do. That story about Amina. The photo of her hand clutching the Thorn. How did Joan get that? There was nothing in the paper to identify the source, but I had a feeling it must have been her.'

'She certainly does have the journalist's instinct for turning up wherever there's trouble. Did she admit it?'

'Not exactly. It may not be admirable, but I got the impression she faked that.'

'I should have guessed.'

'But she did say there was more she could tell me. Something she wanted to show me.'

'If it's anything to do with Amina's murder, she should go straight to the police.'

'Yes, I know. But you have to see it from her point of view. If she's on the brink of another really big story – who killed the mystery Muslim girl in the abbey – she might not want to risk being cut out of it, just as she's about to put the final piece in place.'

'Is that what she said?'

Veronica hesitated. 'Well, not in so many words. But I could tell she was excited. And reading between the lines . . . Anyway, I've said I'll meet her in twenty minutes.'

'Have you, indeed? Where?'

'Apparently there's a sluice gate on one of the drainage channels on the Levels. I think I've got the directions right. I need to take the footpath along the bank. She'll meet me there.'

'Right. It sounds fishy to me, but if there's a chance of finding Amina's killer, it's worth a try.'

She settled herself into the passenger seat and snapped on her seatbelt.

'I'm sorry. I know this sounds odd, but she wants me to come on my own.'

'Why, for heaven's sake?'

Veronica sounded awkward. 'Hilary, dear, I know you think you're the soul of discretion, but Joan can hardly have helped pick up what you think about her.'

'And you're the maternal one, with the journalist daughter.'

'Something like that. At least, I suppose so. Would you mind if I take the car?'

'And leave me at a DIY store for who knows how long? Can't I at least come with you to the start of this footpath and sit in the car?'

Veronica looked unhappy. 'We-ell, I don't suppose it could do any harm.'

A spasm of annoyance came over Hilary. 'All right, all right!

I can tell when I'm not wanted. Run off and exchange secrets with your pathetic protégé.' She struggled to undo the seatbelt. 'Take the wretched car. There's a van over there selling what is probably appalling coffee. Don't mind me.'

She started to march across the car park. Veronica leaned out of the car and called after her. 'No, really, Hilary. I'm sure it will be fine. If you don't mind waiting in the car at the roadside . . .'

Hilary stalked on, fuming. After a little while, she heard the car turn round and watched Veronica drive out on to the road across the pastures of the Levels.

She had almost reached the van selling hot dogs, burgers and drinks when she became aware that she was still clutching something in her hand. She looked down. It was the blue-and-white Arnold's carrier bag.

For a moment she stared at it blankly. Then, unbidden, the picture she had been seeking for so long leaped into her mind.

Joan Townsend, down on her hands and knees among the feet of the midnight dancers. Frantically scrabbling for the fragments of her smashed camera beyond the police tape, as if there was any hope of fitting it together again. Oblivious to the fact that the only thing that mattered was the memory card. She had been clumsily shovelling all the broken pieces into a bag. A white bag, with a blue-and-black logo. A bag identical to the one Hilary held in her hand.

She drew a sharp audible gasp.

Joan Townsend had been shopping in Arnold's hardware store, probably not long ago.

She threw a searching glance back at the shop front, with its stack of shopping carts and its rack of bargain pot plants. Joan Townsend and Amina, both here. Was it possible the two young women had been shopping at the same time? Cold reason was creeping up on her. If Joan had reason to believe that Amina had witnessed what she was buying, and was beginning to put two and two together . . .

The truth came back to hit her. Was it Joan who had told Amina about Rupert Honeydew's midnight dance? Had she lured her out from her lodgings, where she would never otherwise have heard the pipes and drums? What had happened in the churchyard by the Holy Thorn? Or had Amina been killed somewhere else entirely? That street on the far side of the Abbey that went past the retreat house was close to Amina's lodgings. Joan would only have had to drag her victim through the gateway, away from the street lights, and carry her through the gardens of Abbey House. She could have bundled her over that wooden gate and carried her into the undergrowth. For all her plumpness, Joan was sturdily built, and Amina only a light weight. Then she could have left the burka in the churchyard in a bag like this, to lead the police investigation away from Abbey House. While she was there, she could have plucked a sprig of the Thorn as a dramatic image to leave in Amina's dead hand. But she had not been able to resist the temptation to photograph that image. It was chilling to think that photograph might not have been a fake.

Now that she came to think of it, Hilary and Veronica had been watching the midnight dancers for quite some time before Joan burst on the scene with her flash photography.

All these thoughts raced through Hilary's mind. Then the essential truth struck her with the force of a car slamming into a wall.

Veronica had gone off in Hilary's car to meet Joan. By a sluice gate on one of the drainage canals that cut a watery grid across the Somerset Levels. Had Veronica let slip something that made Joan believe that she held the secret to who had killed Amina Haddad?

And who had planted the High Street bomb.

She felt the blood leave her face. Then she pulled herself up short. *Joan Townsend?* The frustrated reporter in the baggy brown cardigan? Was it possible that she could put a bomb together?

But words she had forgotten came back to her. *'I've got a first-class degree.'*

Had Hilary seriously underestimated her? Joan Townsend had made the headlines after all. With a succession of stories, day after day. Part of a carefully planned sequence, to keep the Glastonbury story running.

And Hilary had let Veronica go to meet Joan alone.

THIRTY-TWO

Hilary dashed towards the car. The empty parking space baffled her. She was sure they had left the car just here. It was seconds before her agitated brain registered the fact that Veronica had driven off in it. Hilary had no way of following her.

With shaking hands she rummaged in her bag for her phone. At last the wretched thing might actually prove useful. But the screen remained obstinately blank. Her heart sank further as she remembered that she had let the battery run down.

There was nothing else for it. It was years since she had broken into a run, but she set off racing now towards the open store.

She tore past the checkout, colliding with a man in a paint-stained jumper, who dropped the tin he was carrying. Heads turned, voices shouted, but she disregarded them.

Mercifully, John Arnold in his blue overall was still chatting to a customer in the gardening section. Hilary charged up to him, panting.

'You know you wanted to lynch the person who let off the High Street bomb? Well, I know who it is. And unless we get there fast, I'm very much afraid my friend is going to meet a similarly ghastly end.'

'Excuse me!' John Arnold tore his attention from his customer. His eyes glittered. 'Are you sure about this? Have you told the police?'

'My phone's dead.'

Arnold pulled out his own. He dialled 999, said, 'Police!' and handed it to her.

I must try not to gabble, Hilary thought. She gave her name and location. 'Arnold's DIY store, the industrial estate on the southern edge of Glastonbury. My friend Veronica Taylor has gone to meet a journalist called Joan Townsend at a sluice gate somewhere on the Levels. I have reason to believe this Joan Townsend is the High Street bomber . . . Don't ask how I know.

Just get there. There have been more than enough deaths already. And tell Detective Inspector Fellows . . . No, I *don't* know where this sluice gate is. But she set off driving due south. Apparently it's no more than twenty minutes from here, and that includes walking along a footpath.'

She gave the colour, make and registration number of the car Veronica was driving. Seconds were passing.

At last she handed the phone back. Her cheeks felt flushed. There was something suspiciously like a tear in her eye.

'She said to keep the phone on.'

'Have you got a car?' John Arnold asked.

'Veronica took it. That's what the police are looking for.'

'We'll take mine.'

He strode towards the entrance, flinging off his apron as he went. Hilary hurried after him.

Arnold made for a Land Rover, parked around the corner of the building.

'Get in,' he ordered Hilary.

It was a steep climb up for her short legs, but she made it.

'Now, which way did you say she was headed?'

'She set off straight along this road out of town. I didn't stand and watch her.'

'There are not so many side roads in that direction. If she's going to take a footpath, chances are she'll have parked by the roadside beside one of the rhynes.'

Rhynes. Hilary translated the word into the many canal-like channels that criss-crossed the Levels. She prayed he was right.

They sped down the long straight road. There was no need for winding turns here on this flat farmland, unlike the twisting lanes of Hilary's native Devon. She could see for what seemed like miles ahead. Cars passed, coming towards them. There was no sign of anything parked by the road. Up over the hump where the road crossed the dead straight course of the River Brue.

Over a mile out from Glastonbury, John Arnold slowed the Land Rover to a halt.

'If your friend was going to drive to near the rendezvous and then walk along the footpath to the sluice gate in twenty minutes, we ought to have seen the car by now.'

It was what Hilary had feared.

'Does that mean we have to go back? Take a side road?'

Before he could answer, they were overtaken by a pair of police cars racing past, sirens blaring.

'Looks like they haven't yet reached the same conclusion. Hang on, I'm turning round.'

He swung the car to face back towards Glastonbury. Hilary peered on either side, looking for a possible road, a track, even, where Veronica might have left the main road. She remembered the unpaved cart track to Straightway Farm. If only she had persuaded Veronica to tell her Joan's exact instructions.

White lines, almost obscured by mud, marked the place where a narrow minor road came in to join their own. Arnold stopped the car.

'Hang on a minute.'

Quite deftly for a rather large man, he hauled himself up on to the Land Rover's roof. Hilary got out and watched him. He shaded his eyes as he peered across the flat landscape of meadows and water channels, broken by the occasional flowering hawthorn tree.

Presently he swung himself down to join her. 'There's something catching the light about half a mile along this lane. Might be her car, might be not. Too far away to be sure of the colour. Something light.'

'Mine is silver.'

'You'd better get back to your policeman friend.'

Hilary took the phone he offered and dialled Inspector Fellows' number. The call was picked up with an alacrity which told her the DI was urgently following the case.

'DI Fellows.'

'Hilary Masters. I'm out on the Levels with John Arnold, from Arnold's store. You know the bag you showed me?'

'Yes.'

'I remembered where I'd seen one of them before. Joan Townsend. The reporter behind those sensational stories we've been getting in the papers. Satanists. Islamic woman.'

'Yes, I know the one.'

'I think she may have been to Arnold's to buy some of the things she needed for the bomb.'

'What!'

'Yes. I assume your nine-nine-nine people have passed on my message. Veronica's gone to meet her. Somewhere out here on the Levels. John thinks he can see something which could be my car. We're . . .'

She looked appealingly at John Arnold for help. He took the phone from her.

'Junction of the road that goes due south of Glastonbury. About half a mile past the River Brue. There's something parked on the cross road to our left. Could be another half-mile away.'

He listened for a while longer. 'Right, sir.' He put the phone back in his pocket and turned to her with a grin that did not reach his eyes.

'What you'd expect the police to say. Stay where we are. Wait for the uniforms to arrive. On no account to go any further ourselves.'

'But in the meantime . . .'

'My thinking entirely. I'm going in. You stay here to flag them down.'

'Not likely!'

Hilary swung herself back into the passenger seat and snapped the seat belt on. Her stare challenged him to argue.

'Just drive!'

The glint of metal in the distance resolved itself more certainly into a silver car. The nearer they drove, the more sure Hilary became that it was her Vauxhall. Whatever had she been thinking, to let Veronica drive it here on her own?

She was hoping, praying even, that there would be a figure inside it, that Veronica would be here unhurt.

They had almost reached it before she allowed her hopes to be finally dashed. The parked car was abandoned. No one stood beside it. There was no one in the driver's or passenger seat.

'Hey up,' said John Arnold, 'there's only one car here. So how did that other character get here?'

Hilary looked back along the narrow road and north to the distant roofs of Glastonbury. 'You could walk it, at a pinch. More likely she used a bike.'

Ahead of them, a wide drainage channel passed beneath the road. It led on across the fields in either direction, ruler straight. Tall reeds fringed its banks. A mud-slicked footpath ran alongside it.

'Which way?' John asked.

Hilary felt the shock inside her. She had no idea. She struggled to remember what Veronica had said. But there had been nothing as specific as 'left' or 'right'.

John saw her blank expression. He climbed down and went to examine the path on either side of the road.

'Left,' he announced. 'There's a pretty fresh set of footprints and, yes, you were right, bicycle tyres.'

It was an enormous relief that they did not have to set out in one direction or the other merely praying they had made the right choice.

'Phone, please.' She relayed the information to DI Fellows and cut the call short before he could berate her any further for failing to wait for the police.

When she turned to hand the mobile back to John, he was delving into the back of the Land Rover. When he straightened up, he had a large wrench in his hand.

Panic shot through Hilary. She had a vivid, shocking memory of him saying, '*I'd string them up from the nearest lamp post.*'

'John!'

Suddenly she realized on how flimsy a basis she had made her accusation. The coincidence of two plastic bags bearing the Arnold's logo. The mere speculation that Amina might have seen Joan buying materials that could have been used in bomb-making. Everything else: the attack in the shadowed street past the retreat house, the bundling of the body over the gate, hiding it for a day, so that she could follow one set of dramatic headlines with another, then the placing of Amina's body where it would be found in the Galilee on Friday morning, and inserting that telling image of the Glastonbury Thorn in her hand . . . All of it had been Hilary's own invention, following on that one speculation of the two young women visiting Arnold's store at the same time. She had no proof for any of it.

And here was John Arnold, grim-faced, with a monkey wrench in his hand and murder in his eyes.

Seven people dead in the High Street, and many more in hospital.

Too late she wished, – suddenly, fiercely – that she had heeded Inspector Fellows' advice.

'Look.' She shot out a hand and grabbed his wrist. 'I don't want you to get this wrong. I only *think* Joan Townsend is the High Street bomber. And that she killed the girl they found in the abbey to keep her quiet. I can't prove it.'

'What about your friend, then? You came haring into the shop because you were scared silly she'd gone to meet a murderer and would likely meet the same fate. Are you telling me now that was all made up?'

'No!' She looked frantically down the path where Veronica's footprints led. John was right. She *had* been terrified of what that assignment meant. She still was. 'Just . . . don't do anything hasty. At least give her a fair trial.'

'Like she gave those people blown up in the High Street? Kids, even?'

If it was her. If I haven't stood this whole thing on its head, Hilary thought.

'You stay here, if you can't make your mind up. I'm going after her, before she kills anyone else.'

He set off at a run. Hilary had no choice but to follow him.

John Arnold was a big man, younger and longer-legged than she was. Soon Hilary was falling behind. She stopped to catch her breath. There was a stitch in her side.

What if she was panicking about nothing? Joan must have guessed that Veronica would tell Hilary where she was going, and whom she was going to meet. If Veronica failed to return – or worse – Hilary would be sure to tell the police. Joan would be giving herself away.

Unless . . . What if this was a carefully planned ruse to get each of the two women on their own? Joan could not tackle both of them. But if she killed Veronica, and then waited for the unsuspecting Hilary to follow? Perhaps hidden in the reeds which grew so conveniently tall.

She did not know that Hilary had made the connection between Joan and the Arnold's carrier bag.

She forced herself into a run again. This time she was glad the burly figure of John was in front of her.

The tall reeds shut off a clear view of the channel ahead. Sometimes she glimpsed the watery pathway stretching away through the pastures, then the tassel-headed stems closed in again and she lost the perspective. John's figure was dwindling in the distance. She kept running.

There was a darkness looming across the channel. It stood higher than the reeds. Spanning the sky. Blocking her view of the waterway ahead.

The fringe of reeds ended suddenly. She saw it clearly then, the assignation Joan had given Veronica. A metal gantry spanned the waterway over Hilary's head. Beneath it, massive metal shutters, greasy with green slime, barred the current. One was lifted a little way and the brown water churned under it. Why had Joan wanted to meet Veronica here?

The question was cut short by a sudden cry. Along the footpath, just beyond the gates, the burly store-owner had hold of a shorter figure whom he was dragging out of the weed-grown ditch. There was a heartbeat of anguish as Hilary realized that it was not Veronica. A stockier woman dressed mostly in brown, not the rather elegant grey jacket that Veronica had been wearing. She was struggling wildly in John's grip.

Fear impelled Hilary forward. She hurled herself towards the two.

Just in time, she saw the bicycle wheel projecting from the tall weeds at the side of the path. She almost lost her balance as she swerved.

Now she could hear John Arnold shouting. He had hold of Joan by one massive hand. The other brandished the monkey wrench over her head. Hilary's eyes went past them, searching. She could still see no sign of Veronica.

'Bitch! Tell me what you've done with her! Murderer!' John was beside himself with rage.

Hilary was afraid he would do something irreversible before Joan Townsend said a word about what they desperately needed to know.

The reporter was fighting desperately, trying to pull free. 'I don't know what you're talking about! Let me go!'

'*Joan Townsend!*' Hilary's voice rasped across their shouts with all the authority of a senior teacher with decades of experience with unruly pupils.

Joan's eyes swivelled to her with a different sort of fear.

'John! Drop that wrench! Joan, just tell me. *Where is Veronica?*'

The journalist's eyes shifted away from her. The folds of her pudgy face drooped. 'She . . . slipped.'

A cold horror had hold of Hilary's heart. She had come too late.

THIRTY-THREE

ilary whirled round. Her heart told her it was over, but her brain would not accept it. She was on the brink of the bank, peering over into the churning water on the lower side of the gate. Something grey caught her eye, something that should not be there.

Against the massive greasy door of the sluice, the back and one sleeve of Veronica's jacket swirled in an eddy. Hilary plunged down the slippery bank. Waist deep in muddy water, she reached for the half-submerged cloth.

She had dreaded to feel the dead weight of the body inside it, but the jacket came away easily in her hands. There was nothing inside it. Cold disappointment numbed her. For a moment, she stood there stupidly, looking down at the dripping garment. She was aware of John still shouting at Joan Townsend somewhere above her head.

It was harder to clamber up the muddy bank than it had been to slither down. As she hauled herself clear of the water, she felt her cold wet trousers flapping against her legs. She was panting as she stood on the bank.

She held the sodden jacket up to John, who was still wrestling one-handed with his captive. 'Only this.'

He swore.

His free arm brought the wrench swinging back behind him again. Hilary grabbed it and fought to prise it from his hand. Joan, gripped firmly by his other hand, was now cowering before him, her hands shielding her face. With an effort, Hilary tugged the heavy tool free.

Robbed of his weapon, John brought his broad right hand round to deliver a stinging slap on Joan's face.

'*Where?*' he bellowed.

There were distant shouts behind them. Hilary turned her head. There were figures on the footpath, still dark in the distance, racing towards them.

Another desperate glance down into the water. Hilary could still see no sign of Veronica in the shadowed channel below the sluice where she had found the jacket. The gantry loomed darkly over it.

'I didn't mean to!' Joan was sobbing. 'I didn't mean any of it.'

'Don't be ridiculous!' Hilary exclaimed as she turned. 'You let a bomb off in the High Street in the middle of the afternoon, and you say you didn't mean it! Of course you intended to kill them. *Where's Veronica?*' Her own fist was clenching round the monkey wrench now.

'I . . . it was a mistake,' the terrified girl hiccupped. 'It was meant to go off at half past four in the *morning*. There shouldn't have been anyone there.'

'Don't be ridiculous! There were people living over those shops,' John shouted at her.

'I didn't think about that . . .'

She yelped as he yanked her arm back savagely.

'Just tell me what you've done with Veronica!' Hilary was almost beside herself.

The pounding feet were almost on them. A uniformed policeman seized Joan and dragged her away from the angry John. Handcuffs flashed in the sunlight. The words of the police caution echoed in Hilary's ears.

Behind the tall arresting officer, Hilary saw a sudden blur of movement. A woman, not in uniform, but in a dark trouser suit, had leaped from the bank on the upper side of the sluice gate in an arcing dive. Hilary charged back past the other officers arriving on the crowded footpath to see.

She had been running so hard to catch up with John Arnold and his captive that she had failed to look closely at the sluice gate as she passed it. Only now did she see on the upper side something caught against the massive metal guillotine, over near the opposite bank. Not an empty jacket this time. The white blouse and fair hair of Veronica. Face down in the water. Horror wrenched at Hilary's heart.

The woman in the trouser suit was powering her way across towards her. Hilary dropped the wrench. She clenched her fists, praying. What she was seeing must not be true.

The policewoman caught the inert form under the armpits and towed her to the further bank. Only as she hoisted the limp body up on to the grass did Hilary recognize the swimmer as Detective Sergeant Olive Petersen.

She could only watch helplessly as the sergeant bent to arrange Veronica's limp body on its bed of grass and buttercups and start to administer CPR.

More police officers went running across the gantry, boots hammering the metal bridge. Hilary's legs felt too weak to follow them. She swung back slowly. The policeman who had arrested Joan was already leading her away.

Hilary shot her a look full of scorn and disbelief. 'Veronica tried to help you! She was sorry for you. She even phoned you to come to the High Street because she'd seen Sonia Marsden and you wanted to talk to George. *And you didn't tell her your bomb was about to go off!*'

'I told you! I got the timer wrong. It wasn't *meant* to go off in the afternoon.'

'If Veronica's dead . . .' She cast a fearful look across the channel. Petersen was still at work on the still form.

'I never meant to kill *anybody*.'

'And Amina? The Muslim girl you dumped in the abbey?'

A frightened look replaced the desperate plea in Joan Townsend's eyes.

'I know. You approached her because you thought you could use her for another sensational story. Instead, you discovered that *she* was the one with a story to tell. She'd seen too much. Arnold's hardware store.'

'If you wouldn't mind, ma'am,' the arresting officer interposed. 'We need to get this one back to Glastonbury.'

Hilary stood aside. There were more police haring along the path now. The first arrivals were clattering down the further gantry steps. But only DS Petersen was on the further bank working on Veronica, who might be, but was probably not, still alive.

Someone was talking to Hilary. The voice was unexpectedly gentle. 'If you wouldn't mind answering a few questions, Mrs Masters . . .' She wrenched her eyes away from the only scene that mattered. It was Detective Inspector Fellows.

'In a moment,' she said.

Her gaze went back to the silent drama being played out across the brown water. The other officers had almost reached them now. Presently she saw DS Petersen lean back on her heels and say something into her radio. With a dull certainty Hilary knew that she must be reporting that her efforts were in vain. Veronica Taylor was dead.

Then, as she watched, the inert figure in front of Petersen twitched, rolled over and was sick on the grass.

THIRTY-FOUR

'**H**ilary, promise me you won't tell the children.'

Mercifully, they had been able to get dry clothes from the suitcases in Hilary's car. Hilary looked Veronica over as they sat in the small room in the Baptist hall assigned to Detective Chief Superintendent Allenby.

Veronica had been taken first to the nearest A&E hospital, where they had confirmed, to Hilary's immense relief, that she had suffered no lasting damage. All the same, they had wanted to keep her in overnight for observation. This Veronica had vehemently rejected.

'Just imagine Morag's reaction if I'd had to confess that I was in hospital! After we'd promised them that we'd leave Glastonbury.'

'We did,' Hilary said grimly.

'I know. I was a fool. I really thought this would be a meeting with Joan in which I could make it up to her in some way.'

'She didn't need you. She seems to have carved herself out a fairly meteoric career over the last few days. No, you must have said something to her which convinced her you knew more than you did. And I, fool that I was, didn't make the connection with the Arnold's bag until after you'd gone. And, guess what, my phone battery was flat. I not only couldn't phone you to warn you, but I couldn't even get up your number to ring you on someone else's phone. It had to be nine-nine-nine.'

'It was a very good thing you did,' said DCS Allenby. 'As it was, we got there only just in time.'

Hilary looked across at her friend. The younger woman was dressed in the warmest clothes her holiday packing had allowed. The turtle-neck jumper seemed to swamp her slender form. She looked smaller, so much more vulnerable than Hilary had realized. The DCS was right. It had been a very close-run thing.

Her eyes strayed sideways to DI Fellows and Detective Sergeant Petersen. The latter's black hair still looked damp. Her long face was set in its habitual stern, unsmiling mask. But Hilary remembered the dark-clothed figure leaping from the bank into the muddy water churning through the sluice gate, while her colleague was busy arresting Joan Townsend. The rest of the officers had still been running towards them. Only Olive Petersen had been there first to tow Veronica's water-logged body from the channel and perform the CPR that had restored her to life. Hilary felt a warm rush of gratitude that almost choked her.

'So,' DI Fellows was saying, 'the powers that be, who had me still investigating the Chalice Well bomb while the full murder squad were working all out on the High Street one, were right after all, intentionally or not. There really were two different bombers.'

Veronica frowned. 'She must have worked extremely fast. We found the Chalice Well bomb on Monday afternoon. Over the next forty-eight hours, she'd discovered that a bomb plot really did bring publicity, but only locally, and she wasn't going to benefit from it. So it had to be something bigger. A bomb that really *did* go off. Could she really have found out how to do that, and assembled everything she needed, in such a short time?'

'It's possible,' Fellows said. 'If you know where to look.'

'I don't think her journalism course was intended to equip her for *that*,' Hilary observed.

'And then this stupid, stupid girl never thought about the difference between four-thirty in the morning and four-thirty in the middle of a busy afternoon,' Veronica sighed. 'All those lives, all those injuries, for one idiotic mistake.'

'There were people sleeping over the shops, even at night,' Hilary reminded her.

'So this Honeydew fellow was just a crank?' DS Petersen asked. 'He had nothing to do with the second bomb?'

'Yes and no.' DCS Allenby steepled her fingers. Her dyed blonde hair bent over them. 'If it hadn't been for his little ploy to get more publicity for the Chalice Well, Joan Townsend would never have thought of her own disastrous plan. And he must have been scared out of his wits when he realized that ninety-nine per cent of the population would assume that the two bombers were the same. Crucially Mel Fenwick, who knew about the first one.'

'Would he really have harmed her?' Hilary asked.

'Who's to say? At the very best, he'd have frightened the pants off her to keep her quiet.'

'But where does Amina Haddad come into all this?' Olive Petersen frowned. 'I was tailing her for a while. Well, it seemed an obvious connection. Extreme Islamist, judging by her clothes.'

Hilary felt her lips tighten. It was, after all, going to prove harder to like the detective sergeant than the first warm rush of gratitude had suggested.

'Amina was a devout Muslim. That does *not* make her a cold-blooded murderer.'

'No, but it made her a convenient suspect for Joan Townsend to latch on to, to divert attention from herself,' DI Fellows cut in. 'My guess is that she tried to interview Miss Haddad, to follow up on that prejudicial headline she'd already fed to the press. She may even have let slip that she saw Amina in Arnold's and accused her of buying some of the things she needed for a bomb. Maybe, too late, she realized that the boot was on the other foot. That something in Amina's eyes, through that burka, told her that it was *she* who had guessed why Joan was in that shop. If Joan had paid cash at a self-service till, Amina might have been the only person who could testify to what she bought.'

'So,' said Hilary slowly, 'silence her, and get herself yet another sensational story to report.'

'The Thorn in her hand,' Veronica said. 'We thought she must have been killed in St John's churchyard.'

'But she never got that far,' Fellows added.

'Friday's newspaper story had to be the so-called Satanists dancing in the streets after dark. Joan needed to postpone the finding of Amina's body to hit the headlines again next day. Clever. Just one melodramatic story after another from Glastonbury. The tabloid editors must have loved her.'

They fell silent. Hilary was thinking of the young man Basil, blood pumping from his almost-severed leg. Of Amina's delicate blue-and-gold sandal, all that could be seen of her body under the plastic sheet. Of finding Veronica's empty jacket in the eddy below the sluice gate. Cold horror stalked over her. To have done all that in so short a time, Joan Townsend must have been both very clever and more than a little deranged. Hilary had underestimated her when she had dismissed the would-be reporter as a shambling, rather tiresome failure.

'And George Marsden?'

DCS Allenby sighed. 'Just a loud-mouthed, opinionated bigot, I'm afraid. Not that they can't do their own sort of damage, mind you. But a bomber? No.'

Hilary rose to her feet. 'Well, if you've finished with us, it's high time we were on our way. My phone's flat, and I haven't brought the charger, so goodness knows what messages my family have been stacking up for me. But Veronica can't fend hers off much longer. We promised we'd move out of Glastonbury today, and here we still are. Time to hit the road.'

'Well, thanks from the bottom of my heart.' DI Fellows rose as she did. He cast an apologetic glance at his unsmiling detective sergeant. 'I know we warned you often enough to keep out of this, but in the end, it was your perception that put the vital piece into place.'

'A plastic bag?' Hilary smiled wryly. 'It wouldn't have been enough on its own, and you know it. Just circumstantial evidence. In the end, she shopped herself. One headline story too many.'

'And Mrs Taylor nearly paid the price.'

'I owe Sergeant Petersen a tremendous debt of gratitude.' Veronica smiled.

There was just the hint of a flush in the detective sergeant's face. A twitch of the resolutely set lips.

'I'll be putting her forward for a commendation,' DCS Allenby said.

Out in the fresh air, Veronica turned to Hilary with a more mischievous smile.

'Do you know, just for a few moments, I even wondered whether we'd got the whole thing upside down, and Sister Mary Magdalene was the one. It's amazing what suspicion can do to you.'

'I know,' Hilary agreed. 'Those footsteps behind us in the twilight as we passed the retreat house.'

'Though the real horror was actually Joan's footsteps, catching up with Amina there.'

Hilary shuddered. 'But there was also the fact that Sister Mary Magdalene turned up just when the High Street bomb went off.'

'Only, by that reckoning,' Veronica concluded, 'we should have been prime suspects ourselves.'

Hilary's eyes twinkled. 'Perhaps we were. To DS Petersen, at least. But DI Fellows is far too nice to tell us.

This time, Hilary drove. A little way out of Glastonbury, she pulled over into a lay-by and got out. As she turned to take in the town they were leaving after this turbulent week, the nearest thing that met her eye was the bent back of Wearyall Hill.

'And, after all that, we never did find out who cut down the Thorn tree on the hill and who keeps going back to cut off the new shoots. There was a time when I thought it must be connected with the bombings, but apparently not.'

'I must say I can't see it,' said Veronica, coming to join her. 'Neither of the bombs. Rupert Honeydew may be weird. And scary too. But I can't believe he would damage a tree he almost certainly holds to be sacred. And Joan would still have been at school when the tree was first mutilated.'

'So it stays a mystery.'

'There's a greater mystery,' Veronica said quietly. 'The way the human spirit will not be crushed. People go on grafting cuttings of the Thorn – planting them on Wearyall Hill, in the churchyard, in private gardens, wherever.'

'And the myth of Arthur, the great leader who held the Christian west against the invader. Just when you need him, there's his grave, and his great tree-trunk coffin, at the abbey. And so the story gains power and lives on. And it may be unfashionable to say so, but it *is* a story of heroism to live by.'

'Like Glastonbury Abbey itself. A witness to a greater Resurrection.'

They stood in silence, looking back at the wounded town, where even now people were picking up the threads of their lives.

Hilary found herself brushing away an uncharacteristic tear.

They drove on, over the Levels, where the farmland was springing green again after the floods which had devastated them last winter.

The hills of Devon began to rise in front of them.

Hilary dropped Veronica at her front gate.

'Are you sure you'll be all right? I've told you, you're very welcome to come and spend the night with me.'

A strangely knowing smile flowered in Veronica's face.

'No. I'll be fine. A good bottle of wine and an early night is what I need.'

Hilary watched her walk up the garden path, towing her suitcase. As Veronica stopped to unlock the front door, it struck Hilary with a sharp irony that she had suggested this trip to take her friend's mind off the loss of her husband. Veronica had come close to losing her own life. Hilary was on the point of jumping out of the car and insisting that Veronica change her mind, but the door closed. She could picture her friend relaxing at last in the comfort of her own familiar home.

After a moment, Hilary drove on.

It was her turn now to turn the key of her own front door. The first thing that struck her as she walked inside was that there was not the expected clutter of accumulated mail on the doormat.

She was still trying to puzzle this out when the figure she had least expected strode out of the sitting room and stretched out an arm to hug her.

'David!'

Only one arm, because the left one seemed to be strapped to his chest.

It was a joyful surprise to be enfolded in that lop-sided hug.

'What have you done to yourself?'

The warm voice was caught between laughter and grief. 'A shell hit the hospital. I caught a piece of shrapnel in my side. Nothing too serious, but they sent me home early.'

'Why ever didn't you tell me?' Indignation was warring with delight in his presence and concern for his wound.

'Hilary! Does it never occur to you that a mobile phone is no good unless you switch it on occasionally? I've been trying to get through to you for the last twenty-four hours. In the end, I had to ring Veronica. You gave me her number in case of emergencies. Didn't she tell you I'd rung?'

Hilary remembered the laughter in Veronica's eyes, her insistence that Hilary should go home alone.

'I'll wring her neck!'

'From the sound of it, you two have been in quite enough danger already this week. And Veronica said they still hadn't caught whoever was behind the bomb.'

'They have now.' Suddenly the day's events caught up with Hilary. She sat down suddenly. 'It's a long story.' She drew David down beside her and lifted his right arm aside. 'That was close,' she said, surveying his bandaged chest.

'There were others for whom it was too close. Two patients, one orderly.'

She sat in silence, thinking of all the terrible maybes which had never quite happened.

'We passed the Glastonbury Thorn today. Someone tried to cut it down, eliminate it. But it keeps on putting out shoots, however often the vandal comes back to cut them off. And people have planted slips of it all over the town. It's still alive and blossoming.'

David's hand closed over hers. 'I know what you mean. In all the bombing, the shelling, hope lives on.'

'Well,' said Hilary. 'Veronica talked about cracking open a bottle of wine. That sounds like a very good idea to me.'